Imago

Octavia E. Butler

POPULAR LIBRARY

An Imprint of Warner Books, Inc.

 A Time Warner Company

To Irie Isaacs

POPULAR LIBRARY EDITION

Copyright © 1989 by Octavia E. Butler
All rights reserved.

Popular Library®, the fanciful P design, and Questar® are registered trademarks of Warner Books, Inc.

Cover illustration by Wayne Barlowe

Popular Library books are published by
Warner Books, Inc.
1271 Avenue of the Americas
New York, N.Y. 10020

 A Time Warner Company

Printed in the United States of America

This book was originally published in hardcover by Warner Books.
First Printed in Paperback: March, 1990

10 9 8 7 6 5 4 .

I

Metamorphosis

1

I slipped into my first metamorphosis so quietly that no one noticed. Metamorphoses were not supposed to begin that way. Most people begin with small, obvious, physical changes—the loss of fingers and toes, for instance, or the budding of new fingers and toes of a different design.

I wish my experience had been that normal, that safe.

For several days, I changed without attracting attention. Early stages of metamorphosis didn't normally last for days without bringing on deep sleep, but mine did. My first changes were sensory. Tastes, scents, all sensations suddenly became complex, confusing, yet unexpectedly seductive.

I had to relearn everything. River water, for instance: when I swam in it, I noticed that it had two distinctive major flavors—hydrogen and oxygen?—and many minor flavors. I could separate out and savor each one individually. In fact, I couldn't help separating them. But I learned them quickly and accepted them in their new complexity so that only occasional changes in minor flavors demanded my attention.

Our river water at Lo always came to us clouded with sediment. "Rich," the Oankali called it. "Muddy," the Humans said, and filtered it or let the silt settle to the bottom before they drank it. "Just water," we constructs said, and shrugged. We had never known any other water.

As quickly as I could, I learned again to understand and accept my sensory impressions of the people and things around me. The experience absorbed so much of my attention

3

that I didn't understand how my family could fail to see that something unusual was happening to me. But beyond mentioning that I was daydreaming too much, even my parents missed the signs.

They were, after all, the wrong signs. No one was expecting them, so no one noticed when they appeared.

All five of my parents were old when I was born. They didn't look any older than my adult sisters and brothers, but they had helped with the founding of Lo. They had grandchildren who were old. I don't think I had ever surprised them before. I wasn't sure I liked surprising them now. I didn't want to tell them. I especially didn't want to tell Tino, my Human father. He was supposed to stay with me through my metamorphosis—since he was my same-sex Human parent. But I did not feel drawn to him as I should have. Nor did I feel drawn to Lilith, my birth mother. She was Human, too, and what was happening to me was definitely not a Human thing. Strangely I didn't want to go to my Oankali father, Dichaan, either, and he was my logical choice after Tino. My Oankali mother, Ahajas, would have talked to one of my fathers for me. She had done that for two of my brothers who had been afraid of metamorphosis—afraid they would change too much, lose all signs of their Humanity. That could happen to me, though I had never worried about it. Ahajas would have talked to me and for me, no matter what my problem was. Of all my parents, she was the easiest to talk to. I would have gone to her if the thought of doing so had been more appealing—or if I had understood why it was so unappealing. What was wrong with me? I wasn't shy or afraid, but when I thought of going to her, I felt first drawn, then . . . almost repelled.

Finally there was my ooloi parent, Nikanj.

It would tell me to go to one of my same-sex parents—one of my fathers. What else could it say? I knew well enough that I was in metamorphosis, and that that was one of the few things ooloi parents could not help with. There were still some Humans who insisted on seeing the ooloi as some kind of male-female combination, but the ooloi were no such thing. They were themselves—a different sex altogether.

So I went to Nikanj only hoping to enjoy its company for

a while. Eventually it would notice what was happening to me and send me to my fathers. Until it did, I would rest near it. I was tired, sleepy. Metamorphosis was mostly sleep.

I found Nikanj inside the family house, talking to a pair of Human strangers. The Humans were standing back from Nikanj. The female was almost sheltering behind the male, and the male was making a painful effort to appear courageous. Both looked alarmed when they saw me open a wall and step through into the room. Then, as they got a look at me, they seemed to relax a little. I looked very Human—especially if they compared me to Nikanj, who wasn't Human at all.

The Humans smelled most obviously of sweat and adrenaline, food and sex. I sat down on the floor and let myself work out the complex combinations of scents. My new awareness wouldn't allow me to do anything else. By the time I was finished, I thought I would be able to track those two Humans through anything.

Nikanj paid no attention to me except to notice me when I came in. It was used to its children coming and going as they chose, used to all of us spending time with it, learning whatever it was willing to teach us.

It has an incredibly complex scent because it was ooloi. It had collected within itself not only the reproductive material of other members of the family but cells of other plant and animal species that it had dealt with recently. These it would study, memorize, then either consume or store. It consumed the ones it knew it could re-create from memory, using its own DNA. It kept the others alive in a kind of stasis until they were needed.

Its most noticeable underscent was Kaal, the kin group it was born into. I had never met its parents, but I knew the Kaal scent from other members of the Kaal kin group. Somehow, though, I had never noticed that scent on Nikanj, never separated it out this way.

The main scent was Lo, of course. It had mated with Oankali of the Lo kin group, and on mating, it had altered its own scent as an ooloi must. The word "ooloi" could not be translated directly into English because its meaning was as complex as Nikanj's scent. "Treasured stranger." "Bridge." "Life trader." "Weaver." "Magnet."

Magnet, my birth mother says. People are drawn to ooloi and can't escape. She couldn't, certainly. But then, neither could Nikanj escape her or any of its mates. The Oankali said the chemical bonds of mating were as difficult to break as the habit of breathing.

Scents . . . The two visiting Humans were longtime mates and smelled of each other.

"We don't know yet whether we want to emigrate," the female was saying. "We've come to see for ourselves and for our people."

"You'll be shown everything," Nikanj told them. "There are no secrets about the Mars colony or travel to it. But right now the shuttles allotted to emigration are all in use. We have a guest area where Humans can wait."

The two Humans looked at one another. They still smelled frightened, but now both were making an effort to look brave. Their faces were almost expressionless.

"We don't want to stay here," the male said. "We'll come back when there's a ship."

Nikanj stood up—unfolded, as Humans say. "I can't tell you when there'll be a ship," it said. "They arrive when they arrive. Let me show you the guest area. It isn't like this house. Humans built it of cut wood."

The pair stumbled back from Nikanj.

Nikanj's sensory tentacles flattened against its body in amusement. It sat down again. "There are other Humans waiting in the guest area," it told them gently. "They're like you. They want their own all-Human world. They'll be traveling with you when you go." It paused, looked at me. "Eka, why don't you show them?"

I wanted to stay with it now more than ever, but I could see that the two Humans were relieved to be turned over to someone who at least looked Human. I stood up and faced them.

"This is Jodahs," Nikanj told them, "one of my younger children."

The female gave me a look that I had seen too often not to recognize. She said, "But I thought . . ."

"No," I said to her, and smiled. "I'm not Human. I'm a Human-born construct. Come out this way. The guest area isn't far."

They did not want to follow me through the wall I opened until it was fully open—as though they thought the wall might close on them, as though it would hurt them if it did.

"It would be like being grasped gently by a big hand," I told them when we were all outside.

"What?" the male asked.

"If the wall shut on you. It couldn't hurt you because you're alive. It might eat your clothing, though."

"No, thanks!"

I laughed. "I've never seen that happen, but I've heard it can."

"What's your name?" the female asked.

"All of it?" She looked interested in me—smelled sexually attracted, which made her interesting to me. Human females did tend to like me as long as I kept my few body tentacles covered by clothing and my few head tentacles hidden in my hair. The sensory spots on my face and arms looked like ordinary skin, though they didn't feel ordinary.

"Your Human name," the female said. "I already know . . . Eka and Jodahs, but I'm not sure which to call you."

"Eka is just a term of endearment for young children," I told her, "like lelka for married children and Chka between mates. Jodahs is my personal name. The Human version of my whole name is Jodahs Iyapo Leal Kaalnikanjlo. My name, the surnames of my birth mother and Human father, and Nikanj's name beginning with the kin group it was born into and ending with the kin group of its Oankali mates. If I were Oankali-born or if I gave you the Oankali version of my name, it would be a lot longer and more complicated."

"I've heard some of them," the female said. "You'll probably drop them eventually."

"No. We'll change them to suit our needs, but we won't drop them. They give very useful information, especially when people are looking for mates."

"Jodahs doesn't sound like any name I've heard before," the male said.

"Oankali name. An Oankali named Jodahs died helping

with the emigration. My birth mother said he should be remembered. The Oankali don't have a tradition of remembering people by naming kids after them, but my birth mother insisted. She does that sometimes—insists on keeping Human customs."

"You look very Human," the female said softly.

I smiled. "I'm a child. I just look unfinished."

"How old are you?"

"Twenty-nine."

"Good god! When will you be considered an adult?"

"After metamorphosis." I smiled to myself. Soon. "I have a brother who went through it at twenty-one, and a sister who didn't reach it until she was thirty-three. People change when their bodies are ready, not at some specific age."

She was silent for some time. We reached the last of the true houses of Lo—the houses that had been grown from the living substance of the Lo entity. Humans without Oankali mates could not open walls or raise table, bed, or chair platforms in such houses. Left alone in our houses, these Humans were prisoners until some construct, Oankali, or mated Human freed them. Thus, they had been given first a guest house, then a guest area. In that area they had built their dead houses of cut wood and woven thatch. They used fire for light and cooking and occasionally they burned down one of their houses. Houses that did not burn became infested with rodents and insects which ate the Human's food and bit or stung the Humans themselves. Periodically Oankali went in and drove the non-Human life out. It always came back. It had been feeding on Humans, eating their food, and living in their buildings since long before the Oankali arrived. Still the guest area was reasonably comfortable. Guests ate from trees and plants that were not what they appeared to be. They were extensions of the Lo entity. They had been induced to synthesize fruits and vegetables in shapes, flowers, and textures that Humans recognized. The foods grew from what appeared to be their proper trees and plants. Lo took care of the Humans' wastes, keeping their area clean, though they tended to be careless about where they threw or dumped things in this temporary place.

"There's an empty house there," I said, pointing.

The female stared at my hand rather than at where I pointed. I had, from a Human point of view, too many fingers and toes. Seven per. Since they were part of distinctly Human-looking hands and feet, Humans didn't usually notice them at once.

I held my hand open, palm up so that she could see it, and her expression flickered from curiosity and surprise through embarrassment back to curiosity.

"Will you change much in metamorphosis?" she asked.

"Probably. The Human-born get more Oankali and the Oankali-born get more Human. I'm first-generation. If you want to see the future, take a look at some of the third- and fourth-generations constructs. They're a lot more uniform from start to finish."

"That's not our future," the male said.

"Your choice," I said.

The male walked away toward the empty house. The female hesitated. "What do you think of our emigration?" she asked.

I looked at her, liking her, not wanting to answer. But such questions should be answered. Why, though, were the Human females who insisted on asking them so often small, weak people? The Martian environment they were headed for was harsher than any they had known. We would see that they had the best possible chance to survive. Many would live to bear children on their new world. But they would suffer so. And in the end, it would all be for nothing. Their own genetic conflict had betrayed and destroyed them once. It would do so again.

"You should stay," I told the female. "You should join us."

"Why?"

I wanted very much not to look at her, to go away from her. Instead I continued to face her. "I understand that Humans must be free to go," I said softly. "I'm Human enough for my body to understand that. But I'm Oankali enough to know that you will eventually destroy yourselves again."

She frowned, marring her smooth forehead. "You mean another war?"

"Perhaps. Or maybe you'll find some other way to do it. You were working on several ways before your war."

"You don't know anything about it. You're too young."

"You should stay and mate with constructs or with Oankali," I said. "The children we construct are free of inherent flaws. What we build will last."

"You're just a child, repeating what you've been told!"

I shook my head. "I perceive what I perceive. No one had to tell me how to use my senses any more than they had to tell you how to see or hear. There is a lethal genetic conflict in Humanity, and you know it."

"All we know is what the Oankali have told us." The male had come back. He put his arm around the female, drawing her away from me as though I had offered some threat. "They could be lying for their own reasons."

I shifted my attention to him. "You know they're not," I said softly. "Your own history tells you. Your people are intelligent, and that's good. The Oankali say you're potentially one of the most intelligent species they've found. But you're also hierarchical—you and your nearest animal relatives and your most distant animal ancestors. Intelligence is relatively new to life on Earth, but your hierarchical tendencies are ancient. The new was too often put at the service of the old. It will be again. You're bright enough to learn to live on your new world, but you're so hierarchical you'll destroy yourselves trying to dominate it and each other. You might last a long time, but in the end, you'll destroy yourselves."

"We could last a thousand years," the male said. "We did all right on Earth until the war."

"You could. Your new world will be difficult. It will demand most of your attention, perhaps occupy your hierarchical tendencies safely for a while."

"We'll be free—us, our children, their children."

"Perhaps."

"We'll be fully Human and free. That's enough. We might even get into space again on our own someday. Your people might be dead wrong about us."

"No." He couldn't read the gene combinations as I could. It was as though he were about to walk off a cliff simply because he could not see it—or because he, or rather his descendants, would not hit the rocks below for a long time. And what were we doing, we who knew the truth? Helping him reach the cliff. Ferrying him to it.

"We might outlast your people here on Earth," he said.

"I hope so," I told him. His expression said he didn't believe me, but I meant it. We would not be here—the Earth he knew would not be here—for more than a few centuries. We, Oankali and construct, were space-going people, as curious about other life and as acquisitive of it as Humans were hierarchical. Eventually we would have to begin the long, long search for a new species to combine with to construct new life-forms. Much of Oankali existence was spent in such searches. We would leave this solar system in perhaps three centuries. I would live to see the leave-taking myself. And when we broke and scattered, we would leave behind a lump of stripped rock more like the moon than like his blue Earth. He did not know that. He would never know it. To tell him would be a cruelty.

"Do you ever think of yourself or your kind as Human?" the female asked. "Some of you look so Human."

"We feel our Humanity. It helps us to understand both you and the Oankali. Oankali alone could never have let you have your Mars colony."

"I heard they were helping!" the male said. "Your . . . your parent said they were helping!"

"They help because of what we constructs tell them: that you should be allowed to go even though you'll eventually destroy yourselves. The Oankali believe . . . the Oankali *know to the bone* that it's wrong to help the Human species regenerate unchanged because it *will* destroy itself again. To them it's like deliberately causing the conception of a child who is so defective that it must die in infancy."

"They're wrong. Someday we'll show them how wrong."

It was a threat. It was meaningless, but it gave him some slight satisfaction. "The other Humans here will show you where to gather food," I said. "If you need anything else, ask one of us." I turned to go.

"So goddamn patronizing," the male muttered.

I turned back without thinking. "Am I really?"

The male frowned, muttered a curse, and went back into

the house. I understood then that he was just angry. It bothered me that I sometimes made them angry. I never intended to.

The female stepped to me, touched my face, examined a little of my hair. Humans who hadn't mated among us never really learned to touch us. At best, they annoyed us by rubbing their hands over sensory spots, and once their hands found the spots they never liked them.

The female jerked her hand back when her fingers discovered the one below my left ear.

"They're a little like eyes that can't close to protect themselves," I said. "It doesn't exactly hurt us when you touch them, but we don't like you to."

"So what? You have to teach people how to touch you?"

I smiled and took her hand between my own. "Hands are always safe," I said. I left her standing there, watching me. I could see her through sensory tentacles in my hair. She stood there until the male came out and drew her inside.

2

I went back to Nikanj and sat near it while it took care of family matters, while it met with people from the Oankali homeship, Chkahichdahk, which circled the Earth out beyond the orbit of the moon, while it exchanged information with other ooloi or took biological information from my siblings. We all brought Nikanj bits of fur, flesh, pollen, leaves, seeds, spores, or other living or dead cells from plants or animals that we had questions about or that were new to us.

No one paid any attention to me. There was an odd comfort in that. I could examine them all with my newly sharpened senses, see what I had never seen before, smell what I had never noticed. I suppose I seemed to doze a little. For a time, Aaor, my closest sibling—my Oankali-born sister—came to sit beside me. She was the child of my Oankali mother, and not yet truly female, but I had always thought of her as a sister. She looked so female—or she had looked female before I began to change. Now she . . . Now *it* looked the way it always should have. It looked eka in the true meaning of the word—a child too young to have developed sex. That was what we both were—for now. Aaor smelled eka. It could literally go either way, become male or female. I had always known this, of course, about both of us. But now, suddenly, I could no longer even think of Aaor as she. It probably would be female someday, just as I would probably soon become the male I appeared to be. The Human-born rarely change their apparent sex. In my family, only one Human-born had changed from apparent female to actual male. Several Oankali-born had changed, but most knew long before their metamorphosis that they felt more drawn to become the opposite of what they seemed.

Aaor moved close and examined me with a few of its head and body tentacles. "I think you're close to metamorphosis," it said. It has not spoken aloud. Children learned early that it was ill mannered to speak aloud among themselves if others nearby were having ongoing vocal conversations. We spoke though touch signals, signs, and multisensory illusions transmitted through head or body tentacles—direct neural stimulation.

"I am," I answered silently. "But I feel . . . different."

"Show me."

I tried to re-create my increased sensory awareness for it, but it drew away.

After a time, it touched me again lightly. In tactile signals only, it said, "I don't like it. Something's wrong. You should show Dichaan."

I did not want to show Dichaan. That was odd. I hadn't minded showing Aaor. I felt no aversion to showing Nikanj—except that it would probably send me to my fathers.

"What about me disturbs you?" I asked Aaor.

"I don't know," it answered. "But I don't like it. I've never felt it before. Something is wrong." It was afraid, and that was odd. New things normally drew its attention. This new thing repelled it.

"It isn't anything that will hurt you," I said. "Don't worry."

It got up and went away. It didn't say anything. It just left. That was out of character. Aaor and I had always been close. It was only three months younger than I was, and we'd been together since it was born. It had never walked away from me before. You only walk away from people you could no longer communicate with.

I went over to Nikanj. It was alone now. One of our neighbors had just left it. It focused a cone of its long head tentacles on me, finally noticing that there was something different about me.

"Metamorphosis, Eka?"

"I think so."

"Let me check. Your scent is . . . strange."

The tone of its voice was strange. I had been around when siblings of mine went into metamorphosis. Nikanj had never sounded quite that way.

It wrapped the tip of one sensory arm around my arm and extended its sensory hand. Sensory hands were ooloi appendages. Nikanj did not normally use them to check for metamorphosis. It could have used its head or body tentacles just like anyone else, but it was disturbed enough to want to be more precise, more certain.

I tried to feel the filaments of the sensory hand as they slipped through my flesh. I had never been able to before, but I felt them clearly now. There was no pain, of course. No communication. But I felt as though I had found what I had been looking for. The deep touch of the sensory hand was air after a long, blundering swim underwater. Without thinking I caught its second sensory arm between my hands.

Something went wrong then. Nikanj didn't sting me. It wouldn't do that. But something happened. I startled it. No, I shocked it profoundly—and it transmitted to me the full impact of that shock. Its multisensory illusions felt more real than things that actually happened, and this was worse than an illusion. This was a sudden, swift cycling of its own intense surprise and fear. From me to it to me. Closed loop.

I lost focus on everything else. I wasn't aware of collapsing or of being caught in Nikanj's two almost Human-looking strength arms. Later, I examined my latent memories of this and knew that for several seconds I had been simply held in all four of Nikanj's arms. It had stood utterly still, frozen in shock and fear.

Finally, its shock ebbing, its fear growing, it put me on a broad platform. It focused a sharp cone of head tentacles on me and stood rock still again, observing. After a time it lay down beside me and helped me understand why it was so upset.

But by then, I knew.

"You're becoming ooloi," it said quietly.

I began to be afraid for myself. Nikanj lay alongside me. Its head and body tentacles did not touch me. It offered no comfort or reassurance, no movement, no sign that it was even conscious.

"Ooan?" I said. I hadn't called it that for years. My older siblings called our parents by their names, and I had begun early to imitate them. Now, though, I was afraid. I did not want "Nikanj." I wanted "Ooan," the parent I had most often gone to or been carried to for healing or teaching. "Ooan, can't you change me back? I still *look* male."

"You know better," it said aloud.

"But . . ."

"You were never male, no matter how you looked. You were eka. You know that."

I said nothing. All my life, I had been referred to as "he" and treated as male by my Human parents, by all the Humans in Lo. Even Oankali sometimes said "he." And everyone had assumed that Dichaan and Tino were to be my same-sex parents. People were supposed to feel that way so that I would be prepared for the change that should have happened.

But the change had gone wrong. Until now, no construct had become ooloi. When people reached adulthood and were ready to mate, they went to the ship and found an Oankali ooloi or they signaled the ship and an Oankali ooloi was sent down.

Human-born males were still considered experimental and potentially dangerous. A few males from other towns had been sterilized and exiled to the ship. Nobody was ready for a construct ooloi. Certainly nobody was ready for a Human-born construct ooloi. Could there be a more potentially deadly being?

"Ooan!" I said desperately.

It drew me against it, its head and body tentacles touching, then penetrating my flesh. Its sensory arm coiled around me so that the sensory hand could seat itself at the back of my neck. This was the preferred ooloi grip with Humans and with many constructs. Both brain and spinal cord were easily accessible to the slender, slender filaments of the sensory hand.

For the first time since I stopped nursing, Nikanj drugged me—immobilized me—as though it could not trust me to be still. I was too frightened even to be offended. Maybe it was right not to trust me.

Still, it did not hurt me. And it did not calm me. Why should it calm me? I had good reason to be afraid.

"I should have noticed this," it said aloud. "I should have . . . I constructed you to look very male—so male that the females would be attracted to you and help convince you that you *were* male. Until today, I thought they had. Now I know I was the one who was convinced. I deceived myself into carelessness and blindness."

"I've always felt male," I said. "I've never thought about being anything else."

"I should have sent you to spend more time with Tino and Dichaan." It paused for a moment, rustled its unengaged body tentacles. It did that when it was thinking. A dozen or so body tentacles rubbed together sounded like wind blowing through the trees. "I liked having you around too much," it said. "All my children grow up and turn away from me, turn to their same-sex parents. I thought you would, too, when the time came."

"That's what I thought. I never wanted to do it, though."

"You didn't want to go to your fathers?"

"No. I only left you when I knew I would be in the way."

"I never felt that you were in the way."

"I tried to be careful."

It rustled its tentacles again, repeated, "I should have noticed. . . ."

"You were always lonely," I said. "You had mates and children, but to me, you always tasted . . . empty in some way—as though you were hungry, almost starving."

It said nothing for some time. It did not move, but I felt safely enveloped by it. Some Humans tried to give you that feeling when they hugged you and irritated your sensory spots and pinched your sensory tentacles. Only the Oankali could give it, really. And right now, only Nikanj could give it to me. In all its long life, it had had no same-sex child. It had used all its tricks to protect us from becoming ooloi. It had used all its tricks to keep itself agonizingly alone.

I think I had always known how lonely it was. Surely, of my five parents, I had always loved it best. Apparently my body had responded to it in the way an Oankali child's would. I was taking on the sex of the parent I had felt most drawn to.

"What will happen to me?" I asked after a long silence.

"You're healthy," it said. "Your development is exactly right. I can't find any flaw in you."

And that meant there was no flaw. It was a good ooloi. Other ooloi came to it when they had problems beyond their perception or comprehension.

"What will happen?" I repeated.

"You'll stay with us."

No qualification. It would not allow me to be sent away. Yet it had agreed with other Oankali a century before that any accidental construct ooloi must be sent to the ship. There it could be watched, and any damage it did could be spotted and corrected quickly. On the ship, its every move could be monitored. On Earth, it might do great harm before anyone noticed.

But Nikanj would not allow me to be sent away. It had said so.

3

Quickly Nikanj called all my parents together. I would sleep soon. Metamorphosis is mostly deep sleep while the body changes and matures. Nikanj wanted to tell the others while I was still awake.

My Human mother came in, looked at Nikanj and me, then walked over to me and took my hands. No one had said anything aloud, but she knew something was wrong. She certainly knew that I was in metamorphosis. She had seen that often enough.

She looked closely at me, holding her face near mine, since her eyes were her only organs of sight. Then she looked at Nikanj. "What's wrong with him? This isn't just metamorphosis."

Through her hands, I had begun to study her flesh in a way I never had before. I knew her flesh better than I knew anyone's, but there was something about it now—a flavor, a texture I had never noticed.

She took her hands from me abruptly and stepped away. "Oh, good god. . . ."

Still, no one had spoken to her. Yet she knew.

"What is it?" my Human father asked.

My mother looked at Nikanj. When it did not speak, she said, "Jodahs . . . Jodahs is becoming ooloi."

My Human father frowned. "But that's impos—" He stopped, followed my mother's gaze to Nikanj. "It's impossible, isn't it?"

"No," Nikanj said softly.

He went to Nikanj, stood stiffly over it. He looked more

18

frightened than angry. *"How could you let this happen?"* he demanded. "Exile, for godsake! Exile for your own child!"

"No, Chka," Nikanj whispered.

"Exile! It's your law, you ooloi!"

"No." It focused a cone of head tentacles on its Oankali mates. "The child is perfect. My carelessness has allowed it to become ooloi, but I haven't been careless in any other way." It hesitated. "Come. Know for certain. Know for the people."

My Oankali mother and father joined with it in a tangle of head and body tentacles. It did not touch them with its sensory arms, did not even uncoil the arms until Dichaan took one arm and Ahajas took the other. In unison, then, all three focused cones of head tentacles on my two Human parents. The Humans glared at them. After a time, Lilith went to the Oankali, but did not touch them. She turned and held one arm out to Tino. He did not move.

"Your law!" he repeated to Nikanj.

But it was Lilith who answered. "Not law. Consensus. They agreed to send accidental ooloi to the ship. Nika believes it can change the agreement."

"Now? In the middle of everything?"

"Yes."

"What if it can't?"

Lilith swallowed. I could see her throat move. "Then maybe we'll have to leave Lo for a while—live apart in the forest."

He went to her, looked at her the way he does sometimes when he wants to touch her, maybe to hold her the way Humans hold each other in the guest area. But Humans who accept Oankali mates give up that kind of touching. They don't give up wanting to do it, but once they mate Oankali, they find each other's touch repellent.

Tino shifted his attention to Nikanj. "Why don't you talk to me? Why do you leave her to tell me what's going on?"

Nikanj extended a sensory arm toward him.

"No! Goddamnit, talk to me! Speak aloud!"

". . . all right," Nikanj whispered, its body bent in an attitude of deep shame.

Tino glared at it.

"I cannot restore . . . your same-sex child to you," it said.

"Why did you do this? How could you do it?"

"I made a mistake. I only realized earlier today what I had allowed to happen. I . . . I would not have done it deliberately, Chka. Nothing could have made me do it. It happened because after so many years I had begun to relax about our children. Things have always gone well. I was careless."

My Human father looked at me. It was as though he looked from a long way away. His hands moved, and I knew he wanted to touch me, too. But if he did, it would go wrong the way it had earlier with my mother. They couldn't touch me anymore. Within families, people could touch their same-sex children, their unsexed children, their same-sex mates, and their ooloi mates.

Now, abruptly, my Human father turned and grasped the sensory arm Nikanj offered. The arm was a tough, muscular organ that existed to contain and protect the essential ooloi sensory and reproductive organs. It probably could not be injured by bare Human hands, but I think Tino tried. He was angry and hurt, and that made him want to hurt others. Of my two Human parents, only he tended to react this way. And now the only being he could turn to for comfort was the one who had caused all his trouble. An Oankali would have opened a wall and gone away for a while. Even Lilith would have done that. Tino tried to give pain. Pain for pain.

Nikanj drew him against his body and held him motionless as it comforted him and spoke silently with him. It held him for so long that my Oankali parents raised platforms and sat on them to wait. Lilith came to share my platform, though she could have raised her own. My scent must have disturbed her, but she sat near me and looked at me.

"Do you feel all right?" she said.

"Yes. I'll fall asleep soon, I think."

"You look ready for it. Does my being here bother you?"

"Not yet. But it must bother you."

"I can stand it."

She stayed where she was. I could remember being inside her. I could remember when there was nothing in my universe except her. I found myself longing to touch her. I hadn't felt that before. I had never before been unable to touch her. Now I discovered a little of the Human hunger to touch where I could not.

"Are you afraid?" Lilith asked.

"I was. But now that I know I'm all right, and that you'll all keep me here, I'm fine."

She smiled a little. "Nika's first same-sex child. It's been so lonely."

"I know."

"We all knew," Dichaan said from his platform. "All the ooloi on Earth must be feeling the desperation Nikanj felt. The people are going to have to change the old agreement before more accidents happen. The next one might be a flawed ooloi."

A flawed natural genetic engineer—one who could distort or destroy with a touch. Nothing could save it from confinement on the ship. Perhaps it would even have to be physically altered to prevent it from functioning in any way as an ooloi. Perhaps it would be so dangerous that it would have to spend its existence in suspended animation, its body used by others for painless experimentation, its consciousness permanently shut off.

I shuddered and lay down again. At once, both Nikanj and Tino were beside me, reconciled, apparently, by their concern for me. Nikanj touched me with a sensory arm, but did not expose the sensory hand. "Listen, Jodahs."

I focused on it without opening my eyes.

"You'll be all right here. I'll stay with you. I'll talk to the people from here, and when you've reached the end of this first metamorphosis, you'll remember all that I've said to them—and all they've said." It slipped a sensory arm around my neck and the feel of it there comforted me. "We'll take care of you," it said.

Later, it stripped my clothing from me as I floated atop sleep, a piece of straw floating on a still pond. I could not slip beneath the surface yet.

Something was put into my mouth. It had the flavor and texture of chunks of pineapple, but I knew from tiny differences in its scent that it was a Lo creation. It was almost pure protein—exactly what my body needed. When I had eaten several pieces, I was able to slip beneath the surface into sleep.

4

Metamorphosis is sleep. Days, weeks, months of sleep broken by a few hours now and then of waking, eating, talking. Males and females slept even more, but they had just the one metamorphosis. Ooloi had to go through this twice.

There were times when I was aware enough to watch my body develop. A sair was growing at my throat so that I would eventually be able to breathe as easily in water as in air. My nose was not absorbed into my face, but it became little more than an ornament.

I didn't lose my hair, but I grew many more head and body tentacles. I would not develop sensory arms until my second metamorphosis, but my sensitivity had already been increased, and I would soon be able to give and receive more complex multisensory illusions, and handle them much faster.

And something was growing between my hearts.

Because I was Human-born, internal arrangement was basically Human. Ooloi are careful not to construct children who provoke uncontrollable immune reactions in their birth mothers. Even two hearts seem radical to some Humans. Sometimes they shoot us where they think a heart should be—where their own hearts are—then run away in panic because that kind of thing doesn't stop us. I don't think many Humans have seen what the Oankali look like inside—or what we constructs look like. Two hearts are just double the

Human allotment. But the organ now growing between my hearts was not Human at all.

Every construct had some version of it. Males and females used it to store and keep viable the cells of unfamiliar living things that they sought out and brought home to their ooloi mate or parent. In ooloi, the organ was larger and more complex. Within it, ooloi manipulated molecules of DNA more deftly than Human women manipulated the bits of thread they used to sew their cloth. I had been constructed inside such an organ, assembled from the genetic contributions of my two mothers and my two fathers. The construction itself and a single Oankali organelle was the only ooloi contribution to my existence. The organelle had divided within each of my cells as the cells divided. It had become an essential part of my body. We were what we were because of that organelle. It made us collectors and traders of life, always learning, always changing in every way but one—that one organelle. Ooloi said we *were* that organelle—that the original Oankali had evolved through that organelle's invasion, acquisition, duplication, and symbiosis. Sometimes on worlds that had no intelligent, carbon-based life to trade with, Oankali deliberately left behind large numbers of the organelle. Abandoned, it would seek a home in the most unlikely indigenous life-forms and trigger changes—evolution in spurts. Hundreds of millions of years later, perhaps some Oankali people would wander by and find interesting trade partners waiting for them. The organelle made or found compatibility with life-forms so completely dissimilar that they were unable even to perceive one another as alive.

Once I had been all enclosed within Nikanj in a mature version of the organ I was growing between my hearts. That, I did not remember. I came to consciousness within my Human mother's uterus.

Yashi, the ooloi called their organ of genetic manipulation. Sometimes they talked about it as though it were another person. "I'm going out to taste the river and the forest. Yashi is hungry and twisting for something new."

Did it really twist? I probably wouldn't find out until my second metamorphosis when my sensory arms grew. Until then, yashi would enlarge and develop to become only a little more useful than that of a male or a female.

Other Oankali organs began to develop now as genes, dormant since my conception, became active and stimulated the growth of new, highly specialized tissues. Adult ooloi were more different than most Humans realized. Beyond their insertion of the Oankali organelle, they made no genetic contribution to their children. They left their birth families and mated with strangers so that they would not be confronted with too much familiarity. Humans said familiarity bred contempt. Among the ooloi, it bred mistakes. Male and female siblings could mate safely as long as their ooloi came from a totally different kin group.

So, for an ooloi, a same-sex child was as close as it would ever come to seeing itself in its children.

For that reason among others, Nikanj shielded me.

I felt as though it stood between me and the people so that they could not get past it to take me away.

I absorbed all that happened in the room with me, and all that came through the platform to me from Lo.

"How can we trust you?" the people demanded of Nikanj. Their messages reached us through Lo, and reached Lo either directly from our neighbors or by way of radio signals from other towns relayed to Lo by the ship. And we heard from people who lived on the ship. A few messages came from nearby towns that could make direct undergrown contact with Lo. The messages were all essentially the same. *"How can we possibly trust you? No one else has made such a dangerous mistake."*

Through Lo, Nikanj invited the people to examine it and its findings as though it were some newly discovered species. It invited them to know all that it knew about me. It endured all the tests people could think of and agree on. But it kept them from touching me.

In spite of its mistakes, it was my same-sex parent. Since it said I must not be disturbed in metamorphosis, and since they were not yet convinced that it had lost all competence, they would not disturb me. Humans thought this sort of thing was a matter of authority—who had authority over the child. Constructs and Oankali knew it was a matter of physiology.

Nikanj's body "understood" what mine was going through—
what it needed and did not need. Nikanj let me know that I
was all right and reassured me that I wasn't alone. In the way
of Oankali and construct same-sex parents, it went through
metamorphosis with me. It knew exactly what would disturb
me and what was safe. Its body knew, and no one would
argue with that knowledge. Even Human same-sex parents
seemed to reach an empathy with their children that the
people respected. Without that empathy, some developing
males and females had had a strange time of it. One of my
brothers was completely cut off from the family and from
Oankali and construct companionship during his metamorphosis. He reacted to his unrelated, all-Human companions
by losing all visible traces of his own Human heritage. He
survived all right. The Humans had taken care of him as best
they could. But after metamorphosis he had had to accept
people treating him as though he were an entirely different
person. He was Human-born, but our Human parents didn't
recognize him at all when he came home.

"I don't want to push you toward the Human or the
Oankali extreme," Nikanj said once when the people gave it
a few hours of peace. It talked to me often, knowing that
whether I was conscious or not, I would hear and remember.
Its presence and its voice comforted me. "I want you to
develop as you should in every way. The more normal your
changes are, the sooner the people will accept you as
normal."

It had not yet convinced the people to accept anything
about me. Not even that I should be allowed to stay on Earth
and live in Lo through my subadult stage and second
metamorphosis. The consensus now was that I should be
brought up to the ship as soon as I had completed this first
metamorphosis. Subadults were still seen as children, but
they could work as ooloi in ways that did not involve
reproduction. Subadults could not only heal or cause disease,
but they could cause genetic changes—mutations—in plants
and animals. They could do anything that could be done
without mates. They could be unintentionally deadly, changing insects and microorganisms in unexpected ways.

"I don't want to hurt anything," I said toward the end of

my months-long change when I could speak again. "Don't let me do any harm."

"No harm, Oeka," Nikanj said softly. It had lain down beside me as it often did so that while I slept, it could be with me, yet sink its head and body tentacles into the platform—the flesh of Lo—and communicate with the people. "There is no flaw in you," it continued. "You should be aware of everything you do. You can make mistakes, but you can also perceive them. And you can correct them. I'll help you."

Its words gave a security nothing else could have. I had begun to feel like one of the dormant volcanoes high in the mountains beyond the forest—like a thing that might explode anytime, destroying whatever happened to be nearby.

"There is something that you must be aware of, though," Nikanj said.

"Yes?"

"You will be complete in ways that male and female constructs have not been. Eventually you and others like you will awaken dormant abilities in males and females. But you, as an ooloi, can have no dormant abilities."

"What will it mean . . . to be complete?"

"You'll be able to change yourself. What we can do from one generation to the next—changing our form, reverting to earlier forms or combinations of forms—you'll be able to do within yourself. Superficially, you may even be able to create new forms, new shells for camouflage. That's what we intended."

"If I can change my shape . . ." I focused narrowly on Nikanj. "Could I become male?"

Nikanj hesitated. "Do you still want to be male?"

Had I ever wanted to be male? I had just assumed I *was* male, and would have no choice in the matter. "The people wouldn't be as hard on you if I were male."

It said nothing.

"They haven't accepted me yet," I argued. "They could go on rejecting me until the family had to leave Lo—all because of me."

It continued to focus on me silently. There were times when I envied Humans their ability to shut off their sight by closing their eyes, shut off their understanding by some conscious act of denial that was beyond me.

I closed my throat, then drew and released a noisy, Human breath by mouth. It wasn't necessary now when I wasn't talking, but it filled time.

"I have too many feelings," I said. "I want to be your same-sex child, but I don't want to cause the family trouble."

"What do you want for yourself?"

Now I could not speak. I would hurt it, no matter what I said.

"Oeka, I must know what you want, what you feel, and for your own sake, you must tell me. It will be better for you if the people only see you through me until your metamorphosis is complete."

It was right. The thought of a lot of other people interfering with me now was frightening, terrifying. I hadn't known it would be, but it was. "I wouldn't want to give up being what I am," I said. "I . . . I want to be ooloi. I really want it. And I wish I didn't. How can I want to cause the family so much trouble?"

"You want to be what you are. That's healthy and right for you. What we do about it is our decision, our responsibility. Not yours."

I might not have believed this if a Human had said it. Humans said one thing with their bodies and another with their mouths and everyone had to spend time and energy figuring out what they really meant. And once you did understand them, the Humans got angry and acted as though you had stolen thoughts from their minds.

Nikanj, on the other hand, meant what it said. Its body and its mouth said the same things. It believed that I should want to be what I was. But . . .

"Ooan, could I change if I wanted to?"

It smoothed its head and body tentacles flat against its skin, accepting my curiosity with amusement. "Not now. But when you're mature, you'll be able to cause yourself to look male. You wouldn't be satisfied with a male sexual role, though, and you wouldn't be able to make a male contribution to reproduction."

I tried to move, tried to reach toward it, but I was still too weak. Talking was exhausting, most other movement was impossible. My head tentacles swept toward it.

It moved closer and let me touch it, let me examine its flesh so that I could begin to understand the difference between its flesh and my own. I would be the most extreme version of a construct—not just a mix of Human and Oankali characteristics, but able to use my body in ways that neither Human nor Oankali could. Synergy.

I studied a single cell of Nikanj's arm, comparing it with cells of my own. Apart from my Human admixture, the main difference seemed to be that certain genes of mine had activated and caused my metamorphosis. I wondered what might happen if these genes activated in Nikanj. It was mature. Were there other changes it might undergo?

"Stop," Nikanj said quietly. It signaled silently and spoke aloud. Its silent signal felt urgent. What was I doing?

"Look what you've done." Now it spoke only silently.

I reexamined the cell I had touched and realized that somehow I had located and activated the genes I had been curious about. These genes were trying to activate others of their kind in other cells, trying to cause Nikanj's body to begin the secretion of inappropriate hormones that would cause inappropriate growth.

What would grow?

"Nothing would grow in me," Nikanj said, and I realized it had perceived my curiosity. "The cell will die. You see?"

The cell died as I watched.

"I could have kept it alive," Nikanj said. "By a conscious act, I could have prevented my body from rejecting it. Without you, though, I could not have activated the dormant genes. My body rejects that kind of behavior as . . . deeply self-destructive."

"But it didn't seem wrong or dangerous," I said. "It just felt . . . out of place."

"Out of place, out of its time. In a Human, that could be enough to kill."

I couldn't think of anything to say. My curiosity burned away in fear.

"When you touch them, never withdraw without checking to see whether you've done harm."

"I won't touch them at all."

"You won't be able to resist them."

It didn't doubt or guess or suspect. It knew. "What shall I do?" I whispered aloud. It couldn't be wrong about such things. It had lived too long, seen too much.

"For now you can only be careful. After your second metamorphosis, you'll mate and you won't be quite so interested in investigating people who aren't your mates."

"But that could be two or three years from now."

"Less, I think. Your body feels as though it will develop quickly now. Until it has, you know how careful you'll have to be."

"I don't know whether I can do it. To be so careful of every touch . . ."

"Only deep touches." Touches that penetrated flesh with sensory tentacles or, later, sensory arms. Only Humans could be satisfied with less than deep touches.

"I don't see how I can be that careful," I said. "But I have to."

"Yes."

"Then I'll do it."

It touched my head tentacles with several of its own, agreeing. Then it examined the rest of my body closely, again checking for dangerous flaws, gathering information for the people. I relaxed and let it work, and it said instantly, "No!"

"What?" I asked. I really hadn't done anything this time. I knew I hadn't.

"Until you know yourself a great deal better, you can't afford to relax that way while you're in contact with another person. Not even with me. You're too competent, too well able to make tiny, potentially deadly changes in genes, in cells, in organs. What males, females, and even some ooloi must struggle to perceive, you can't fail to perceive on one level or another. What they must be taught to do, what they must strain to do, you can do almost without thought. You have all the sensitivity I could give you, and that's a great deal. And you have the latent abilities of your Human ancestors. In you, those abilities are no longer latent. That's why you were able to activate genes in me that even I can't reawaken. That's why the Humans are such treasure. They've given us regenerative abilities we had never been able to trade for before, even though we've found other species that had such abilities. I'm here because a Human was able to share such ability with me."

It meant Lilith, my birth mother. Every child in the family had heard that story. One of Nikanj's sensory arms had been all but severed from its body, but Lilith allowed it to link into her body and activate certain of her highly specialized genes. It used what it learned from these to encourage its own cells to grow and reattach the complex structures of the arm. It could not have done this without the triggering effect of Lilith's genetic help.

Lilith's ability had run in her family, although neither she nor her ancestors had been able to control it. It had either lain dormant in them or come to life in insane, haphazard fashion and caused the growth of useless new tissue. New tissue gone obscenely wrong.

Humans called this condition cancer. To them, it was a hated disease. To the Oankali, it was treasure. It was beauty beyond Human comprehension.

Nikanj might have died without Lilith's help. If it had lived, maimed, it could not have functioned as an ooloi. Its mates would have had to find another ooloi. They were young then. They might have survived the break and managed to accept someone else. But then we wouldn't exist—we, the children Nikanj had constructed gene by gene, chromosome by chromosome. A different ooloi would have chosen a different mix, would have manufactured a different series of genes to patch the created whole together and make it viable. All our construct uniqueness was the work of our ooloi parent. Until Nikanj's mistake with me, it had been known for the beauty of its children. It had shared all that it knew about mixing construct children, and it had probably saved other people from pain, trouble, and deadly error. It had been able to do all this because, thanks to Lilith, it had two functioning sensory arms.

"You could give Humans back their cancers," it said, rousing me from my thoughts. "Or you could affect them genetically. You could damage their immune systems, cause neurological disorders, glandular problems. . . . You could give them diseases they don't have names for. You could do all that with just a moment's inattention." It paused, wholly focused on me. "Humans will attract you and seduce you without realizing what they're doing. But they'll have no defense against you. And you're probably as sexually precocious as any Human-born construct."

"I don't have sensory arms," I said. "What can I do sexually until they grow?" I had nothing between my legs anymore. No one could see me naked and mistake me for male—or female. I was an ooloi subadult, and I would be one for years—or perhaps only for months if Nikanj was right about the speed of my maturing.

"You'll be able to take pleasure in new sensation," Nikanj said. "Especially in the complex, frightening, promising taste of Humans. I didn't enjoy them often when I was subadult because I could give little in return. I tasted Lilith when I could heal her or make necessary changes. But I couldn't give pleasure until I was adult. You may be able to give it now with sensory tentacles."

I drew my sensory tentacles tight against me, wondering. There had been that Human couple I met just before I fell asleep months ago. They were on their way to Mars by now. But what would they have tasted like? The female might have let me find out. But the male . . .? How did any ooloi seduce Human males? Males were suspicious, hostile, dangerous. I suddenly wanted very much to taste one. I had touched my Human father and other mated males before my change, but I wasn't as perceptive then. I wanted to touch an unmated stranger—perhaps a potential mate.

"Precocious," Nikanj said flatly. "Stick to constructs for a while. They aren't defenseless. But even they can be hurt. You can damage them so subtly that no one notices the problem until it become serious. Be more careful than you have ever been."

"Will they let me touch them?"

"I don't know. The people haven't decided yet."

I thought about what it might be like to spend all my subadulthood alone in the forest with only my parents and unmated siblings as company. A shudder went through my body and Nikanj touched its sensory tentacles to mine, concerned.

"I want them to accept me," I said unnecessarily.

"Yes. I can see that any exile could be hard on you, bad for you. But . . . perhaps Chkahichdahk exile would be least hard. My parents are still there. They would take you in."

Ship exile. "You said you wouldn't let them take me!"

"I won't. You'll stay with us for as long as you want to stay."

It meant as long as I was not more miserable alone with the family than it believed I would be if I were cut off from the family and sent to the ship. Humans tended to misunderstand ooloi when ooloi said things like that. Humans thought the ooloi were promising that they would do nothing until the Humans said they had changed their minds—told the ooloi with their mouths, in words. But the ooloi perceived all that a living being said—all words, all gestures, and a vast array of other internal and external bodily responses. Ooloi absorbed everything and acted according to whatever consensus they discovered. Thus ooloi treated individuals as they treated groups of beings. They sought a consensus. If there was none, it meant the being was confused, ignorant, frightened, or in some other way not yet able to see its own best interests. The ooloi gave information and perhaps calmness until they could perceive a consensus. Then they acted.

If, someday, Nikanj saw that I needed mates more than I needed my family, Nikanj would send me to the ship no matter what I said.

5

As the days passed, I grew stronger. I hoped, I wished, I pleaded with myself for Nikanj to have no reason ever to seek a consensus within me. If only the people would trust me, perceive that I was no more interested in using my new abilities to hurt other living things than I was in hurting myself.

Unfortunately I often did both. Every day, at least, Nikanj had to correct some harm that I had done to Lo—to the living platform on which I lay. Lo's natural color was gray-brown. Beneath me, it turned yellow. It developed swellings. Rough, diseased patches appeared on it. Its odor changed, became foul. Parts of it sloughed off. Sometimes it developed deep, open sores.

And all that I did to Lo, I also did to myself. But it was Lo that I felt guilty about. Lo was parent, sibling, home. It was the world I had been born into. As an ooloi, I would have to leave it when I mated. But woven into its genetic structure and my own was the unmistakable Lo kin group signature. I would have done anything to avoid giving Lo pain.

I got up from my platform as soon as I could and collected dead wood to sleep on.

Lo ate the wood. It was not intelligent enough to reason with—would not be for perhaps a hundred years. But it was self-aware. It knew what was part of it and what wasn't. I was part of it—one of its many parts. It would not have me with it, yet so distant from it, separated by so much dead matter. It preferred whatever pain I gave it to the unnatural itch of apparent rejection.

So I went on giving it pain until I was completely

recovered. By then, I knew as well as anyone else that I had to go. The people still wanted me to go to Chkahichdahk because the ship was a much older, more resistant organism. It was as able as most ooloi to protect and heal itself. Lo would be that resistant someday, but not for more than a century. And on the ship, I could be watched by many more mature ooloi.

Or I could go into exile here on Earth—before I did more harm to Lo or to someone in Lo. Those were my only choices. Through Lo, Nikanj had kept a check on the air of my room. It had seen that I did not change the microorganisms I came into contact with. And outside, insects avoided me as they avoided all Oankali and constructs. The people would permit me Earth exile, then.

With no real discussion, we prepared to go. My Human parents made packs for themselves, wrapping Lo cloth hammocks around prewar books, tools, extra clothing, and food from Lilith's garden—food grown in the soil of Earth, not from the substance of Lo. Both Lilith and Tino knew that their Oankali mates would provide for all their physical needs, yet they could not easily accept being totally dependent. This was a characteristic of adult Humans that the Oankali never understood. The Oankali simply accepted it as best they could and were pleased to see that we constructs understood.

I went to my Human mother and watched her assemble her pack. I did not touch her—had not touched any Human since my metamorphosis ended. As a reminder of my unstable condition, I had developed a rough, crusty growth on my right hand. I had deliberately reabsorbed it twice, but each night it grew again. I saw Lilith staring at it.

"It will heal," I told her. "Nikanj will help me with it."

"Does it hurt?" she asked.

"No. I just feels . . . *wrong*. Like a weight tied there where it shouldn't be."

"Why is it wrong?"

I looked at the growth. It was red and broken in places, crusty with distorted flesh and dried blood. It always seemed to be bleeding a little. "I caused it," I said, "but I don't understand how I did it. I fixed a couple of obvious problems, but the growth keeps coming back."

"How are you otherwise?"

"Well, I think. And once Ooan shows me how to take care of this growth, I'll remember."

I think my scent was beginning to bother. She stepped away, but looked at me as though she wanted to touch me. "How can I help you?" she asked.

"Make a pack for me."

She looked surprised. "What shall I put in it?"

I hesitated, afraid my answer would hurt her. But I wanted the pack, and only she could put it together as I wished. "I may not live here again," I said.

She blinked, looked at me with the pain I had hoped not to see.

"I want Human things," I said. "Small Human things that you and Tino would leave behind. And I want yams from your garden—and cassava and fruit and seed. Samples of all the seed or whatever is needed to grow your plants."

"Nikanj could give you cell samples."

"I know. . . . But will you?"

"Yes."

I hesitated again. "I would have to leave Lo anyway, you know. Even without this exile, I couldn't mate here where I'm related to almost everyone."

"I know. But it will be a while before you mate. And if you were leaving to do that, we'd see you again. If you have to go to the ship . . . we may not."

"I belong to this world," I said. "I intend to stay. But even so, I want something of yours and Tino's."

"All right."

We looked at one another as though we were already saying goodbye—as though only I were leaving. I did leave her then, to take a final walk around Lo to say goodbye to the people I had spent my life with. Lo was more than a town. It was a family group. All the Oankali males and females were related in some way. All constructs were related except the few males who drifted in from other towns. All the ooloi had become part of Lo when they mated here. And any Human who stayed long in a relationship with an Oankali family was related more closely than most Humans realized.

It was hard to say goodbye to such people, to know that I might not see them again.

It was hard not to dare to touch them, not to allow them to touch me. But I would certainly do to some of them what I kept doing to Lo—change them, damage them as I kept changing and damaging myself. And because I was ooloi and construct, theoretically I could survive more damage than they could. I was to let Nikanj know if I touched anyone.

Everywhere I went, ooloi watched me with a terrible mixture of suspicion and hope, fear and need. If I didn't learn control, how long would it be before they could have same-sex children? I could hurt them more than anyone else they knew. The sharp, attentive cones of their head tentacles followed me everywhere and weighed on me like logs. If there were anything I would be glad to be away from, it was their intense, sustained attention.

I went to our neighbor Tehkorahs, an ooloi whose Human mates were especially close to my Human parents. "Do you think I should go into exile on the ship?" I asked it.

"Yes." Its voice was softer than most soft ooloi voices. It preferred not to speak aloud at all. But signs were sterile without touch to supplement them, and even Tehkorahs would not touch me. That hurt because it was ooloi and safe from anything I was likely to do. "Yes," it repeated uncharacteristically.

"Why! You know me. I won't touch people. And I'll learn control."

"If you can."

". . . yes."

"There are resisters in the forest. If you're out there long enough, they'll find you."

"Most of them have emigrated."

"Many. Not most."

"I won't touch them."

"Of course you will."

I opened my mouth, then closed it in the face of Tehko-rahs's certainty. There was no reserve in it, no concealment. It was speaking what it believed was the truth.

After a time, it said, "How hungry are you?"

I didn't answer. It wasn't asking me how badly I wanted food, but when I'd last been touched. Just before I would have walked away, it held out all four arms. I hesitated, then stepped into its embrace.

It was not afraid of me. It was a forest fire of curiosity, longing, and fear, and I stood comforted and reassured while it examined me with every sensory tentacle that could reach me and both sensory arms.

We fed each other. My hunger was to be touched and its was to know everything firsthand and understand it all. Observing it, I understood that it was looking mainly for reassurance of its own. It wanted to see from an understanding of my body that I would gain control. It wanted me to be a clear success so that it would know it would be allowed to have its own same-sex children. Soon.

When it let me go, it was still uncomprehending. "You were very hungry," it said. "And that after only a day or two of being avoided." It knotted its head and body tentacles hard against its flesh. "You know something of what we can do, we ooloi, but I think you had no idea how much we need contact with other people. And you seem to need it more than we do. Spend more time with your paired sibling or you could become dangerous."

"I don't want to hurt Aaor."

"Nikanj will heal it until you learn to. If you learn to."

"I still don't want to hurt it."

"I don't think you can do it much harm. Not being able to go to anyone for comfort, though, can make you like the lightning—mindless and perhaps deadly."

I looked at it, my own head tentacles swept forward, focused. "What did you learn when you examined me? You weren't satisfied. Does that mean you think I can't learn control?"

"I don't know whether you can or not. I couldn't tell. Nikanj says you can, but that it will be hard. I don't know what it sees to draw that conclusion. Perhaps it only sees its first same-sex child."

"Do you still think I should go to the ship?"

"Yes. For your sake. For everyone's." It rubbed its right

hand, and I saw that it had developed a duplicate of my crusty, running tumor.

"I'm sorry," I said. "Do you know what I did wrong to cause that?"

"A combination of things. I don't understand all of them yet. You should take this to Nikanj, *now*."

"Will you be all right?"

"Yes."

I looked at it, missing it already—a smaller than average pale gray ooloi from the Jah kin group. It uncoiled one sensory arm and touched a sensory spot on my face. It could see the spots—as I could now. Their texture was slightly rougher than the skin around them. Tehkorahs made the contact a sharp, sweet shock of pleasure that washed over me like a sudden, cool rain. It ebbed slowly away. A goodbye.

6

It was raining when we left. Pouring. A brief waterfall from the sky. Lilith said rains like this happened to remind us that we lived in a rain forest. She had been born in a desert place called Los Angeles. She loved sudden, drenching rains.

There were eleven of us. My five parents, Aaor and me, Oni and Hozh, Ayodele and Yedik. These last four were my youngest siblings. They could have been left behind with some of our adult siblings, but they didn't want to stay. I didn't blame them. I wouldn't have wanted to part with our parents at that premetamorphosal state either. Even now, between metamorphoses, I needed them. And the family would have felt wrong without the younger siblings. My parents had only one pair per decade now. Ordinarily they would already have begun the next pair. But during the months of my methamorphosis, they had decided to wait until they could return to Lo—with or without me.

We headed first toward Lilith's garden to gather a few more fresh fruits and vegetables. I think she and Tino just wanted to see it again.

"It's time to rest this land anyway," Lilith said as we walked. She changed the location of her garden every few years, and let the forest reclaim the land. With these changes and with her habit of using fertilizer and river mud, she had used and reused the land beyond Lo for a century. She abandoned her gardens only when Lo grew too close to them.

But this garden had been destroyed.

It had not simply been raided. Raids happened occasionally. Resisters were afraid to raid Oankali towns—afraid the Oankali would begin to see them as real threats and transfer them permanently to the ship. But Lilith's gardens were clearly not Oankali. Resisters knew this and seemed to feel free to steal fruit or whole plants from them. Lilith never seemed to mind. She knew resisters thought of her—of any mated Human—as a traitor to Humanity, but she never seemed to hold it against them.

This time almost everything that had not been stolen had been destroyed. Melons had been stomped or smashed against the ground and trees. The line of papaya trees in the center of the garden had been broken down. Beans, peas, corn, yams, cassava, and pineapple plants had been uprooted and trampled. Nearby nut, fig, and breadfruit trees that were nearly a century old had been hacked and burned, though the fire had not destroyed most of them. Banana trees had been hacked down.

"Shit!" Lilith whispered. She stared at the destruction for a moment, then turned away and went to the edge of the garden clearing. There, she stood with her back to us, her body very straight. I thought Nikanj would go to her, offer comfort. Instead, it began gathering and trimming the least damaged cassava stalks. These could be replanted. Ahajas found an undamaged stalk of ripening bananas and Dichaan found and unearthed several yams, though the aboveground portions of the plants had been broken and scattered. Oankali and constructs could find edible roots and tubers easily by sitting on the ground and burrowing into it with the sensory tentacles of their legs. These short body tentacles could extend to several times their resting length.

It was Tino who went to Lilith. He walked around her, stood in front of her, and said, "What the hell? You know you'll have other gardens."

She nodded.

His voice softened. "I think we met in this one. Remember?"

She nodded again, and some of the rigidity went out of her posture. "How many kids ago was that?" she asked softly. The humor in her voice surprised me.

"More than I ever expected to have," he said. "Perhaps not enough, though."

And she laughed. She touched his hair, which he wore long and bound with a twist of grass into a long tail down his back. He touched hers—a soft black cloud around her face. They could touch each other's hair without difficulty because hair was essentially dead tissue. I had seen them touch that way before. It was the only way left to them.

"As much as I've loved my gardens," she said, "I never raised them just for myself or for us. I wanted the resisters to take what they needed."

Tino looked away, found himself staring at the downed papaya trees, and turned his head again. He had been a resister—had spent much of his life among people who believed that Humans who mated with Oankali were traitors, and that anything that could be done to harm them was good. He had left his people because he wanted children. The Mars colony did not exist then. Humans either came to the Oankali or lived childless lives. Lilith had told me once that Tino did not truly let go of his resister beliefs until the Mars colony was begun and his people could escape the Oankali. She had never been a resister. She had been placed with Nikanj when it was about my age. She did not understand at the time what that meant, and no one told her. Nikanj said she did not stop trying to break away until one of my brothers convinced the people to allow resisting Humans to settle on Mars.

In one way, the Mars colony freed both my Human parents

to find what pleasure they could find in their lives. In another it hadn't helped at all. They still feel guilt, feel as though they've deserted their people for aliens, as though they still suspect that they are the betrayers the resisters accused them of being. No Human could see the genetic conflict that made them such a volcanic species—so certain to destroy themselves. Thus, perhaps no Human completely believed it.

"I was always glad when they took whole plants," Lilith was saying, "Something to feed them now and something to transplant later."

"There are some peanuts here that survived," Tino said. "Do you want them?" He bent to pull a few of the small plants from the loose soil I had watched Lilith prepare for them.

"Leave them," she said. "I have some." She turned back to face the garden, watched the Oankali members of the family place what they had gathered on a blanket of overlapping banana leaves. Ahajas stopped Oni from eating a salvaged papaya and sent her to tell Lo what had happened and that the food was being left. Oni was Human-born, and so deceptively Human-looking that I had gone on thinking of her as female—though it would be more than ten years before she would have any sex at all.

"Wait," Lilith said.

Oni stopped near her, stood looking up at her.

Lilith walked over to Dichaan. "Will you go instead?" she asked him.

"The people who did this are gone, Lilith," he told her. "They've been gone for over a day. There's no sound of them, no fresh scent."

"I know. But . . . just for my peace of mind, will you go?"

"Yes." He turned and went. He would go only to the edge of Lo where some of the trees and smaller plants were not what they appeared to be. There he could signal Lo by touch, and Lo would pass the message on exactly to the next several people to open a wall or request food or in some other way come into direct contact with the Lo entity. Lo would pass the message on eight or ten times, then stop and store the message away. It couldn't forget any more than we could, but unless someone requested the memory, it would never bother anyone with it again. Humans could neither leave nor receive such messages. Even though Lilith and a few others had learned some of what they called Oankali codes, their fingers were not sensitive enough to receive messages or fine and penetrating enough to send them.

Oni watched Dichaan go, then returned to Hozh, who had finished her papaya. She stood close to him. He was no more male than she female, but it was easier to go on thinking of them the way I always had. The two of them slipped automatically into silent communication. Whenever they stood close together that way, Hozh's sensory tentacles immediately found Oni's sensory spots—she had very few sensory tentacles of her own—and established communication. Paired siblings.

Watching them made me lonely, and I looked around for Aaor. I caught it watching me. It had avoided me carefully since I go up from my metamorphosis. I had let it keep its distance in spite of what Tehkorahs had told me because Aaor obviously did not want contact. It did not seem to need me as much as I needed it. As I watched, it turned away from me and focused its attention on a large beetle.

Lilith and Tino joined the family group where it had settled to wait for Dichaan. "This is just the beginning," Lilith said to no one in particular. "We'll be meeting people like the ones who destroyed this garden. Sooner or later they'll spot us and come after us."

"You have your machete," Nikanj said.

It could not have gotten more attention if it had screamed. I focused on it to the exclusion of everything, felt pulled around to face it. Oankali did not suggest violence. Humans said violence was against Oankali beliefs. Actually it was against their flesh and bone, against every cell of them. Humans had evolved from hierarchical life, dominating, often killing other life. Oankali had evolved from acquisitive life, collecting and combining with other life. To kill was not simply wasteful to the Oankali. It was as unacceptable as slicing off their own healthy limbs. They fought only to save their lives and the lives of others. Even then, they fought to subdue, not to kill. If they were forced to kill, they resorted to biological weapons collected genetically on thousands of worlds. They could be utterly deadly, but they paid for it later. It cost them so dearly that they had no history at all of striking out in anger, frustration, jealousy, or any other emotion, no matter how keenly they felt it. When they killed even to save life, they died a little themselves.

I knew all this because it was as much a part of me as it was of them. Life was treasure. The only treasure. Nikanj was the one who had made it part of me. How could Nikanj be the one to suggest that anyone kill?

". . . Nika?" Ahajas whispered. She sounded the way I felt. Uncomprehending, disbelieving.

"They have to protect their lives and the family," Nikanj whispered. "If this were only a journey, we could guard them. We've guarded them before. But we're leaving home. We'll live cut off from others for . . . I don't know, perhaps a long time. There will be times when we aren't with them. And there are resisters who would kill them on sight."

"I don't want anyone to die because of me," I said. "I thought we were leaving to save life."

It focused on me, reached out a sensory arm, and drew me to its side. "We're leaving because the forest is the only place where we can live together as a family," it said. "No one will die because of you."

"But—"

"If they die, it will only be because they work very hard to make us kill them."

My siblings and other parents began to focus away from it. It had never said such things before. I stared at it and saw what they had missed. It was almost making itself sick with this talk. It would have been happier holding its hand in fire.

"There are easier ways to say these things," it admitted. "But some things shouldn't be said easily." It hesitated as Dichaan rejoined us. "We will leave the group only in pairs. We won't leave if it isn't necessary. You children—all of you—look out for one another. There will be new things everywhere to taste and understand. If your sibling is tasting something, you stand guard. If you see or smell Humans, hide. If you're caught in the open, run—even if it means being shot. If you're brought down, scream. Make as much noise as you can. Don't let them carry you away. Struggle. Make yourselves inconvenient to hold. If they seem intent on killing you, sting."

My siblings stood with head and body tentacles hanging undirected. The stings of males, females, and children were lethal.

"Once you're free, come to me or call me. I may be able to save whoever you've stung." It paused. "These are terrible things. If you stay with the group and stay alert, you won't have to do them."

They began to come alive again, focusing a few tentacles on it and understanding why it was speaking so bluntly to them. We were all hard to kill. Even our Human parents had been modified, made strong, more able to survive injury. The main danger was in being overwhelmed and abducted. Once we were taken away from the family, anything could be done to us. Perhaps Oni and Hozh would only be adopted for a time by Humans who were desperate for children. The rest of us looked too much like adult Humans—or adult Oankali. Those who looked female would be raped. Those who looked male would be killed. The Humans would have all the time they needed to beat, cut, and shoot us until we died. Unless we killed them.

Best never to get into such a position.

Nikanj focused on Lilith and Tino for several seconds, but said nothing. It knew them. It knew they would make every effort not to kill their own people—and it knew they would resent being told to take care. I had seen Oankali make the mistake of treating Humans like children. It was an easy mistake to make. Most Humans were more vulnerable than their own half-grown children. The Oankali tried to take care of them. The Humans reacted with anger, resentment, and withdrawal. Nikanj's way was better.

Nikanj focused for a moment on me. I still stood next to it, a coil of its right sensory arm around my neck. With its left sensory arm, it gestured to Aaor.

"No!" I whispered.

It ignored me. Aaor came toward us slowly, its whole body echoing my "no." It was afraid of me. Afraid of being hurt?

"Do you understand what you feel?" Nikanj asked when

Aaor was close enough for it to loop its left sensory arm around Aaor's neck.

Aaor shook its head Humanly. "No. I don't want to avoid Jodahs. I don't know why I do it."

"I understand," Nikanj said. "But I don't know whether I can help you. This is something new."

That caught Aaor's attention. Anything new was of interest.

"Think, Eka. When has an ooloi ever had a paired sibling?"

I almost missed seeing Aaor's surprise, I was so involved with my own. Of course ooloi did not have paired siblings in the usual sense. In Oankali families, females had three children, one right after the other. Once became male, one female, and one ooloi. Their own inclinations decided which became which. The male and the female metamorphosed and found an unrelated ooloi to mate with. The ooloi still had its subadult phase to mature through. It was still called a child—the only child who knew its sex. And it was alone until it neared its second metamorphosis and found mates. I should have had only my parents around me now. But where would that leave Aaor?

"Stop running away from one another," Nikanj said. "Find out what's comfortable for you. Do what your bodies tell you is right. This is a new relationship. You'll be finding the way for others as well as for yourselves."

"If it touches me, you'll have to heal it," I said.

"I know." It flattened its head and body tentacles in something other than amusement. "Or at least, I think I know. This is new to me, too. Aaor, come to me every day for examination and healing. Come even if you believe nothing is wrong. Jodahs can make very subtle, important changes. Come immediately if you feel pain or if you notice anything wrong."

"Ooan, help me understand it," Aaor said. "Let me reach it through you."

"Shall I?" Nikanj asked me silently.

"Yes," I answered in the same way.

It wove us into seamless neurosensory union.

And it was as though Aaor and I were touching again with

nothing between us. I savored Aaor's unique taste. It was like part of me, long numb, long out of touch, yet so incredibly welcome back that I could only submerge myself in it.

Aaor said nothing to me. It only wanted to know me again—know me as an ooloi. It wanted to understand as deeply as it could the changes that had taken place in me. And I came to understand from it without words how lonely it had been, how much it wanted me back. It was totally unnatural for paired siblings to be near one another, and yet avoid touching.

Aaor asked wordlessly for release, and Nikanj released us both. For a second I was aware only of frog and insect sounds, the rain dropping from the trees, the sun breaking through the clouds. No one in the family moved or spoke. I hadn't realized they were all focused on us. I started to look around, then Aaor stepped up to me and touched me. I reached for it with every sensory tentacle I had, and its own more numerous tentacles strained toward me. This was normal. This was what paired siblings were supposed to be able to do whenever they wanted to.

For a moment relief overwhelmed me again. My underarms itched just about where my sensory arms would grow someday. If I had already had the arms, I couldn't have kept them off Aaor.

"It's about time," Ahajas said. "You two look after each other."

"Let's go." Tino said.

We followed him out of the ruined garden, moving single file through the forest. He knew of a place that sounded as though it would make a good campsite—plenty of space, far from other settlements of any kind. Everyone's fear was that I would make changes in the plant and animal life. These changes could spread like diseases—could actually be diseases. The adults in the family did not know whether they could detect and disarm every change. Sooner or later other people would have to deal with some of them. The idea was for us to isolate ourselves, to minimize and localize any cleaning up that would have to be done later. The place Tino had found years before was an island—a big island with a new growth of cecropia trees at one end and a mix of old growth over the rest. It was moving slowly downstream the way river islands did—mud taken from one end was deposited downstream at the other. All the adults remembered a place like this created aboard the ship and used to train Humans to live in the forest. None of them had liked it. Now they were headed for the real thing—because of me.

Sometime during the afternoon, Aaor's underarms began to itch and hurt. By the time it went to Nikanj for healing, swellings had begun to appear. I had apparently caused Aaor's unsexed, immature body to try to grow sensory arms. Instead, it was growing potentially dangerous tumors.

"I'm sorry," I said when Nikanj had finished with it.

"Just figure out what you did wrong," it said unhappily. "Find out how to avoid doing it again."

That was the problem. I hadn't been aware of doing anything to Aaor. If I had felt myself doing it, I would have stopped myself. I thought I had been careful. I was like a blind Human, trampling what I could not see. But a blind Human's eyesight could be restored. What I was missing was something I had never had—or at least, something I had never discovered.

"Learn as quickly as you can so we can go home," Aaor said.

I focused on the trail ahead—on scenting or hearing strangers. I couldn't think of anything to say.

7

The island should have been three days' walk upriver. We thought we might make it in five days, since we had to circle around Pascual, an unusually hostile riverine resister settlement. People from Pascual were probably the ones who had destroyed Lilith's garden. Now we would go far out of our way to avoid repaying them. Too many of them might not survive contact with me.

We never thought we were in danger from Pascual because its people knew better than most resisters what happened to anyone who attacked us. Their village, already shrunken by emigration, would be gassed, and the attackers hunted out by scent. They would be found and exiled to the ship. There, if they had killed, they would be kept either unconscious or drugged to pleasure and contentment. They would never be allowed to awaken completely. They would be used as teaching aids, subjects for biological experiments, or reservoirs of Human genetic material. The people of Pascual knew this, and thus committed only what Lilith called property crimes. They stole, they burned, they vandalized. They had not come as close to Lo as the garden before. They had confined their attentions to travelers.

We did not understand how extreme their behavior had become until we met some of them on our first night away from Lo. We stopped walking at dusk, cooked and ate some of the food Lilith and Tino had brought, and hung our hammocks between trees. We didn't bother erecting a shelter, since the adults agreed that it wasn't going to rain.

Only Nikanj cleared a patch of ground and spread its hammock on the bare earth. Because of the connections it had to make with sensory arms and tentacles, it was not comfortable sharing a hanging hammock with anyone. It wanted us to feel free to come to it with whatever wounds, aches, or pains we had developed. It gestured to me first, though I had not intended to go to it at all.

"Come every night until you learn to control your abilities," it told me. "Observe what I do with you. Don't drowse."

"All right."

It could not heal without giving pleasure. People tended simply to relax and enjoy themselves with it. Instead, this time I observed, as it wished, saw it investigate me almost cell by cell, correcting the flaws it found—flaws I had not noticed. It was as though I had gained an understanding of the complexity of the outside world and lost even my child's understanding of my inner self. I used to notice quickly when something was wrong. Now my worst problem was uncontrolled, unnecessary cell division. Cancers. They began and grew very quickly—many, many times faster than they could have in a Human. I was supposed to be able to control and use them in myself and in others. Instead, I couldn't even spot my own when they began. And they began with absolutely no conscious encouragement from me.

"Do you see?" Nikanj asked.

"Yes. But I didn't before you showed me."

"I've left one."

I hunted for it and after some time found it growing in my throat, where it would surely kill me if it were allowed to continue. I did not readjust the genetic message of the cells and deactivate the part that was in error. That was what Nikanj had done to the others, but I did not trust my ability to follow its example. I might accidentally reprogram other genes. Instead, I destroyed the few malignant cells.

Then I put my head against Nikanj, let my head tentacles link with its own. I spoke to It silently.

"I'm not learning. I don't know what to do."

"Wait."

"I don't want to keep being dangerous, hurting Aaor, being afraid of myself."

"Give yourself time. You're a new kind of being. There's never been anyone like you before. But there's no flaw in you. You just need time to find out more about yourself."

Its certainty fed me. I rested against it for a while, enjoying the easy, safe contact—my only one now. It nudged me after a while, and I went back to my hammock. Lilith was lying with it when the resisters made themselves known to us.

First they screamed. A female Human screamed again and again, first cursing someone, then begging, then making hoarse, wordless noises. There were also male voices—at least three of them shouting, laughing, cursing.

"Real and not real," Dichaan said when the screaming began.

"What is it?" Oni demanded.

"The female is being hurt now," Nikanj said. "And she's

afraid. But something is wrong about this. Her first screams were false. She was not afraid then."

"If she's being hurt now, that's enough!" Tino said. He was on his feet, staring at Nikanj, his posture all urgency and anger.

"Stay here," Nikanj said. It stood up and grasped. Tino with all four arms. "Protect the children." It shook him once for emphasis, then ran into the forest. Ahajas and Dichaan followed. Oankali were much less likely to be killed even if the shouting Humans made a serious effort.

Our Human parents gathered us together and drew us into thicker forest, where we could see and resisters could not. Lilith and Tino had been modified so that, like us, they could see by infrared light—by heat. For us all, the living forest was full of light.

And the air was full of scents. Humans coming. Not close yet, but coming. Several of them. Eight, nine of them. Males.

Lilith and Tino freed their machetes and backed us farther into the forest.

"Do nothing unless they come after us," Lilith said. "If they do come, run. If they catch you, kill."

She sounded like Nikanj. But from Nikanj, the words had sounded like cries of pain. From her they were cries of fear. She feared for us. I could not remember ever seeing her afraid for herself. Years before, concealed high in a tree, I watched her fight off three male resisters who wanted to rape her. She hadn't been afraid once she saw that they weren't aware of me. She even managed not to hurt them much. They ran away, believing she was a construct.

The resisters who were hunting us now would not run from us, and both Lilith and Tino knew it. They watched as the resisters discovered the camp, tried to tear down the hammocks, tried to burn them. But Lo cloth would not burn, and no normal Human could cut or tear it.

They stole Lilith's and Tino's packs, hacked down the smaller trees we'd tied our hammocks to, ground exposed food into the dirt, and set fire to the trees. They looked for us in the light of the fire, but they were afraid to venture too far into the forest, afraid to scatter too much yet, afraid to seem to huddle together. Perhaps they knew what would happen to them if they found us. Perhaps destroying our belongings would be enough—though they did have guns.

They had not gotten the pack Lilith had made for me. While she and Tino were gathering my siblings, I had grabbed my pack and run with it. I meant to help if there was fighting. I wouldn't run with my younger siblings. But I also meant to keep what might be my last bit of Lo. No one would steal it.

The fire spread slowly, and the resisters had to leave our campsite. They went back into the trees the way they'd come. We stayed where we were, knowing that the river was nearby. We would run for that if we had to.

But the fire did not spread far. It singed a few standing trees and consumed the few that had been cut. My Oankali parents came back wounded and already healing, carrying a living burden.

The danger seemed past. We smelled nothing except smoke, heard nothing except the crackling of the dying fire and natural sounds. We went out to meet the three Oankali.

As I stepped into the open, into the firelight, I was in front of my Human parents and my siblings. That was good because as an ooloi, I was theoretically more able to survive gunshot wounds than any of them. Now I would find out whether that was true.

I was shot three times. The first two shots came from slightly different directions at almost the same instant. To me, they were a single blow, slamming into me, spinning me all the way around. The first two shots hit me in the left shoulder and left lower back. The third hit me in the chest as I spun. It knocked me down.

I rolled and came to my feet just in time to see my Oankali parents go after the resisters. The resisters stopped firing abruptly and scattered. I could hear them—nine males fleeing in nine directions, knowing that three Oankali could not catch them all.

Nikanj and Dichaan each caught one of them. Ahajas, larger, and apparently unwounded, caught two. Each of those caught had fired their rifles. They smelled of the powder they used to shoot. They also smelled terrified. They were being held by the people they feared most. They struggled desperately. One of them wept and cursed and stank more than the others. This was one of those held by Ahajas.

Silently Nikanj took that one from Ahajas and passed her the one he'd caught. The male who had been given to Nikanj began to scream. Blood spilled out of his nose, though no one had touched his face.

Nikanj touched his neck with a sensory tentacle and injected calmness.

The male shouted, "No, no, no, no." But the last "no" was a whimper. He drew a deep breath, choked on his own blood, and coughed several times. After a while, he was quiet and calm. Nikanj let him wipe his nose on the cloth of his shirt at the shoulder. Nikanj touched his neck once more and the male smiled. Nikanj took him to a large tree and made him sit down against it.

"Stay there," Nikanj said.

The male looked at it, smiled, and nodded. Even in the leaping fire shadows, he looked peaceful, relaxed.

"Run!" one of his companions shouted to him.

The male put his head back against the tree and closed his eyes. He wasn't unconscious. He was just too comfortable, too relaxed to worry about anything.

Nikanj went to each prisoner and gave comfort and calmness. When there was no need for anyone to hold them, it came to examine me.

I had sat down against a tree myself, glad for the support it gave. I was having a lot of pain, but I had already expelled the two bullets that hadn't gone all the way through me and I had stopped the bleeding. By the time Nikanj reached me, I was slowly, carefully encouraging my body to repair itself. I had never been injured this badly before, but my body seemed to be handling it. Here was its chance to grow tissue quickly to fulfill need rather than to cause trouble.

"Good," Nikanj said. "You don't need me right now." It stood back from me. "Is anyone else hurt?"

No one was except the Human woman my Oankali parents had rescued. I could have used some help with my pain, but Nikanj had perceived that and ignored it. It wanted to see what I could do on my own.

Nikanj went to the bloody, unconscious Human woman and lay down beside her.

The woman had been beaten about the face, and from her scent, two males had recently had sex with her. I was too involved with my own healing to detect anything else.

Aaor came to sit next to me. It did not touch me, but I was glad it was there. My other siblings and Dichaan kept watch for resisters.

Ahajas spoke to one of the captives—the one who had been so frightened.

"Why did you attack us?" she asked, sitting down in front of him.

The male stared at her, seemed to examine her very carefully with his eyes. Finally he reached out and touched a sensory tentacle on her arm. Ahajas allowed this. He had not been able to hurt her when she captured him. Now that he was drugged, he was not likely even to try.

After a time, he let the tentacle go as though he did not like it. Humans compared ooloi sensory arms to the appendages of extinct animals—elephant trunks. They compared sensory tentacles to large worms or snakes—like the slender, venomous vine snakes of the forest, perhaps, though sensory tentacles could be much more dangerous, more sensitive, and more flexible than vine snakes, and they were not independent at all.

"You were coming to raid us," the male said. "One of our hunters saw you and warned us."

"We would not have attacked you," Ahajas protested. "We've never done such a thing."

"Yes. We were warned. A gang of Oankali and half-Oankali coming to take revenge for the garden."

"Did you destroy the garden?"

"Some of us did. Not me." That was true. People drugged the way he was did not bother to lie. It didn't occur to them. "We thought your animals shouldn't have real Human food."

"Animals . . .?"

"Those!" He waved a hand toward Lilith and Tino.

Ahajas had known. She had simply wanted to know whether he would say it. He looked with interest at Oni and Ayodele. Since my metamorphosis, they were the most

Human-looking members of the family. Children born of Lilith-the-animal.

Aaor and I got up in unison and moved to the other side of the tree we had been leaning against. I was still in pain and I had to watch my healing flesh closely to see that it did not go wrong. It could go very wrong if I kept paying attention to the captive and his offensive nonsense.

8

Sometime later the rescued female made a small, wordless noise, and without thinking, I left Aaor and went over to where she lay on the ground alongside Nikanj. I stood, looking down at them. The female was completely unconscious now, and Nikanj was busy healing her. I almost lay down on her other side, but Lilith called my name, and I stopped. I stood where I was, confused, not knowing why I stood there, but not wanting to leave.

Some of Nikanj's body tentacles lifted toward me. Gradually it detached itself from the female and focused on me. It sat up and extended its sensory tentacles toward me. "Let me see what you've done for yourself," it said.

I stepped around the female, who was still unconscious, and let Nikanj examine me.

"Good," it said after a moment. "Flawless." It was clearly surprised.

"Let me touch her," I said.

"I haven't finished with her." Nikanj smoothed its tentacles flat to its body. "There's work for you to do if you want it."

I did. That was exactly what I wanted. Yet I knew I

shouldn't have been allowed to touch her. I hesitated, focusing sharply on Nikanj.

"I'll have to check her afterward," it said. "You'll find you won't like that. But for the sake of her health, I have to do it. Now go ahead. Help her."

I lay down alongside the female. I don't think I could have refused Nikanj's offer. The pull of the female, injured, alone, and in no way related to me was overwhelming.

I was too young to give her pleasure. That disturbed me, but there was nothing I could do about it. When I had something to work with besides sensory tentacles, I could give pleasure. Now, at least, I could give relief from pain.

The female's face, head, breasts, and abdomen were bruised from blows and would be painful if I woke her. I could find no other injuries. Nikanj had not left me anything serious. I went to work on the bruises.

I held the female close to me and sank as many head and body tentacles into her as I could, but I couldn't get over the feeling that I was somehow not close enough to her, not linked deeply enough into her nervous system, that there was something missing.

Of course there was—and there would be until my second metamorphosis. I understood the feeling, but I couldn't make it go away. I had to be especially careful not to hold her too tightly, not to interfere with her breathing.

The beauty of her flesh was my reward. A foreign Human as incredibly complex as any Human, as full of the Human Conflict—dangerous and frightening and intriguing—as any Human. She was like the fire—desirable and dangerous, beautiful and lethal. Humans never understood why Oankali found them so interesting.

I took my time finishing with the woman. No one hurried me. It was a real effort for me to move aside and let Nikanj check her. I didn't want it to touch her. I didn't want to share her with it. I had never felt that way before.

I stood with my arms tightly folded and my attention on the now silent male prisoners. I think Nikanj worked quickly for my sake. After a very short time, it stood up and said, "I think she's inspired you to get control of your abilities. Stay with her until she wakes. Don't call me unless she seems likely to hurt herself or to run away."

"Was she working with them?" I asked, gesturing with head tentacles toward the males.

"She was a captive of their friends. I don't think she knew what was going to happen to her." It hesitated. "They've learned that false screams won't lure us away. Her first screams sounded false because she wasn't frightened yet. Probably they told her to scream. Then they began to beat her."

The female moaned. Nikanj turned and went to help Lilith and Tino, who had begun to pull undamaged Lo cloth hammocks and pieces of clothing from the ashes. The fire had not gone completely out, but it was burning down rather than spreading. We didn't seem to be in any danger. I went over and borrowed one of Tino's salvaged shirts. He rarely wore them himself, but now, for a while, they would conceal some of my new body tentacles. The more familiar I seemed to the female, the less likely she would be to panic. I was gray-brown now. She would know I was a construct. But not such a startling construct.

She awoke, sat up abruptly, looked around in near panic.

"You're safe," I said to her. "You're not hurt and no one here will hurt you."

She drew back from me, scrambled away, then froze when she saw my parents and siblings.

"You're safe," I repeated. "The people who hurt you are not here."

That seemed to catch her attention. After all, Humans had injured her, not Oankali. She looked around more carefully, jumped when she saw the Human males sitting nearby.

"They can't hurt you," I said. "Even if they've hurt you before, they can't now."

She stared at me, watched my mouth as I spoke.

"What's your name?" I asked.

She didn't answer.

I sighed, watched her for a while without speaking. She understood me. It was as though it had suddenly occurred to her to pretend not to understand. I had spoken to her in English and her responses had shown me she understood. She had very black hair that reminded me of Tino's. But hers was loose and uncombed, hanging lank around her narrow, angular brown face. She had not gotten enough to eat for many days. Her body had told me that clearly. But for most of her life, she had been comfortably well nourished. Her body was small, quick, harder muscled than most Human female bodies. Not only had it done hard work, it was probably comfortable doing hard work. It liked to move quickly and eat frequently. It was hungry now.

I went to the tree I had leaned against while I was healing. I'd left my pack there. I found it and brought it back to where the female sat on her knees, watching me. From it I gave her two bananas and a handful of shelled nuts. She didn't even make a pretense of not wanting them.

I watched her eat and wondered what it would be like to be in contact with her while she ate. How did the food taste and feel to her?

"Why are you staring at me?" she demanded. Fast, choppy English like the firing of guns.

"My name is Jodahs," I offered. "What's yours?"

"Marina Rivas. I want to go to Mars."

I looked away from her, suddenly weary. One more small, thin-boned female to be sacrificed to Human stubbornness. I recalled from examining her that she had never had a child. That was good because her narrow hips were not suitable to bearing children. If her fertility were restored and nothing else changed, she would surely die trying to give birth to her first child. She could be changed, redesigned. I wouldn't trust myself to do such substantial work, but she must have it done.

"Were you on your way to Lo?" I asked.

"Yes. The ships leave from there, don't they?"

"Yes."

"You're from there?"

"Yes."

"Can I go back with you?"

"We'll see that you get there. Did your people beat you because you wanted to go to Mars?" Such things had happened. Some resisters killed their "deserters," as they called those who wanted to emigrate.

"Do they look like my people!" the female demanded harshly. "I was on my way to Lo. When I passed their village, they took me from my canoe and raped me and called me stupid names and made me stay in their pigsty village. The men kept me shut up in an animal pen and they raped me. The women spat on me and put dirt or shit in my food because the men raped me."

There was so much hatred and anger in her face and voice that I drew back. "I know Humans do such things," I said. "I understand the biological reasons why they do them, but . . . I've never seen them done."

"Good. Why should you? Do you have anything else to eat?"

I gave her what I had. She needed it.

"Where did you live before the war?" I asked. She was brown and narrow-eyed and her English was accented in a way I had not heard before. I had siblings who looked a little like her—children of Lilith's first postwar mate who had come from China. He had been killed by people like the resisters who had shot me.

Aaor came up and stood close so that it could link with me. It was intensely curious about the female. The female stared at it with equal curiosity, but spoke to me.

"I'm from Manila." Her voice had gone harsh again, as though the words hurt her. "What can that mean to you?"

"The Philippines?" I asked.

She looked surprised. "What do you know about my country?"

I thought for a moment, remembering. "That it was made up of islands, warm and green—some of them like this, I think." I gestured toward the forest. "That it could have fed everyone easily, but didn't because some Humans took more than they needed. That it took no part in the last war, but it died anyway."

"Everything died," the female said bitterly. "But how do you know even that much? Have you known another Filipina?"

"No, but a few people from the Philippines have come through Lo. Some of my adult siblings told me about them."

"Do you know any names?"

"No."

She sighed. "Maybe I'll see them on Mars. Who is this?" She looked at Aaor.

"My closest sibling, Aaor."

She stared at us both and shook her head. "I could almost stay," she said. "It doesn't seem as bad as it once did—the Oankali, the idea of . . . different children. . . ."

"You should stay," I told her. "Mars may not be green during your lifetime. You won't be able to go outside the shelters unprotected. Mars is cold and dry."

"Mars is Human. Now."

I said nothing.

"I'm tired," she said after a while. "Does anyone care if I sleep?"

I cleared some ground for her and spread a piece of Lo cloth on it.

"You two are children, aren't you?" she asked Aaor.

"Yes," Aaor answered.

"So? Will you be a woman someday?"

"I don't know."

"I don't understand that. It bothers me more than most things about you people. Come and lie here. I know your kind like to touch everyone. If you want to, you can touch me."

I took that to include me, too, and pressed two pieces of Lo cloth edge-to-edge so that we could have a wider sleeping mat.

"I didn't invite you," she said to me. "You look too much like a man."

"I'm not male," I said.

"I don't care. You look male."

"Let it sleep here," Aaor said. "The insects won't come near you with one of us on either side."

She stared at me. "Really? You scare the bugs away?"

"Our scent repels them."

She sniffed, trying to smell us. In fact, she did smell me—unconsciously. I smelled ooloi. Interesting, perhaps attractive to an unmated person.

"All right," she said. "I've never yet caught an Oankali or

a construct in a lie. Come and sleep here. You're honestly not male?"

"I'm honestly not male."

"Come keep the bugs off, then."

We kept the bugs off and kept her warm and investigated her thoroughly, though we were careful not to touch her in any way that would alarm her. I thought hands would alarm her, so I only touched her with my longest sensory tentacles. This startled her at first, but once she realized she wasn't being hurt, she put up with our curiosity. She never knew that I helped her fall asleep.

And I never knew how it happened that during the night she moved completely out of contact with Aaor and against me so that I could reach her with most of my head and body tentacles.

I discovered that I had slightly altered the structure of her pelvis during the night. I hadn't intended to try such a thing. It wouldn't have occurred to me to try it. Yet it was done. The female could bear children now.

I detached myself from her and sat up, missing the feel of her at once. It was dawn and my parents were already up. Nikanj and Ahajas were cooking something in a suspended pot made of layers of Lo cloth. Lilith was looking through the ashes of the night's fire. Tino and Dichaan where out of sight, but I could hear and smell them nearby. Last night, once my attention was on Marina Rivas, I had almost stopped sensing them. I had not known then how completely she had absorbed my attention.

Nikanj left the belly of cloth and its weight of cooking food—nut porridge. The Humans would not want it until they had tasted it. Then they would not be able to get enough of it. It might actually contain some nuts from wild trees. Lilith or Tino might have gathered some. More likely, though, all the nuts had been synthesized by Nikanj and Ahajas from the substance of Ahajas's body. We could eat a great many things that Humans could not or would not touch. Then we could use what we'd eaten to create something more palatable for Humans. My Human parents shrugged and said this was no more than Lo did every day—which was true. But resisters were always repelled if they knew. So we didn't tell them unless they asked directly.

Nikanj came over to me and checked me carefully.

"You're all right," it said. "You're doing fine. The female is good for you."

"She's going to Mars."

"I heard."

"I wish I could keep her here."

"She's very strong. I think she'll survive Mars."

"I changed her a little. I didn't mean to, but—"

"I know. I'm going to check her very thoroughly just before we leave her, but from what I've seen in you, you did a good job. I wish she were not so old. If she were younger, I would help you persuade her to stay."

She was as old as my Human mother. She might live a century more here on Earth where there was plenty to eat and drink and breathe, where there were Oankali to repair her injuries. I could live five times that long—unless I mated with someone like Marina. Then I would live only as long as I could keep her alive.

"If she were younger, I would persuade her myself," I said.

Nikanj coiled a sensory arm around my neck briefly, then went to give the male captives their morning drugging. Best to do that before they woke.

Marina was already awake and looking at me. "There's food," I said. "It doesn't look very interesting, but it tastes good."

She extended a hand. I took it and pulled her to her feet. Four bowls from Lo had been salvaged from the fire. We took two of them down to the river, washed them, washed ourselves, and swam a little. This was my first experience with breathing underwater. I slipped into it so naturally and comfortably that I hardly noticed that I was doing something new.

I heard Marina's voice calling me and I realized I'd drifted some distance downstream. I turned and swam back to her. She had not taken off her clothing—short pants that had once been longer and a ragged shirt much too big for her.

I had taken off mine. She had stared at me then. Now she

stared again. No visible genitals. In fact, no reproductive organs at all.

"I don't understand," she said as I walked out of the water. "You must not care what I see or you wouldn't have undressed. I don't understand how you can have . . . nothing."

"I'm not an adult."

"But . . ."

I put my shorts and Tino's shirt back on.

"Why do you wear clothes?"

"For Humans. Don't you feel more comfortable now?"

She laughed. I hadn't heard her laugh before. It was a harsh, sharp shout of joy. "I feel more comfortable!" she said. "But take your clothes off if you want to. What difference does it make?"

My underarms itched painfully. Because there was nothing else for me to do, I took her hand, picked up the bowls, and headed back toward camp and breakfast.

She walked close to me and didn't shrink away from my sensory tentacles.

"I don't think you have to worry about becoming a woman," she said.

"No."

"You're almost a man now."

I stepped in front of her and stopped. She stopped obligingly and watched me, waiting.

"I'm not male. I never will be. I'm ooloi."

She almost leaped away from me. I saw the shadow of abrupt movement, not quite completed in her muscles. "How *can* you be?" she demanded. "You have two arms, not four."

"So far," I said.

She stared at my arms. "You . . . You're truly ooloi?"

"Yes."

She shook her head. "No wonder I had dreams about you last night."

"Oh? Did you like them?"

"Of course I liked them. I liked you. And I shouldn't have. You look too male. Nothing male should have been appealing to me last night—after what those bastards did to me.

Nothing male should be appealing to me for a long, long time."

"You're healed."

"Yes. You did that?"

"Part of it."

"There's more to healing than just closing wounds."

"You're healed."

She looked at me for a time, then looked away at the trees. "I must be," she said.

"More than healed."

She put her head to one side. "What?"

"When your fertility is restored, you'll be able to have children without trouble. You couldn't have done that before."

Her expression changed to one of remembered pain. "My mother died when I was born. People said she should have had a cesarean, you know?"

"Yes."

"She didn't. I don't know why."

"You need to be changed a little genetically so that your daughters will be able to give birth safely."

"Can you do that?"

"I won't have time. We'll be escorting you and the male prisoners to Lo today. I'm not experienced enough to do that kind of work anyway."

"Who'll do it?"

"An adult ooloi."

"No!"

"Yes," I said, taking her by the arms. "Yes. You can't condemn your daughters to die the way your mother did. Why do adult ooloi frighten you?"

"They don't frighten me. My response to them frightens me. I feel . . . as though I'm not in control of myself anymore. I feel drugged—as though they could make me do anything."

"You won't be their prisoner. And you won't be dealing with unmated ooloi. The ooloi who changes you won't want anything from you."

"I would rather have you do it—or someone like you."

"I'm a construct ooloi. The first one. There is no one else like me."

She looked at me for a little longer, then pulled me closer to her and drew a long, weary breath. "You're beautiful, you know? You shouldn't be, but you are. You remind me of a man I knew once." She sighed again. "Damn."

9

Back to Lo.

We gave the drugged prisoners to the people of Lo. A house would be grown for them from the substance of Lo and they would not be let out of it until a shuttle came for them. Then they would be transferred to the ship. They understood what was to happen to them, and even drugged, they asked to be spared, to be released. The one who had called Lilith and Tino animals began to cry. Nikanj drugged him a little more and he seemed to forget why he had been upset. That would be his life now. Once he was aboard the ship, one ooloi would drug him regularly. He would come to look forward to it—and he would not care what else was done with him.

I took Marina to the guest area before Nikanj was free to check her. I didn't want to watch it examine her. I got the impression that it was perfectly willing not to touch her. There must have been too much of my scent on her to make her seem still alone and unrelated.

She kissed me before I left her. I think it was an experiment for her. For me it was an enjoyment. It let me touch her a little more, sink filaments of sensory tentacles into her along the lengths of our bodies. She liked that. She shouldn't have. I was supposed to be too young to give pleasure. She liked it anyway.

"I'll send someone to change you genetically," I said after a time. "Don't be afraid. Let your children have the same chance you have."

"All right."

I held her a little longer, then left her. I asked Tehkorahs to check her and make the necessary adjustment.

It stood with Wray Ordway, its male Human mate, and Wray smiled and gave me a look of understanding and amusement. He was one of the few people in Lo to speak for me when the exile decision was being made. "A child is a child," he said through Tehkorahs. "The more you treat it like a freak, the more it will behave like one." I think people like him eased things for me. They made Earth exile feel less objectionable to the truly frightened people who wanted me safely shut away on the ship.

"You know I'll take care of the female," Tehkorahs said. "She seemed to like you very much."

I felt my head and body tentacles flatten to my skin in remembered pleasure. "Very much."

Wray laughed. "I told you it would be sexually precocious—just like the construct males and females."

Tehkorahs looped a sensory tentacle around his neck. "I'm not surprised. Every gene trade brings change. Jodahs, let me check you. The female won't want to see me for a while. You've left too much of yourself with her."

I stepped close to it and it released Wray and examined me quickly, thoroughly. I felt its surprise before it let me go. "You're much more in control now," it said. "I can't find anything wrong with you. And if your memories of the female are accurate—"

"Of course they are!"

"Then I probably won't find anything wrong with her either. Except for the genetic problem."

"She'll cooperate when you're ready to correct that."

"Good. You look like her, you know."

"What?"

"Your body has been striving to please her. You're more brown now—less gray. Your face is changed subtly."

"You look like a male version of her," Wray said. "She probably thought you were very handsome."

"She said so," I admitted amid Wray's laughter. "I didn't know I was changing."

"All ooloi change a little when they mate," Tehkorahs said. "Our scents change. We fit ourselves into our mates' kin group. You may fit in better than most of us—just as your descendants will fit more easily when they find a new species for the gene trade."

If I ever had descendants.

The next day, the family gathered new supplies and left Lo for the second time. I had had one more night to sleep in the family house. I slept with Aaor the way I always used to before my metamorphosis. I think I made it as lonely as I felt myself now that Marina was gone. And that night I gave Aaor, Lo, and myself large, foul-smelling sores.

II

Exile

1

We didn't stop at the island we had intended to live on. It was too close to Pascual. Living there would have made us targets for more Human fear and frustration. We followed the river west, then south, traveling when we wanted to, resting when we were tired—drifting, really. I was restless, and drifting suited me. The others simply seemed not content with any likely campsite we found. I suspected that they wouldn't be content again until they returned to Lo to stay.

We edged around Human habitations very carefully. Humans who saw us either stared from a distance or followed us until we left their territory. None approached us.

Twelve days from Lo, we were still drifting. The river was long with many tributaries, many curves and twists. It was good to walk along the shaded forest floor, following the sound and smell of it, and thinking about nothing at all. My fingers and toes became webbed on the third day, and I didn't bother to correct them. I was wet at least as often as I was dry. My hair fell out and I developed a few more sensory tentacles. I stopped wearing clothing, and my coloring changed to gray-green.

"What are you doing?" my Human mother asked. "Letting your body do whatever it wants to?" Her voice and posture expressed stiff disapproval.

"As long as I don't develop an illness," I said.

She frowned. "I wish you could see yourself through my eyes. Deformity is as bad as illness."

I walked away from her. I had never done that before.

Fifteen days out of Lo, someone shot at us with arrows. Only Lilith was hit. Nikanj caught the archer, drugged him unconscious, destroyed all his weapons, and changed the color of his hair. It had been deep brown. It would be colorless from now on. It would look all white. Finally Nikanj encouraged his face to fall into the permanent creases that this male's behavior and genetic heritage had dictated for his old age. He would look much older. He would not be weaker or in any way infirm, but appearances were important to Humans. When this male awoke—sometime then next day—his eyes and his fingers would tell him he had paid a terrible price for attacking us. More important, his people would see. They would misunderstand what they saw, and it would frighten them into letting us alone.

Lilith had no special trouble with the arrow. It damaged one of her kidneys and gave her a great deal of pain, but her life was in no danger. Her improved body would have healed quickly even without Nikanj's help, since the arrow was not poisoned. But Nikanj did not leave her to heal herself. It lay beside her and healed her completely before it returned to whiten the drugged archer's hair and wrinkle his face. Mates took care of one another.

I watched them, wondering who I would take care of. Who would take care of me?

Twenty-one days out, the bed of our river turned south and we turned with it. Dichaan veered off the trail, and left us for some time, and came back with a male Human who had broken his leg. The leg was grotesque—swollen, discolored, and blistered. The smell of it made Nikanj and me look at one another.

We camped and made a pallet for the injured Human. Nikanj spoke to me before it went to him.

"Get rid of your webbing," it said. "Try to look less like a frog or you'll scare him."

"Are you going to let me heal him?"

"Yes. And it will take a while for you to do it right. Your

first regeneration. . . . Go eat something while I ease his pain."

"Let me do that," I said. But it had already turned away and gone back to the male. The male's leg was worse than worthless. It was poisoning his body. Portions of it were already dead. Yet the thought of taking it disturbed me.

Ahajas and Aaor brought me food before I could look around for it, and Aaor sat with me while I ate.

"Why are you afraid?" it said.

"Not exactly afraid, but . . . To take the leg . . ."

"Yes. It will give you a chance to grow something other than webbing and sensory tentacles."

"I don't want to do it. He's old like Marina. You don't know how I hated letting her go."

"Don't I?"

I focused on it. "I didn't think you did. You didn't say anything."

"You didn't want me to. You should eat."

When I didn't eat, it moved closer to me and leaned against me, linking comfortably into my nervous system. It had not done that for a while. It wasn't afraid of me anymore. It had not exactly abandoned me. It had allowed me to isolate myself—since I seemed to want to. It let me know this is in simple neurosensory impressions.

"I was lonely," I protested aloud.

"I know. But not for me." It spoke with confidence and contentment that confused me.

"You're changing," I said.

"Not yet. But soon, I think."

"Metamorphosis? We'll lose each other when you change."

"I know. Share the Human with me. It will give the two of us more time together."

"All right."

Then I had to go to the Human. I had to heal him alone. After that, Aaor and I could share him.

People remembered their ooloi siblings. I had heard Ahajas and Dichaan talk about theirs. But they had not seen it for decades. An ooloi belonged to the kin group of its mates. Its siblings were lost to it.

The Human male had lost consciousness by the time I lay down beside him. The moment I touched him, I knew he must have broken his leg in a fall—probably from a tree. He had puncture wounds and deep bruises on the left side of his body. The left leg was, as I had expected, a total loss, foul and poisonous. I separated it from the rest of his body above the damaged tissue. First I stopped the circulation of bodily fluids and poisons to and from the leg. Then I encouraged the growth of a skin barrier at the hip. Finally I helped his body let go of the rotting limb.

When the leg fell away, I withdrew enough of my attention from the male to ask the family to get rid of it. I didn't want the male to see it.

Then I settled down to healing the many smaller injuries and neutralizing the poisons that had already begun to destroy the health of his body. I spent much of the evening healing him. Finally I focused again on his leg and began to reprogram certain cells. Genes that had not been active since well before the male was born had to be awakened and set to work telling the body how to grow a leg. A leg, not a cancer. The regeneration would take many days and would have to be monitored. We would camp here and keep the man with us until regeneration was complete.

It had been dark for some time when I detached myself from the male. My Human parents and my siblings were asleep nearby. Ahajas and Dichaan sat near one another guarding the camp and conversing aloud so softly that even I could not hear all they said. A Human intruder would have heard nothing at all. Oankali and construct hearing was so acute that some resisters imagined we could read their thoughts. I wished we could have so that I would have some idea how the male I had healed would react to me. I would have to spend as much time with him as new mates often spent together. That would be hard if he hated or feared me.

"Do you like him, Oeka?" Nikanj asked softly.

I had known it was behind me, sitting, waiting to check my work. Now it came up beside me and settled a sensory arm around my neck. I still enjoyed its touch, but I held stiff against it because I thought it would next touch the male.

"Thorny, possessive ooloi child," it said, pulling me

against it in spite of my stiffness. "I must examine him this once. But if what you tell me and show me matches what I find in him, I won't touch him again until it's time for him to go—unless something goes wrong."

"Nothing will go wrong!"

"Good. Show me everything."

I obeyed, stumbling now and then because I understood the working of the male's body better than I understood the vocabulary, silent or vocal, for discussing it. But with neurosensory illusions, I could show it exactly what I meant.

"There are no words for some things," Nikanj told me as it finished. "You and your children will create them if you need them. We've never needed them."

"Did I do all right with him?"

"Go away. I'll find out for sure."

I went to sit with Ahajas and Dichaan and they gave me some of the wild figs and nuts they had been eating. The food did not take my mind off Nikanj touching the Human, but I ate anyway, and listened while Ahajas told me how hard it had been for Nikanj when its ooan Kahguyaht had had to examine Lilith.

"Kahguyaht said ooloi possessiveness during subadulthood is a bridge that helps ooloi understand Humans," she said. "It's as though Human emotions were permanently locked in ooloi subadulthood. Humans are possessive of mates, potential mates, and property because these can be taken from them."

"They can be taken from anyone," I said. "Living things can die. Nonliving things can be destroyed."

"But Human mates can walk away from one another," Dichaan said. "They never lose the ability to do that. They can leave one another permanently and find new mates. Humans can take the mates of other Humans. There's no physical bond. No security. And because Humans are hierarchical, they tend to compete for mates and property."

"But that's built into them genetically," I said. "It isn't built into me."

"No," Ahajas said. "But, Oeka, you won't be able to bond with a mate—Human, construct, or Oankali—until you're adult. You can feel needs and attachments. I know you feel more at this stage than an Oankali would. But until you're mature, you can't form a true bond. Other ooloi can seduce potential mates away from you. So other ooloi are suspect."

That sounded right—or rather, it sounded true. It didn't make me feel any better, but it helped me understand why I felt like tearing Nikanj loose from the male and standing guard to see that it did not approach him again.

Nikanj came over to me after a while, smelling of the male, tasting of him when it touched me. I flinched in resentment.

"You've done a good job," it said. "How can you do such a good job with Humans and such a poor one with yourself and Aaor?"

"I don't know," I said bleakly. "But Humans steady me somehow. Maybe it's just that Marina and this male are alone—mateless."

"Go rest next to him. If you want to sleep, sleep linked with him so that he won't wake up until you do."

I got up to go.

"Oeka."

I focused on Nikanj without turning.

"Tino made crutches for him to use for the next few days. They're near his foot."

"All right." I had never seen a crutch, but I had heard of them from the Humans in Lo.

"There's clothing with the crutches. Lilith says put some of it on and give the rest to him."

Now I did turn to look at it.

"Put the clothing on, Jodahs. He's a resister male. It will be hard enough for him to accept you."

It was right, of course. I wasn't even sure why I had stopped wearing clothes—except perhaps that I didn't have anyone to wear them for. I dressed and lay down alongside the male.

2

The male and I awoke together. He saw me and tried at once to scramble away from me. I held him, spoke softly to him. "You're safe," I said. "No one will hurt you here. You're being helped."

He frowned, watched my mouth. I could read no understanding in his expression, though the softness of my voice seemed to ease him.

"*Español?*" I asked.

"*Português?*" he asked hopefully.

Relief. "*Sim, senhor. Falo português.*"

He sighed with relief of his own. "Where am I? What has happened to me?"

I sat up, but with a hand on his shoulder encouraged him to go on lying down. "We found you badly injured, alone in the forest. I think you had fallen from a tree."

"I remember . . . my leg. I tried to get home."

"You can go home in a few days. You're still healing now." I paused. "You did a great deal of damage to yourself, but we can fix it all."

"Who are you?"

"Jodahs Iyapo Leal Kaalnikanjlo. I'm the one who has to see that you walk home on two good legs."

"It was broken, my leg. Will it be crooked?"

"No. It will be new and straight. What's your name?"

"Excuse me. I am João. João Eduardo Villas da Silva."

"João, your leg was too badly injured to be saved. But your new leg has already begun to grow."

He groped in sudden terror for the missing leg. He stared at me. Abruptly he tried again to scramble away.

75

I caught his arms and held him still, held him until he stopped struggling. "You are well and healthy," I told him softly. "In a few days you will have a new leg. Don't do yourself any more harm now. You're all right."

He stared at my face, shook his head, stared again.

"It is true," I said. "A few days of crutches, then a whole leg again. Look at it."

He looked, twisting so that I could not see—as though he thought his body still held secrets from me.

"It doesn't look like a new leg," he said,.

"It's only a few hours old. Give it time to grow."

He sat where he was and looked around at the rest of the family. "Who are you all? Why are you here?"

"We're travelers. One family from Lo, traveling south."

"My home is to the west in the hills."

"We won't leave you until you can go there."

"Thank you." He stared at me a little longer. "I mean no offense, but . . . I've met very few of your people—Human and not Human."

"Construct."

"Yes. But I don't know . . . Are you a man or a woman?"

"I'm not an adult yet."

"No? You appear to be an adult. You appear to be a young woman—too thin, perhaps, but very lovely."

I wasn't surprised this time. My body wanted him. My body sought to please him. What would happen to me when I had two or more mates? Would I be like the sky, constantly changing, clouded, clear, clouded, clear? Would I have to be hateful to one partner in order to please the other? Nikanj looked the same all the time and yet all four of my other parents treasured it. How well would my looks please anyone when I had four arms instead of two?

"No male or female could regenerate your leg," I told João. "I am ooloi."

It was as though the air between us became a crystalline wall—transparent, but very hard. I could not reach him through it anymore. He had taken refuge behind it and even if I touched him, I would not reach him.

"You have nothing to fear from us," I said, meaning he

had nothing to fear from me. "And even though I'm not adult, I can complete your regeneration."

"Thank you," he said from behind his cold new shield. "I'm very grateful." He was not. He did not believe me.

My head and body tentacles drew themselves into tight prestrike coils, and I moved back from João. It would have been easier if he had leaped away from me the way Marina had almost done. Fear was easier to deal with than this . . . this cold rejection—this revulsion.

"Why do you hate me?" I whispered. "You would have died without an ooloi to save your life. Why do you hate me for saving your life?"

João'a face underwent several changes. Surprise, regret, shame, anger, renewed hatred and revulsion. "I did not ask you to save me."

"Why do you hate me?"

"I know what you do—your kind. You take men as though they were women!"

"No! We—"

"Yes! Your kind and your Human whores are the cause of all our trouble! You treat all mankind as your woman!"

"Is that how I've treated you?"

He became sullen. "I don't know what you've done."

"Your body tells you what I've done." I sat for a time and looked at him with my eyes. When he looked away, I said, "That male over there is my Human father. The female is my Human mother. I came from her body. I didn't heal you so that you could insult these people."

He only stared at me. But there was doubt in him now. Lilith was putting something into a Lo cloth pot that she had suspended between two trees. She had not yet made a fire beneath it. Tino was some distance away cutting palm branches. We would build a shelter of sapling trees, Lo cloth, and palm branches and hang our hammocks in it. We had not done that for a while.

My Human parents must have looked much like the people of João's home village. When lone resisters had to live among us, they usually found themselves identifying with the mated Humans around them and choosing an Oankali or a construct "protector." They became temporary mates or temporary adopted siblings. Marina had chosen a kind of temporary mate status, staying with me and hardly speaking at all to anyone else except Aaor. That was what I wanted of João, too. But I would have to encourage him more, and at the same time convince him that his manhood was not threatened. I had heard that males often felt this way about ooloi. I would have to talk to Tino. He could help me understand the fear and ease it. Reason would clearly not be enough.

"No one will guard you," I told João. "You are not a prisoner. But I have to monitor your leg. If you leave before the regeneration is complete, before I make certain the growth process had stopped, you could wind up with a monstrous tumor. It would eventually kill you. If someone cut it away for you, it would grow again."

He did not want to believe me, but I had frightened him. I had intended to. All that I'd said was true.

I stood up and pointed. "Your crutches are there. And my Human mother has left you clean clothing." I paused. "Anyone here will give you any help you need if you don't insult them."

I wanted to hold my hand out to him, but all of his body language said he would not take it as Marina had. He sat where he was, staring at the place where his leg had been. He made no effort to get up.

I brought him a bowl of fruit and nut portridge and he only sat staring at it. I sat with him and ate mine, but he hardly moved. No, he moved once. When I touched him, he flinched and turned to stare at me. There was nothing in his expression except hatred.

I went away and bathed in the river. Aaor was with João when I got back to camp. They were not talking, but the stiffness had gone out of João's back. Perhaps he was simply tired.

I saw Aaor push the bowl of porridge toward him. He took the bowl and ate. When Aaor touched him, he did not flinch.

3

João chose Aaor. He accepted help from it and talked to it and caressed its small breasts once he realized that neither it nor anyone else minded this. The breasts did not represent true mammary glands. Aaor would probably lose them when it metamorphosed. Most constructs did, even when they became female. But João liked them. Aaor simply enjoyed the contact.

At night, João endured me. I think his greatest shame was that his body did not find me as repellent as he wanted to believe I was. This frightened him as much as it shamed him. Perhaps it told him what I had already realized—that given time he could learn to accept me, to enjoy me very much. I think he hated me more for that than for anything.

In twenty-one days João's leg had grown. I had made him eat huge amounts of food—had stimulated his appetite so that he could not stubbornly refuse meals. Also, I chemically encouraged him to be sedentary. He needed all his energy to grow his leg.

I had grown breasts myself, and developed an even more distinctly Human female appearance. I neither directed my body nor attempted to control it. It developed no diseases, no abnormal growths or changes. It seemed totally focused on João, who ignored it during the day, but caressed it at night and investigated it before I put him to sleep.

I kept him with me for three extra days to help him regain his strength and to be absolutely certain the leg had stopped growing and worked as well as his old one. It was smooth and soft-skinned and very pale. The foot was so tender that I folded lengths of Lo cloth and pressed them together to make sandals for him.

"I haven't worn anything on my feet since long before you were born," he told me.

"Wear these back to your home or you'll damage the new foot badly," I said.

"You're really going to let me go?"

"Tomorrow." It was our twenty-fifth night together. He still pretended to ignore me during the day, but it had apparently become so much trouble for him to manufacture hatred against me at night. He accepted what I did for him and he did not insult me. He didn't insult anyone. Once I found him telling Aaor, Lilith, and Tino about São Paulo, where he had been born. He had been only nineteen when the war came. He had been a student. He would have become a doctor like his father. "People shook their heads over the war at first," he told them. "They said it would kill off the north—Europe, Asia, North America. They said the northerners had lost their minds. No one realized we would suffer from sickness, hunger, blindness. . . ."

He had known I was listening. He hadn't cared, but he would not have volunteered to tell me anything of his past. He answered my questions, but he volunteered nothing.

The name of his resister village was São Paulo, in memory of his home city, which had once existed far to the east. He had just traveled back to the site of the city—through thick forests and hostile people, across many rivers. Before the war and the coming of the Oankali, São Paulo was a city of millions of Humans and forests of buildings, large and small. But what the war and its aftermath had not destroyed, the Oankali fed to their shuttles. Shuttles ate whatever they landed on. There were a few ruins left, but the forest now covered most of what had been São Paulo.

João had talked about his past to Ahajas and Dichaan as well. He avoided Nikanj, at least. I could accept everything he did as long as he avoided Nikanj.

"Tomorrow," he repeated now, lying beside me. He moved warningly, then sat up. I had told him always to move a little to warn me that he intended to change position or get up—in case I had sensory tentacles linked into him. He had ignored me once. The pain of that had made him scream aloud and roll himself into a tight fetal knot for some time, sweating and gasping. He hurt me as badly as he hurt himself, but I managed not to react as much. I never said anything, but he always made me a small, warning move after that.

He looked down at me. "I didn't believe you."

"Your leg is complete and strong. It's tender. You need to protect it. But you're whole. Why shouldn't you leave?"

His mouth said nothing. His face said he wasn't sure he wanted to go. He wasn't even sure he appreciated my telling him he could go. But his pride kept him silent.

"All right!" he said finally. "Tomorrow I go. Tomorrow morning."

I drew him down to our pallet and kissed his face, then his mouth. "I won't be glad to see you go," I said. "If you were younger . . ." I rubbed the back of his neck. My underarms didn't itch. They hurt.

"I didn't know my age was important," he said. He sighed. "I shouldn't care. I should be grateful. I haven't changed my opinion . . . of ooloi."

"You have, I think."

"No. I've only changed my feelings toward you. I wouldn't have believed I could do even that."

"Before you leave, go to Nikanj. Have it check you to be certain that I haven't missed anything."

"No!"

"It will only touch you for a moment. Only for a moment. Come to me afterward . . . to say goodbye."

"No. I can't let that thing touch me. I would rather trust you."

"It's one of my parents."

"I know. I mean no offense. But I cannot do that."

"I won't sent you away to die from some mistake of mine that could have been corrected. You *will* let it touch you."

Silence.

"Do it for my sake, João. Don't leave me wondering whether I've killed you."

He sighed. After a moment, he nodded.

I put him to sleep. He did not realize it, but I was

responsible for strengthening his aversion to Nikanj. No male or female who spent as much time with an ooloi as he had with me would feel comfortable touching another ooloi. João was not bound to me, but he was chemically oriented toward me and away from others. And adult ooloi could seduce him from me if he truly disliked me and was interested in finding another ooloi. But otherwise, he would stay with me. Lilith had begun this way with Nikanj.

The next morning, I took João to Nikanj. As I had promised, Nikanj touched him briefly, then let him go.

"You've done nothing wrong with him," he told me. "I wish he could stay and keep you from becoming a frog again." I was grateful that it spoke in English and João did not understand.

I gave João food and a hammock and my machete. He had lost whatever gear he had had with him when he fell.

"There are older Oankali who would mate with you," I told him. "They could give you pleasure. You could have children."

"Which of them would look like someone I used to dream about when I was young?" he asked.

"I don't really look like this, João. You know I don't. I didn't look this way when we met."

"You look like this for me," he said. "Tell me who else could do that?"

I should my head. "No one."

"You see?"

"Then go to Mars. Find someone who does really look this way. Have Human children."

"I've thought about Mars. It seemed a fantasy, though. To live on another world. . . ."

"Oankali have lived on many other worlds. Why shouldn't Humans live on at least one other?"

"Why should the Oankali have the one world that's ours?"

"They do have it. And you can't take it back from them. You can stay here and die uselessly, resisting. You can go to Mars and help found a new Human society. Or you can join us in the trade. We will go to the stars eventually. If you join us, your children will go with us."

He shook his head. "I don't know. I've been among

Oankali before. We all have, we resisters. Oankali never made me doubt what I should do." He smiled. "Before I met you, Jodahs, I knew myself much better."

He went away undecided. "I don't even know what I want from you," he said as he was leaving. "It isn't the usual thing, certainly, but I don't want to leave you." He left.

4

Two days after João had gone, Aaor went into metamorphosis. It did not seem to edge in slowly as I had—though I had been so preoccupied with João that I could easily have missed the signs. It simply went to its pallet and went to sleep. I was the one who touched it and realized that it was in metamorphosis. And that it was becoming ooloi.

There would be two of us, then. Two dangerous uncertainties who might never be allowed to mate normally, who might spend the rest of our lives in one kind of exile or another.

We had not begun to travel again on the day João left us. Now we could not. There was no good reason to carry Aaor through the forest, forcing it to assimilate new sensations when it should be isolated and focusing inward on the growth and readjustment of its own body.

We could have put together a raft and traveled down the river to Lo in a fraction of the time it had taken us to reach this point. In an emergency, Nikanj could even signal for help. But what help? A shuttle to take us back to Lo, where we could not stay? A shuttle to take us to Chkahichdahk, where we did not want to go?

We sat grouped around the sleeping Aaor and agreed to do the only thing we really could do: move to higher ground to avoid the rainy season floods and build a more permanent house. My Human mother said it was time to plant a garden.

Nikanj and I stayed with Aaor while the others went to find the site of our new home.

"Do you realize you've already lost most of your hair?" Nikanj asked me as we sat on opposite sides of Aaor's sleeping body.

I touched my head. It still had a very thin covering of hair, but as Nikanj had said, I was nearly bald. Again. I had not noticed. Now I could see that my skin was changing, too, losing the softness it had taken on for João, losing its even brown coloring. I could not tell yet whether I would return to my natural gray-brown or take on the greenish coloring I'd had just before João.

"You should be at least as good at monitoring your own body as you are at monitoring a Human," Nikanj said.

"Will Aaor be like me?" I asked.

It let all its sensory tentacles hang limp. "I'm afraid it might be." It was silent for a while. "Yes, I believe it will be," it said finally.

"So now you have two same-sex children to need you . . . and to resent you."

It focused on me for a long time with an intensity that first puzzled me, then began to scare me. It had rested one sensory arm across Aaor's chest, examining, checking.

"Is it all right?" I asked.

"As much as you are." It rustled its tentacles. "Perfect, but imperfect. It has all that it should have. It can do all that it should be able to do. But that won't be enough. You'll have to go to the ship, Oeka. You and Aaor."

"No!" I felt the way I had once when an apparently friendly Human had hit me in the face.

"You need mates," it said softly. "No one will mate with you here except old Humans who would steal perhaps four fifths of your life. On the ship, you may be able to get young mates—perhaps even young Humans."

"And bring them back to Earth?"

"I don't know."

"I won't go then. I won't take the chance of being held there. I don't think Aaor will either."

"It will. You both will when it finishes its metamorphosis."

"No!"

"Oeka, you've seen it yourself. With a potential mate—even a very unsuitable one—your control is flawless. Without a potential mate, you have no control. You were surprised when I told you you were losing your hair. You've been surprised by your body again and again. Yet nothing it does should surprise you. Nothing it does should be beyond your control."

"But I didn't even grow that hair deliberately. I just . . . On some level I realized João would like it. I think I became all the things he liked, even though he never told me what they were."

"His body told you. His every look, his reactions, his touch, his scent. He never stopped telling you what he wanted. And since he was the sole focus of your attention, you gave him everything he asked for." It lay down beside Aaor. "We do that, Jodahs. We please them so that they'll stay and please us. You're better at it with Humans than I ever was. I was bred for this trade, but you, you're part of the trade. You can understand both Human and Oankali by looking inside yourself." It paused, rustled its tentacles. "I don't believe we would have had many resisters if we had made construct ooloi earlier."

"You think that, and you still want to send me away?"

"I believe it, yes. But no one else does. We must teach them."

"I don't want to teach—. We? We, Ooan?"

"For a while, we'll all relocate to the ship."

I almost said no again, but it wouldn't have paid any attention to me. When it began telling me what I *would* do, it had decided. Our interests—Aaor's and mine—and our needs would be best served on Chkahichdahk, even if we were never allowed to come home. The family would stay with us until we were adults, but then it would leave us on the ship. No more forests or rivers. No more wildness filled with things I had not yet tasted. The planet itself was like one of my parents. I would leave it, and I would gain nothing.

No, that wasn't true. I would gain mates. Eventually.

Perhaps. Nikanj would do all it could to get the mates. There were young Humans born and raised on the ship because there had been so few salvageable Humans left after their war and their resulting disease and atmospheric disturbances. There had not been enough for a good trade. Also most of those who wanted to return to Earth had been allowed to return. That left the Toaht Oankali—those who wanted to trade and to leave with the ship—too few Human mates. They had been breeding more Humans as well as accepting violent ones from Earth. But even so, there were not enough for everyone who wanted them. Not yet. How likely would the Toaht be to let me mate with even one?

I shook my head. "Don't desert me, Ooan."

It focused on me, its manner questioning. "You know I won't."

"I won't go to Chkahichdahk. I won't take what they decide to give me and stay if they decide to keep me. I would rather stay here and mate with old Humans."

It did not shout at me as my Human parents would have. It did not tell me what I already knew. It did not even turn away from me.

"Lie here with me," it said softly.

I went over and lay down next to it, felt it link into me with more sensory tentacles than I had on my entire body. It looped a sensory arm around my neck.

"Such despair in you," it said silently. "You could not throw away so much life."

"Your life will be shorter because of Tino and Lilith," I told it. "Do you feel that you're throwing something away?"

"On Chikahichdahk, there are Humans who will live as long as you would normally."

"So many that a pair would be allowed to come to me? And what about Aaor?"

It began to feel despair of its own. "I don't know."

"But you don't think so. Neither do I."

"You know I'll speak for you."

"Ooan . . ."

"Yes. I know. I've produced two construct ooloi children. No one else has produced any. Who will listen to me?"

"Will anyone?"

"Not many."

"Why did you threaten to send me to Chkahichdahk, then?"

"You will go, Oeka. There's not place for you here, and you know it."

"*No!*"

"There's life there for you. *Life!*" It paused. "You're more adaptable than you think. I made you. I know. You could live there. You could find construct or Oanakali mates and learn to be content with shipboard life."

I spoke aloud. "You're probably right. There used to be Humans who adapted to not being able to see or hear or walk or move. They adapted. But I don't think any of them chose to be so limited."

"But think!" It tightened its grip on me. "Where will you live with old Human mates? Will resisters let you join them in one of their villages? How many attacks on you will it take for them to force a lethal response from you? What will happen then? And, Jodahs, what will happen to your children—your Human children? Will you make them sterile or let them mate together without an ooloi and create deformity and disease? Will you try to force them to go to one of our villages? They may not want to join us any more than you want to go to Chkahichdahk. They'll want the land and the people they know. And if you do a good job when you make them, they could outlive all other resisters. They could outlive this world. If they manage to elude us, they could die when we break the Earth and go our ways."

I withdrew from it, signaling it to withdraw from me. When the Earth was divided and the new ship entities scattered to the stars, Nikanj would be long dead. If I mated with an Old Human, I would be dead, too. I would not be able to safeguard my children even if they were willing, as adults, to be guided by a parent.

I went away from Nikanj, into the forest. I didn't go far. Aaor was helpless and Nikanj might need help protecting it. Aaor was more my paired sibling now than ever. Had it known what was happening to it? Had it wanted to be ooloi? Since it was Oankali-born, would it be willing to live on Chkahichdahk?

What difference would it make what Aaor wanted—or what I wanted? We would go to Chkahichdahk. And we would probably not be allowed to come home.

When my parents and siblings returned to move Aaor to the new home site they had chosen, I went down to the river, went in, and crossed.

I wandered for three days, my body green, scaly, and strange. No one came near me. I lived off the plants I found, picking and choosing according to the needs of my body. I ate everything raw. Humans liked fire. They valued cooked food much more than we did. Also, Humans were less able to get the nutrition they needed from the leaves, grasses, seeds, and fungi that were so abundant in the forest. We could digest what we needed from wood if we had to.

I wandered, tasting the forest, tasting the Earth that I would soon be taken from.

After three days, I went back to the family. I spent a couple of days sitting with Aaor, then left again.

That was my pattern during the rest of Aaor's metamorphosis. Sometimes I brought Nikanj a few cells of some plant or animal that I had run across for the first time. We all did that—brought the adult ooloi of the family living samples of whatever we encountered. Ooloi generally learned a great deal from what their mates and unmated children brought them. And whatever we gave Nikanj, it remembered. It could still recall and re-create a rare mountain plant that one of my brothers had introduced it to over fifty years before. Someday it was supposed to duplicate the cells of its vast store of biological information and pass the copies along to its same-sex children. We were to receive it when we were fully adult and mated. What would that mean, really, for Aaor and me? Someday on Chkahichdahk? Never?

I had always enjoyed bringing Nikanj things. I had enjoyed sharing the pleasure it felt in new tastes, new sensations. Now I needed contact with it more than ever. But I no longer enjoyed the contact. I didn't blame it for pointing out the obvious: that Aaor and I had to to go the ship. It was our same-sex parent, doing its duty. But every time it touched me, all I could feel was stress. Distress. Its own and mine. I brought out the worst in it.

I began to stay away even longer.

I met resisters occasionally, but I looked so un-Human and so un-Oankali most of the time that they fled. Twice they shot me, then fled. But no matter how my body distorted itself, I could always heal wounds.

My family never tried to control my goings and comings. They accepted my feelings whether they understood them or not. They wanted to help me, and suffered because they could not. When I was at home I sat with them sometimes—with Ayodele and Yedik when they guarded at night. People guarded in pairs except for Nikanj, who stayed with Aaor, and Oni and Hozh, who were too young to guard.

But I could touch Oni and Hozh. I could touch Ayodele and Yedik. They were still children, neutral-scented, and not yet forbidden to me. When I came out of the forest, looking like nothing anyone on Earth would recognize, one or the other pair of them took me between them and stayed with me until I looked like myself again. If I touched only one of them, I would change that one, make it what I was. But if they both stayed with me, they changed me.

"We shouldn't be able to do this to you," Yedik said as we guarded one night.

"You make it easy for me not to wander," I told it. "My body wanders. Even when I come home, it wants to go on wandering."

"We shouldn't be able to stop it," Yedik insisted. "We shouldn't influence you at all. We're too young."

"I want you to influence me." I looked from one of them to the other. Ayodele looked female and Yedik looked male. I hoped they would be more strongly influenced by the way they looked than I had. Humans said they were beautiful.

"I can change myself," I told them. "But it's an effort. And it doesn't last. It's easier to do as water does: allow myself to be contained, and take on the shape of my containers."

"I don't understand," Ayodele said.

"You help me do what I want to do."

"What do Humans do?"

"Shape me according to their memories and fantasies."

"But—" They both spoke at once. Then, by mutual

consent, Ayodele spoke. "Then you're either out of control or contained by us or forced into a false Human shape."

"Not forced."

"When can you be yourself?"

I thought about that. I understood it because I remembered being their age and having a strong awareness of the way my face and body looked, and of that look being *me*. It never had been, really.

"Changing doesn't bother me anymore," I said. "At least, not this kind of deliberate, controlled changing. I wish it didn't bother other people. I've never deformed plants or animals the way people said I might."

"Just people," Yedik said quietly. "People and Lo."

"Lo was barely annoyed. It would have survived that war the Humans killed each other with."

"It's part of you and vulnerable to you. You hurt it."

"I know. And I confused it. But I don't think I could injure it seriously if I tried—and I wouldn't try. As for people, have you noticed that the Humans, the people I'm supposed to be the greatest danger to, are the ones I've never hurt?"

Silence.

"Does it bother you to have me here with you?"

"It did," Ayodele said. "We thought your life must be terrible. We can feel your distress when we link with you."

"This is my place," I told them. "This world. I don't belong on the ship—except perhaps for a visit. People go there to absorb more of our past sometimes. I wouldn't mind that. But I can't live there. No matter what Ooan says, I can't live there. It's a finished place. The people are still making themselves, but the place . . ."

"It's still dividing in two to make a ship for the Toaht and a ship for the Akjai."

"And the two halves will be smaller finished places. No wildness. No newness. I'm Dinso like you, not Toaht or Akjai."

Again they were silent.

"You two sit together." I withdrew from them and started to get up.

They watched me with their eyes and their few sensory tentacles. Silently they took my hands and drew me down to sit between them again. They acted more in perfect unison than any of my siblings. Ahajas said they would certainly become mates if they developed as male and female. They did not want me between them. I made them uncomfortable because they wanted to help me and couldn't help much. On the other hand, they *did* want me between them because they could help a little, and they knew they would lose me soon, and they liked the way I made their bodies feel. I wasn't as able to make people feel good as Nikanj was, but I could give them something. And I was old enough to read internal and external body language and understand more of what they were feeling.

I liked that. I liked a lot of what I had been able to do recently. It was only the thought of going to Chkahichdahk, and being kept there, that made me feel caged and frantic.

The next morning that thought drove me into the forest again.

5

Aor had a long metamorphosis. Eleven months. I was afraid every time I went home that it would be awake and the family would be building a raft.

I began to seek out Humans. I avoided large parties of them, but it was easy to find individuals and small groups.

I followed them silently, dissected and enjoyed their scents, listened to their conversations. Sometimes they became aware that they were being followed, though they never saw me. My coloring had darkened and I hid easily in the shadows. The forest understory was usually wet or at least damp, and it was easy for me to move silently. The Humans I followed often made much more noise than I did. I watched a Human hunter make so much noise that the feeding peccary he was stalking heard him and ran away. The Human went to the place where the peccary had been feeding and he cursed and kicked the fruit the animal had been feeding on. It never occurred to him to eat the fruit or to collect some for his people. I ate some when he was gone.

Once three people stalked me. I considered letting them catch me. But I circled around to have a look at them first, and I heard them talking about opening me up and seeing how I looked inside. Since they all had guns and machetes, I decided to avoid them. Three were too many for a subadult to subdue safely.

I was moving upriver—farther upriver than I had been before—well into the hills. The forest was less varied here, but I had no trouble finding enough to eat, and occasional plants and animals that were new to me. But I found few people in the hills. For several days, I found no one at all. No breeze brought me a Human scent.

I began to feel loneliness as an almost physical pain. I hadn't realized how much seeing Humans every few days had meant to me.

Now I had to go home. I didn't want to. Surely Aaor would be awake this time. The thought panicked me, brought back the caged feeling so strongly that I could not think.

I stayed where I was for a while, cleared a space, made a fire, though I did not need one. It comforted me and reminded me of Humans. I let the fire burn down and roasted several wild tubers in the coals. The smell of the food wasn't enough to mask the smell of the two Humans when they approached. No doubt it was the food smell that drew them.

They were a male and a female and they smelled . . . very strange. Wrong. Injured, perhaps. They were armed. I could smell gunpowder. They might shoot me. I decided to risk it. I would not move. I would let them surprise me.

My body at this time was covered with fingernail-sized, overlapping scales. It was also inclined to be quadrapedal, but I had resisted that. Hands were much more useful than clawed forefeet.

Now, while the Humans approached very carefully, very quietly, I prepared for them. My bald, scaly head and scaly face had to look more Human. I didn't have time to change the rest of me. I could look as though I were wearing unusual clothing, perhaps. In fact, I didn't wear clothing at all on these trips. It just got in the way.

The Humans kept to cover and circled around, watching me. They wanted to be behind me. I decided to play dead if they shot me. Best to lure them close and disarm them as quickly as possible.

Perhaps they would not shoot me. I used a stick to uncover one of the tubers and roll it out of the coals. It was too hot to eat, but I brushed it off and broke it open. It was well cooked, steaming hot, spicy, and sweet. It had not existed before the Humans had their war. Lilith said it was one of the few good-tasting mutations she had eaten. She called it an applesauce fruit. Apples were an extinct fruit that she had especially liked. She didn't like the taste of the tubers raw, but sometimes when she had baked one she went away by herself to eat it and remember a different time.

One of the Humans made a small noise behind me—a moan.

I ran a hand over my face. The hand was more clawlike than I would have preferred, but the face was clear and soft now. If it wasn't beautiful, it was, at least, not terrifying.

"Come join me," I said loudly. It felt unnatural to talk aloud. I hadn't spoken at all for about thirty days. "There's more food. You're welcome to it." I repeated the words in Spanish, Portuguese, and Swahili. Those, together with French and English, were the most widely known languages. Most people were fluent in at least one of them. Most survivors were from Africa, Australia, and South America.

The two Humans did not answer me. They did not move, but their heartbeats speeded up. They had heard me and they probably understood that I was talking to them. When had their heartbeats increased? I focused on my memories for a moment. My speaking at all had startled them, but my Spanish had excited them more. My other languages had provoked no further reaction. Spanish, then. I repeated my invitation in Spanish.

They did not come. I thought they understood, but they did not answer, and they remained hidden.

I took the rest of the tubers from the coals and put them on a platter of large leaves.

"They're yours if you would like them," I said. I cleared a place well away from the food and lay down to rest. I had not slept in two days. Humans liked regular periods of sleep—preferably at night. Oankali slept when they needed rest. I needed rest now, but I would not sleep until the Humans made some decision—either to go away or to come satisfy their hunger and their curiosity. But I could be still in the Oankali way. I could lie awake using the least possible energy, and as Lilith and Tino said, looking dead. I could do this very comfortably for much longer than most Humans would willingly sit and watch.

The male left cover first. I watched him with a few of my sensory tentacles. All his body language told me he meant to grab the food and run with it. I was prepared to let him do that until I got a good look at him.

He was diseased. His face was half obscured by a large growth. He wore no shirt and I could see that his back and chest were covered with tumorous growths, large and small. One of his eyes was completely covered. The other seemed endangered. If the facial tumor continued to grow, he would soon be unable to see.

I couldn't let him go. I don't think any ooloi could have let him go. No living being should be left to wander without care in his condition.

I waited until his attention was totally focused on the food. At first he kept flickering back and forth between the food and me. Finally, though, the food was in reach. He put out his hands to take it.

I had him before he realized I was up. At once, I turned him to face the female, whom I could see now. She was aiming a rifle at me. Let her aim it at him.

He struggled, first wildly, then with calculation, meaning to hurt me and get free. I held him still and investigated him quickly.

He had a genetic disorder. Its effects were worsening slowly. As I had suspected, he would be blind if it were allowed to continue. The disorder had deformed even the bones of his face. He was deaf in one ear. Eventually he would be deaf in the other. His spine was becoming involved. Already he could not turn his head freely. One shoulder was completely covered with fleshy growths. The arm was still useful, but it wouldn't be for long. And there was something else wrong. Something I didn't understand. This man was already dying. He was using up his life the way mice did, swallowing it in a few quick gulps, then dying. The disorder threatened to invade his brain and spine. But even without continued tumor growth, he would die in just a few decades. He was genetically programmed to use himself up obscenely quickly.

How could he have such a disorder? An ooloi had examined him before he was set free. Ooloi had examined every Human, correcting defects, slowing aging, strengthening resistance to disease. But perhaps the ooloi had only controlled the disorder—imperfectly—and not tried to correct it. Ooloi had done that with some genetic disorders. Such disorders were complicated and best corrected by mates. Resisters had been altered so that they could not have children without ooloi mates, and thus could not pass their disorder on. Controlling it should have been enough.

I spoke into the male's one good ear as I held him. "You'll be completely blind soon. After that you'll go deaf. Eventually you won't be able to use your right arm—and that's the arm you prefer to use. That's not all. That's not even the worst. Do you understand me?"

He had stopped struggling. Now he rocked back, trying to get a look at me in spite of his uncooperative neck.

"I can help you," I said. "I will help you if you let me. And if your friend doesn't shoot me." I would help him whether the female shot me or not, but I wanted to avoid being shot if I could. Bullet wounds hurt more than I wanted to think about, and I still wasn't very good at controlling my own pain.

The man was feeling calmer now. I did not dare drug him much. I could please him a little, relax him a little, but I could not put him to sleep. If he lost consciousness in my arms, the female would surely misunderstand, and shoot me.

"I can help," I repeated. "All I ask in return is that you not try to kill me."

"Why should you do anything?" he demanded. "Just let me go!"

I shifted to a more comfortable grip. "Why should you become more and more disabled?" I asked. "Why should you die when you can live and be well? Let me help you."

"Let go of me!"

"Will you stay, and at least hear me?"

He hesitated. "Yes. All right." His body was tense—ready to run.

I made a sighing sound so that he would hear it. "If you lie to me, I can't help knowing."

That frightened him and made him stiffly resentful in my grasp, but he said nothing.

The female came completely out of her cover and faced us. I kept the male's body between my own and her rifle. Looking at her, I had absolutely no doubt that she would shoot. But I needed a few moments more with the male before I could have anything serious to show them. The female had tumors, too, though hers were not as big as the male's. Her face, arms, and legs—all that was visible of her—were covered with small irregularly spaced growths.

"Let him go," she said quietly. "I won't shoot you if you let him go." That was true at least. She was afraid, but she meant what she said.

I nodded to her, then spoke to the male. "I haven't hurt you. What will you do if I let you go?"

Now the male gave a real sigh. "Leave."

"You're hungry. Take the food with you."

"I don't want it." He no longer trusted it—probably because I wanted him to have it.

"Do one thing for me before I let you go."

"What?"

"Move your neck."

I kept a firm hold on him, but drew back slightly to let him turn and twist the neck that had been all but frozen in place before I touched him. He swore softly.

"Tomás?" the female said, her voice filled with doubt.

"I can move it," he said unnecessarily. He had not stopped moving it.

"Does it hurt?"

"No. It just feels . . . normal. I had forgotten how it felt to move this way."

I let him go and spoke softly. "Perhaps when you've been blind for a while, you'll forget how it feels to see."

He almost fell turning to look at me. When he'd gotten a good look, he took a step back. "You won't touch me again until I see you heal yourself," he said. "What . . . Who are you?"

"Jodahs," I said. "I'm a construct, Human and Oankali."

He looked startled, then moved around so that he could get a look at all sides of me. "I never heard that they had scales." He shook his head. "My god, man, you must frighten more people than we do!"

I laughed. I could feel my sensory tentacles flattening against my scales. "I don't always look this way," I said. "If you stay to be healed, I'll begin to look more like you. More like the way you will look when you're healed."

"We can't be healed," the female said. "The tumors can be cut off, but they grow back. The disease . . . we were born with it. No one can heal it."

"I know you were born with it. You'll give it to at least some of your children if you decide to go where you can have them. I can correct the problem."

They looked at each other. "It isn't possible," the male said.

I focused on him. He had been such a pleasure to touch. Now there was no need to hurry back home. No need to hurry at anything. Two of them. Treasure.

"Move your neck," I said again.

The male moved it, shaking his misshapen head. "I don't understand," he said. "What did you say you were called?"

"Jodahs."

"I'm Tomás. This is Jesusa." No other names. Very deliberately, no other names. "Tell us how you did this."

I took sticks from the pile I had gathered and built up the fire. The two Humans obligingly sat down around it. The male picked up a baked tuber. The female caught his arm and looked at him, but he only grinned, broke open the tuber, and bit into it. His single visible eye opened wide in surprise and pleasure. The tuber was new to him. He ate a little more, then gave a piece to the female. She scooped out a little with one finger and tasted it. She did not take on the same look of surprised pleasure, but she ate, then examined the peeling carefully in the firelight. It was dark now for resisters. The sun had gone down.

"I haven't tasted this before. Is it only a lowland plant?"

"It grows here. I'll show you tomorrow morning."

There was a silence. Of course they would stay the night in this place. Where else could they go in the dark?

"You're from the mountains?" I asked softly.

More silence.

"I won't get to the mountains. I wish I could."

They were both eating tubers now, and they seemed content to eat and not talk. That was surprising. Nervousness alone should have made at least one of them talkative. How many times had they sat alone in the forest at night with a scaly construct?

"Will you let me begin to heal you tonight?" I asked Tomás.

"Thank you for healing my neck," Tomás said aloud while his entire body recoiled from me in tiny movements.

"It may fuse again if your disorder isn't cured."

He shrugged. "It wasn't that bad. Jesusa says it kept me working instead of looking around daydreaming."

Jesusa touched his forearm and smiled. "Nothing would keep you from daydreaming, brother."

Brother? Not mate—or husband, as the Humans would say. "Blindness will be bad," I said. "Deafness will be even worse."

"Why do you say he'll go blind or deaf?" Jesusa demanded. "He may not. You don't know."

"Of course I know. I couldn't touch him and not know. And I know there was a time when he could see out of his right eye and hear with his right ear. There was a time when the mass on his shoulder was smaller and his arm wasn't involved at all. He will be blind and deaf and without the use of his right arm—and he knows it. So do you."

There was a very long silence. I lay down on the cleared ground and closed my eyes. I could still see perfectly well, and most Humans knew it. Somehow, though, they felt more at ease when they were observed only with sensory tentacles. They *felt* unobserved.

"Why do you want to heal us?" Jesusa asked. "You waylay us, feed us, and want to heal us. Why?"

I opened my eyes. "I was feeling very lonely," I said. "I would have been glad to see . . . almost anyone. But when I realized you had something wrong, I wanted to help. I need to help. I'm not an adult yet, but I can't ignore illness. I'm ooloi."

Their mild reaction surprised me. I expected anything from João's prejudiced rejection to actually running away into the forest. Only ooloi interacted directly with Humans *and* produced children. Only ooloi interacted directly with Humans in an utterly non-Human way.

And only ooloi needed to heal. Males and females could learn to heal if they wanted to. Ooloi had no choice. We exist to make the people and to unite them and to maintain them.

Jesusa grabbed Tomás's hand and stared at me with terror. Tomás looked at her, touched his neck thoughtfully, and looked at her again. "So it isn't true, what they say," he whispered.

She gave him a look more forceful than a scream.

He drew back a little, touched his neck again, and said nothing else.

"I had thought . . ." Jesusa's voice shook and she paused for a moment. When she began again, the quiver was gone. "I thought that all ooloi had four arms—two with bones and two without."

"Strength arms and sensory arms," I said. "Sensory arms come with maturity. I'm not old enough to have them yet."

"You're a child? A child as big as an adult?"

"I'm as big as I'll get except for my sensory arms. But I still have to develop in other ways. I'm not exactly a child, though. Young children have no sex. They're potentially any sex. I'm definitely ooloi—a subadult, or as my parents would say, an ooloi child."

"Adolescent," Jesusa decided.

"No. Human adolescents are sexually mature. They can reproduce. I can't." I said this to reassure them, but they didn't seem to be reassured.

"How can you heal us if you're just a kid?" Tomás asked.

I smiled. "I'm old enough to do that." My gaze seemed to confuse him, but it only annoyed her. She frowned at me. She would be the difficult one. I looked forward to touching her, learning her body, curing the disorder she never should have had. Some ooloi had wronged her and Tomás more than I would have imagined was possible.

I changed the subject abruptly. "Tomorrow I'll show you some of the things you can eat here in the forest. The tuber was one of many. If you keep moving, the forest will sustain you very comfortably." I paused. "Can you see well enough to make pallets for yourselves or will you sleep on the bare ground?"

Tomás sighed and looked around. "Bare ground, I suppose. We'll do the local insects a good turn." The pupil of his eye was large, but I doubted that he could see beyond the light of the fire. The moon had not yet risen, and starlight was useful to Humans only in boats on the rivers. Very little of it reached the forest understory.

I got up and stepped around the fire to them. "Let me have your machete for a few moments."

Jesusa grabbed Tomás's arm to stop him, but he simply handed me the machete. I took it and went into the forest. Bamboo was plentiful in the area so I cut that and a few stalks from saplings. I would cover these with palm and wild banana leaves. I also took a stem of bananas. They could be cooked for breakfast. They weren't ripe enough for Humans to eat raw. And there was a nut tree nearly—not to mention more tubers. All this so close, and yet Tomás had been very hungry when I touched him.

"You haven't cut anything for yourself," Jesusa said as I handed back the machete. It meant a great deal to her to get the knife back and to get a comfortable pallet to sleep on. She was still wary, but less obviously on edge.

"I'm used to the ground," I said. "No insect will bother me."

"Why?"

"I don't smell good to them. I would taste even worse."

She thought for a moment. "That would protect you against biting insects, but what about those that sting?"

"Even those. I smell offensive and dangerous. Humans don't notice my scent in any negative way, but insects always do."

"Oh, I would be willing to stink if it would keep them off me," Tomás said. "Can you make me immune to them?"

Jesusa turned to frown at him.

I smiled to myself. "No, I can't help you with that." Not until they let me sleep between them. But insects would bother them less while I healed them. If someday they mated with an adult ooloi, insects would hardly bother them at all. There was time enough for them to learn that. I lay down again beside the dying fire.

Jesusa and Tomás lay quietly, first awake, then drifting into sleep. I did not sleep, though I lay still, resting. The scent of the Humans was a mild torment to me because I could not touch them—would not touch them until they had learned to trust me. There was something strange about them—about Tomás, anyway—something I didn't yet understand. And my failure to understand was unusual. Normally if I touched someone to correct a flaw, I understood that person's body completely. I had to get my hands on Tomás again. And I had to touch Jesusa. But I wanted them to let me do it. Immature as I was, my scent must be working on them. And Tomás's healed neck must be working on him. He couldn't possibly like his growing disabilities—and surely other Humans did not like the way he looked. Humans cared very much how other people looked. Even Jesusa must seem grotesquely ugly to them—though neither Tomás nor Jesusa acted as though they cared how they looked. Very unusual. Perhaps it was because there were two of them. If they were siblings they had been together most of their lives. Perhaps they sustained one another.

6

They awoke just before dawn the next morning. Jesusa awoke first. She shook Tomás awake, then put a hand over his mouth so that he would not speak. He took her hand from his mouth and sat up. How much could they see? It was still fairly dark.

Jesusa pointed downriver through the forest.

Tomás shook his head, then glanced at me and shook his head again.

Jesusa pulled at him, both her face and her body language communicating pleading and terror.

He shook his head gain, tried to take her arms. His manner was reassuring, but she evaded him. She stood up, looked down at him. He would not get up.

She sat down again, touching him, her mouth against his ear. It was more as though she breathed the words. I heard them, but I might not have if I hadn't been listening for them.

"For the others!" she whispered. "For *all* of the others, we *must* go!"

He shut his eyes for a moment, as though the soft words hurt him.

"I'm sorry," she breathed. "I'm so sorry."

He got up and followed her into the forest. He did not look at me again. When I couldn't see them any longer, I got up. I was well rested and ready to track them—to stay out of sight and listen and learn. They were going downriver as I had to do to get home. That was convenient, though the truth was, I would have followed them anywhere. And when I spoke to them again, I would know the things they had not wanted me to know.

I followed them for most of the day. Whatever was driving them, it kept them from stopping for more than a few minutes to rest. They ate almost nothing until the end of the day when, with metal hooks they had not shown me, they managed to catch a few small fish. The smell of these cooking was disgusting, but the conversation, at least, was interesting.

"We should go back," Tomaś said. "We should cross the river to avoid Jodahs, then we should go back."

"I know," Jesusa agreed. "Do you want to?"

"No."

"It will rain soon. Let's make a shelter."

"Once we're home, we'll never be free again," he said. "We'll be watched all the time, probably shut up for a while."

"I know. Cut leaves from that plant and that one. They're big enough for good roofing."

Silence. Sounds of a machete hacking. And sometime later, Tomás's voice. "I would rather stay here and be rained on every day and starve every other day." There was a pause. "I would almost rather cut my own throat than go back."

"We will go back," Jesusa said softly.

"I know." Tomás sighed. "Who else would have us anyway—except Jodah's people."

Jesusa had nothing to say on that subject. They worked for a while in silence, probably erecting their shelter. I didn't mind being rained on, so I stretched out silently and lay with most of my attention focused on the two Humans. If someone approached me from a different direction, I would notice, but if people or animals were simply moving around nearby, not coming in my direction, I would not be consciously aware of them.

"We should have let Jodahs teach us about safe, edible plants," Tomás said finally. "There's probably food all around us, but we don't recognize it. I'm hungry enough to eat that big insect right there."

Jesusa said, with amusement in her voice, "That is a very pretty red cockroach, brother. I don't think I'd eat it."

"At least there will be fewer insects when we get home."

"They'll separate us." Jesusa became grim again. "They'll

make me marry Dario. He has a smooth face. Maybe we'll have mostly smooth-faced children." She sighed. "You'll choose between Virida and Alma."

"Alma," he said wearily. "She wants me. How do you think she will like leading me around? And how will we speak to one another when I'm deaf?"

"Hush, little brother. Why think about that?"

"You don't have to think about it. It won't happen to you." He paused, then continued with sad irony. "That leaves you free to worry about bearing child after child after child, watching most of them die, and being told by some smooth-faced elder who looks younger than you do that you're ready to do it all again—when she's never done it at all."

Silence.

"Jesusita."

"Yes?"

"I'm sorry."

"Why? It's true. It happened to Mama. It will happen to me."

"It may not be so bad. There are more of us now."

In a tone that made a lie of every word she said, Jesusa agreed. "Yes, little brother. Perhaps it will be better for our generation."

They were quiet for so long, I thought they wouldn't speak again, but he said, "I'm glad to have seen the lowland forest. For all its insects and other discomforts, it's a good place stuffed with life, drunk with life."

"I like the mountains better," she said. "The air is not so thick or so wet. Home is always better."

"Maybe not if you can't see it or hear it. I don't want that life, Jesusa. I don't think I can stand it. Why should I help give the people more ugly cripples anyway? Will my children thank me? I don't think they will."

Jesusa made no comment.

"I'll see that you get back," he said. "I promise you that."

"We'll both get back," she said with uncharacteristic harshness. "You know your duty as well as I know mine."

There was no more talk.

There was no more need for talk. *They were fertile!* Both of them. That was what I had spotted in Tomás—spotted, but not recognized. He was fertile, and he was young. *He was young!* I had never touched a Human like him before—and he had never touched an ooloi. I had thought his rapid aging was part of his genetic disorder, but I could see now that he was aging the way Humans had aged before their war—before the Oankali arrived to rescue the survivors and prolong their lives.

Tomás was probably younger than I was. They were both probably younger than I was. *I could mate with them!*

Young Humans, born on Earth, fertile among themselves. A colony of them, diseased, deformed, but breeding!

Life.

I lay utterly still. I had all I could do to keep myself from getting up, going to them at once. I wanted to bind them to me absolutely, permanently. I wanted to lie between them tonight. Now. Yet if I weren't careful, they would reject me, escape me. Worse, their hidden people would have to be found. I would have to betray them to my family, and my family would have to tell others. The settlement of fertile Humans would be found and the people in it collected. They would be allowed to choose Mars or union with us or sterility here on Earth. They could not be allowed to continue to reproduce here, then to die when we separated and left an uninhabitable rock behind.

No Human who did not decide to mate with us was told this last. They were given their choices and not told why.

What could Tomás and Jesusa be told? What should they be told to ease the knowledge that their people could not remain as they were? Obviously Jesusa, in particular, cared deeply about these people—was about to sacrifice herself for them. Tomás cared enough to walk away from certain healing when it was what he desperately wanted. Now, clearly, he was thinking about death, about dying. He did not want to reach his home again.

How could either of them mate with me, knowing what my people would do to theirs?

And how should I approach them? If they were potential mates and nothing more, I would go to them now. But once Jesusa understood that I knew their secret, her first question would be, "What will happen to our people?" She would not accept evasion. If I lied to her, she would learn the truth eventually, and I did not think she would forgive me for the lies. Would she forgive me for the truth?

When she and Tomás saw that they had given their people away, would they decide to kill me, to die themselves, or to do both?

7

The next day, Jesusa and Tomás crossed the river and began their journey home. I followed. I let them cross, waited until I could no longer see or hear them, then swam across myself. I swam upriver for a while, enjoying the rich, cool water. Finally I went up the bank and sorted their scent from the many.

I followed it silently, resting when they rested, grazing on whatever happened to be growing nearby. I had not decided what I would do, but there was comfort for me just being within range of their scent.

Perhaps I should follow them all the way to their home, see its location, and take news of it back to my family. Then other people, Oankali and construct, would do what was necessary. I would not be connected with it. But I also might not be allowed to mate with Jesusa and Tomás. I might be sent to the ship in spite of everything. Jesusa and Tomás might choose Mars once others had healed them and explained their choices to them. Or they might mate with others. . . .

The more I followed them, the more I wanted them, and the more unlikely it seemed that I would ever mate with them.

After four days, I couldn't stand it any longer. I just joined them. If I could not have them as mates permanently, I could enjoy them for a while.

They had caught no fish that night. They had found wild figs and eaten them, but I doubted that these had satisfied them.

I found nuts and fruit for them, and root stalks that could be roasted and eaten. I wrapped all this in a crude basket I had woven of thin lianas and lined with large leaves. I could only do this by biting through the lianas in a way that would have disturbed the resisters, so I was glad they could not see me. A resister had said to me years before that we constructs and Oankali were supposed to be superior beings, but we insisted on acting like animals. Oddly both ideas seemed to disturb him.

I took my basket of food and went quietly into Jesusa and Tomás's camp. It was dark and they had built a small shelter and made a fire. Their fire still burned, but they had lain down on their pallets. Jesusa's even breathing said she was asleep, but Tomás lay awake. His eyes was open, but he did not see me until I was beside him.

Then before he could get up, before he could shout, I was down beside him, one hand over his mouth, the other grasping his hand and forcing it to maintain its hold on the machete, but to be still.

"Jodahs," I whispered, and he stopped struggling and stared at me.

"It *can't* be you!" he whispered when I let him speak. He remembered a scaly Jodahs, like a humanoid reptile. But I could not stay within range of their scent for four days and go on looking that way. Now I was brown-skinned and black-haired and I thought it was likely that I looked the way Tomás would when I healed him. He was the one I had touched and studied.

He let me take the machete from his hand and put it aside. I already had several body tentacles linked into his nervous system. I put him to sleep so that I could take care of Jesusa before she awoke.

From the moment I said my name, he was never afraid. "Will you heal me?" he whispered in his last moments of consciousness.

"I will," I said. "Completely."

He closed his eye, trusting himself to me in a way that made it hard for me to withdraw from him and turn to attend to Jesusa.

When I did turn, it was almost too late. She was awake, her eyes full of confusion and terror. She drew back as I turned, and she almost pulled the trigger on the rifle she was holding.

"I'm Jodahs," I told her.

She shot me.

The bullet went through one of my hearts and I had all I could do to stop myself from lunging at her reflexively and stinging her to death. I grabbed the gun from her and threw it against a nearby tree. It broke into two pieces, the wooden stock splintering and separating from the metal, and the metal bending.

I grasped her wrists so she couldn't run. I couldn't trust myself to put her to sleep until I had my own problem under control.

She struggled and shouted for Tomás to wake up and help her. She managed to bite me twice, managed to kick me between the legs, then stopped her struggling for a moment to absorb the reality that I had only smooth skin between my legs, and that her kick did not bother me at all.

She twisted frantically and tried to gouge my eyes. I held on. I had to hold her. She couldn't see in the dark. She might run into the surrounding forest and hurt herself—or run toward the river and fall down the high, steep bluff there. Or perhaps she meant to try to shoot me again with what was left of the gun or use the machete on me. I could not let her hurt herself or hurt me again and perhaps make me kill her. Nothing would be more irrational than that.

She stopped struggling abruptly and stared at one of the bite wounds she had inflicted on my left arm. In the firelight, even Human eyes could see it. It was healing, and that seemed to fascinate her. She watched until there was no visible sign of injury. Just a little smeared blood and saliva.

"You're doing that inside," she said, "healing your wound."

I lay down, dragging her with me. She lay facing me, watching me with fear and distrust.

"I can heal myself as well as most adults," I said. "I'm not very good at controlling pain in myself, though."

She looked concerned, then deliberately hardened her expression. "What did you do to Tomás?"

"He's only asleep."

"No! He would have awakened."

"I drugged him a little. He didn't mind. I promised I would heal him."

"We don't want your healing!"

The worst of the pain from my wound was over. I relaxed in relief and drew a long breath. I let go of her hands and she drew them away, looked at them, then back to me.

I grinned at her. "You're not afraid of me now. And you don't want to hurt me again."

I could feel her face grow warmer. She sat up abruptly, very much against her own will. My scent was at work on her. She would probably have difficulty resisting it because she was not consciously aware of it.

"We truly don't want your healing," she repeated. "Though . . . I'm sorry I shot you." She sat still, looking down at me. "You look like Tomás, you know? You look the way he should look. You could be our brother—or perhaps our sister."

"Neither."

"I know. Why did you follow us?"

"Why did you run from me?"

She stared at the machete. She would have to get over or around both Tomás and me to get it.

"No, Jesusa," I said. "Stay here. Let me talk to you."

"You know about us, don't you?" she demanded.

"Yes."

"I knew you would—once you'd touched us both."

"I should have known from your scent alone. I let your disorder and my own inexperience confuse me. But, no, I didn't learn what I know from touching you just now. I learned it from following you and hearing you and Tomás talk."

Her face took on a look of outrage. "You listened? You hid in the bushes and listened to what I said to my brother!"

"Yes. I'm sorry. We don't usually do such things, but I needed to know about you. I needed to understand you."

"You needed nothing!"

"You were new to me. New, different, in need of help with your genetic disorder, and alone. You knew I could help you, yet you ran away. When you know us better, you may understand that it was as though you were dragging me by several ropes. The question wasn't whether I would follow you, but how long I could follow before I joined you again."

She shook her head. "I don't think I like your people if you're all compelled to do such things."

"It's been a century since anyone in my family has seen anyone like you. And you . . . perhaps you won't have to worry about attracting the attention of others of my people."

"What will you do, now that you know about us? What do you want of us?"

"That we must talk about," I said, "you, Tomás, and me. But I wanted to talk to you first."

"Yes?" she said.

I looked at her for some time, simply enjoying the look and the scent of her. She still might leave me. She no longer wanted to, but she was capable of causing herself pain if she thought it was the right thing to do.

"Lie here with me," I said, knowing she would not. Not yet.

"Why?" she asked, frowning.

"We're very tactile. We don't just enjoy contact, we need it."

"Not with me."

At least she did not move away from me. My left heart was not yet healed so I did not get up. I took her hand and held it for a while, examined it with body tentacles. This startled her, but did not bring out the phobic terror some Humans are subject to when we touch them that way. Instead, she bent to get a better look at my body tentacles. They were widely scattered now, and the same brown as the rest of my skin. My head tentacles, all hidden in my hair now, were as black as my hair.

"Can you move them all at will?" she asked.

"Yes. As easily as you move your fingers. You've never seen them before, have you?"

"I've hear of them. All my life, I've heard that they were like snakes and the Oankali were covered with them."

"Some are. No Oankali has as few of them as I do now. Even I have the potential to develop a great many more."

She looked at her own arm and its dozens of small tumors. "Actually I think mine are uglier," she said.

I laughed and, with great relief, pulled her down beside me again. She didn't really mind. She was wary, but not afraid.

"You have to tell me what will happen," she said. "I'm afraid for my people. You have to tell me."

I put her head on my shoulder so that I could reach her with both head and body tentacles. She let me position her, then lay relaxed and alert against me. I eased her weariness, but did not let her become drowsy. She was younger than I had thought. She had never had a mate in the Human way. Now she never would. I felt as though I could absorb her into myself. And yet she seemed too far away. If I could just bring her closer, touch her with more sensory tentacles, touch her with . . . with what I did not yet possess.

"This is wonderful," she said. "But I don't know why it should be." She said nothing for a while. On her own, she discovered that if she touched me now with her hand, she felt the touch as though on her own skin, felt pleasure or discomfort just as she made me feel.

"Touch me," she said.

I touched her thigh, and her body flared with sexual feeling. This surprised and frightened her and she caught my free hand and held it in her own. "You haven't told me anything," she said.

"In a way, I've told you everthing," I said, "and all without words."

She let go of my hand and touched me again, let the sensation we shared guide her so that her fingertips slid around the bases of some of my sensory tentacles. She stopped an instant before I would have stopped her. The sensation was too intense.

She took my hand and put it on her breasts, and I

remembered what it had been like to have breasts for João, and to drink from Lilith's breasts. Jesusa's breasts, covered by rough cloth that scratched against the top of my hand, were small and wonderfully sensitive. How had she become accustomed to the rough cloth? Probably she had never worn anything else.

She moaned and shared with me the pleasure of her body until I took my hand away and reluctantly detached from her.

"No!" she said.

"I know. We'll sleep together tonight. I have to talk to you, though, and I wanted you to experience a little of that first. I wanted you to live in my skin for a while."

She sat up and glanced at Tomás, who slept on. "Is that what you do?" she asked. She meant was that all I did.

"For now. When I'm an adult, I'll be able to do more. And also . . . even now, if I spend much time with you, I'll heal you. I can't help it."

"I can't go home if you heal me."

"Jesusa . . . that doesn't really matter."

"My people matter. They matter very much to me."

"Your people are tormenting themselves unnecessarily. They don't even know about the Mars colony, do they?"

"The what?"

"I thought not. And with their background in high-altitude living, they may be better suited to it than most Humans. The Mars colony is exactly what it sounds like: a colony of Humans living and reproducing on the planet Mars. We transport them and we've given them the tools to make Mars livable."

"Why?"

"There are no Oankali living on Mars. It's a Human world."

"*This* should be a Human world!"

"It isn't anymore. It won't ever be again."

Silence.

"That's a hard thing to think about, but it's true. Humans who are sent to Mars are healed completely of any disease or defect. They'll pass only good health on to their children."

"What else had been done to them?"

"Nothing. Not even what I've already done with you.

Their healing won't be done by some hungry ooloi child. It will be done by people who are adult and mated and not especially interested in them. That's good if they want to go to Mars. That's safe."

"And I think what we did is not safe."

"Not safe at all."

"Then you must tell me what you want of me—and of Tomás?"

I turned my face away from her for a moment. I could still lose her. I stood a good chance of losing her. "You know what I want of you. Your people must have warned you. I want to mate with you. With both of you. I want you to stay with me."

"To . . . to marry? But you're . . . we're strangers."

"Are we? Not really. Not after what we've shared. I don't think one of your priests would make us a marriage ceremony, but Oankali and constructs don't have much of a ceremony. For us, mating is biological . . . neuro-chemical."

"I don't understand."

"Our bodies please one another and depend on one another. We keep one another well and make children together. We—"

"Have children with my brother!"

"Jesusa . . ." I shook my head. "Your flesh is so like his that I could transplant some of it to his body, and with only a small adjustment, it would live and grow on him as well as it does on you. Your people have been breeding brother to sister and parent to child for generations."

"Not anymore! We don't have to do that anymore!"

"Because there are more of you now—all closely related. Isn't that so?"

She said nothing.

"And unfortunately there was a mutation. Or perhaps one of your founding parents had a serious genetic defect that was controlled, but not corrected. That wouldn't have mattered if they'd had an ooloi to clear the way for them, but they didn't." I touched her face. "You have one now, so why should you be separated from Tomás?"

She drew back from me. "We've never touched one another that way!"

"I know."

"People had to do what they did in the past. Like the children of Adam and Eve. There wasn't anyone else."

"On Mars there are already a great many others. Why should your people want to stay here and breed dead children or disabled children? They should go to Mars or come to us. We would welcome them."

She shook her head slowly. "They told us you were of the devil."

Now it was my turn to keep quiet. She didn't believe in devils. In spite of her name, she probably didn't believe strongly in gods. She believed in her people and in what her senses told her.

"Your people won't be hurt," I assured her. "People who spend as much time as we do living inside one another's skins are very slow to kill. And if we injure people, we heal them."

"You should let them alone."

"No. We shouldn't."

"They own themselves. They don't belong to you."

"They can't survive as they are. Their gene pool is too small. It's only a matter of time before some disease or effect wipes them out." I stopped for a moment, thinking. "I'm Human enough to understand what they're trying to do. One of my brothers began the Mars colony because he understood the need of Humans to live as themselves, not to blend completely with the Oankali."

"You have brothers?" She was frowning at me as though it had never occurred to her that she and I had anything in common.

"I have brothers and sisters. I even have one ooloi sibling." Had it completed its first metamorphosis yet? Was the family simply waiting for me to return so that Aaor and I could begin our extraterrestrial exile? Let them wait.

I focused on Jesusa. I couldn't lie to her, yet I couldn't tell her everything. I was desperate to keep her and Tomás with me. The people would almost certainly not allow me to find Human mates on the ship, but they would not take away mates I had found on my own. And perhaps they would not exile me at all if they saw that with these two Human, I was stable—not changing others, not changing myself except in a deliberate, controlled way. And Aaor could get mates from among Jesusa's people. It would want them. I had no doubt of that.

So what to do?

"My people will fight," Jesusa said.

"They'll be gassed and taken," I said. "My people like to get that kind of thing over quickly so that they don't have to hurt anyone."

She looked at me with anger—almost with hatred. "I won't tell you where my people are. I would drown myself before I would tell you."

"I wouldn't have asked."

"Why? How will you find out?"

"I won't. My people will. Once they know that your people exist, they'll find them."

She did not look toward the broken gun. She probably could not have seen it in the darkness now, but her body wanted to turn and look. Her hands wanted the gun. Her muscles twitched. If she killed me, no one would find out what I knew. No one would look for her hidden people.

I made up my mind abruptly. She had to know everything or she might die defending her people. She probably could not kill me, but she could force me to act reflexively and kill her.

"Jesusa," I said, "come over here."

She stared at me with hostility.

"Come. I'm going to tell you something my own Human mother didn't learn until she had given birth to two construct children. Your people are not usually told this at all. I . . . I should not tell it to you, but I think I have to. Come."

Her muscles wanted to move her toward me. My scent and her memory of comfort and pleasure drew her, but she moved deliberately away. "Tell me," she said. "Just tell me. Don't touch me again."

I said nothing for a while. It would be easier for her to believe what I said if we were in contact. Humans did not usually understand why being linked into our nervous systems enabled them to feel the truth of what we said, but they did feel it. Now she would not. All her body language told me she would not be persuaded.

Should she still be told?

She had to be.

I spoke to her very softly. "You and your brother mean life to me." I paused. "And in a different way, I mean life to your people. They'll die if they stay where they are. *They'll all die.*"

"Some of us die. Some live." She shook her head. "I don't care what you say. Nothing will kill us if your people let us alone. We're strong enough to stand anything else."

"No."

"You don't know—"

"Jesusa! Listen." When she had settled into an angry silence, I told her what would happen to the Earth, what would be left of it when we were gone. "Nothing will be able to live on what we leave," I said. "If your people stay where they are and keep breeding, they'll be destroyed. Every one of them. There's life for them on Mars, and there's life here with us. But if they insist on staying where they are . . . they won't be allowed to keep having children. That way, by the time we break away from Earth, your people will have died of age."

She shook her head slowly as I spoke. "I don't believe you. Even your people can't destroy all the Earth."

"Not all of it, no. It's like . . . when you eat a piece of fruit that has an inedible core or inedible seeds. There will be a rocky core of the Earth left—a great mass of material, useful for mining, but not for living on. We'll be scattering in a great many ships. Each one will have to be self-sustaining in interstellar space perhaps for thousands of years.

"Self-sustaining in . . . ?"

"Just think of it as being beyond any possible help or dependable resupply."

"In space . . . between the stars. That's what you mean. No sun. Almost nothing."

"Yes."

"The elders who raised us when our mother died . . . they knew about such things. One used to write about them before the war to help others understand."

I said nothing. Let her think for a while.

She sat silent, frowning, sometimes shaking her head. After a while, she rubbed her face with both hands and moved to sit next to Tomás.

"Shall I wake him?" I asked.

She shook her head.

I went into the forest and brought back a few sticks of dry wood. The rain began just as I returned. Jesusa sat where I had left her, rocking back and forth a little. I hung the basket of food that I had brought on the stump of a branch that had been left on one of the support saplings. Jesusa was hungry, but she did not want to eat now. I could satisfy the needs of her body without getting her to eat. Linked with her, I could transfer nourishment to her.

I fed the fire, then went to sit with her, Tomás lying between us.

"I don't know what to think," she said softly. "My brother was going to die, you know." She stroked his black hair. "Someone is always going to die." She paused. "He was going to kill himself as soon as he got me within sight of home. I don't know whether I could have stopped him this time."

"He tried before?" I asked.

She nodded. "That was the reason for this trip. To keep him alive a little longer." She looked at me solemn-faced. "We didn't need you to tell us he was becoming disabled. We've watched it happen to too many of our people. And . . . they just go on having children until they die or it becomes physically impossible." She touched his misshapen face. "Last year, he broke his leg and had to lie on his back with his leg splinted and attached to weights for weeks. He told the elders he didn't remember what happened. I told them he fell. They would have locked him up otherwise. We both knew he'd jumped. He meant to die. That long fall down to the river should have killed him. Thank god it didn't. I promised him we would make this trip before they married us off. I said when his leg was strong, we would slip away. He had wanted to do that for years. Only I knew. It was wrong, of course. Fertile young people risking themselves in the lowland forests, risking the welfare of everyone. . . . I did it for him. I didn't even want to come here." Tears streamed down her face, but she made no sound of crying, no move to wipe her face.

I reached over Tomás, caught her by the waist, and lifted her. She wasn't heavy at all. I put her down beside me so that I was between the two of them—where I belonged.

"You've saved him," I said. "You've saved his life and your people's lives. You've saved yourself from a life of unnecessary misery."

"Have I done so much good? Then how is it that my people would kill me if they found out?"

She believed me. It didn't make her feel any better, but she did believe.

"We can't go home," she said. "The elders always told us that if even one of your people learned the truth about us, they would find us, and the thing we were trying to rebuild would be destroyed."

"Perhaps it will only be healed and transported to Mars. Everyone who wants to go will be sent."

"They won't believe you. They wouldn't even believe me. Even if I went home now, when your people came to collect us, my people would know who had betrayed them."

"That's not what you've done. Anyway, I want you to stay with me."

She studied me, vertical frowns forming between her eyes where there was a small expanse of clear skin. "I don't know if I can do that," she said.

"You're with me now." I lay down and moved close against Tomás so that all the sensory tentacles on his side of my body could reach him. Linking into him was such a sharp, sweet shock that for a moment, I could not see. When the shock had traveled through me, I became aware of Jesusa watching. I reached up and pulled her down with us. She gasped as the contact was completed. Then she groaned and twisted her body so that she could bring more of it into contact with me. Tomás, not really awake yet, did the same, and we lay utterly submerged in one another.

8

By the next morning, most of Jesusa's small tumors had vanished, reabsorbed into her body. She was not truly healed yet, but her skin was soft and smooth for the first time since her early childhood. She cried as she ate the breakfast I prepared from my basket. She examined herself over and over.

Tomás's tumors had been bigger and would take longer to get rid of, but they had clearly begun to shrink.

We had all awakened together—which meant they had awakened when I did. I didn't want to take a chance on Jesusa rationalizing and running again, or worse, deciding to try to kill me again.

They awoke content and rested and in better physical shape than they'd been in for years. Both were fascinated by the obvious changes in Jesusa.

I lay between them, comfortably exhausted on a brand-new level. My body had been working hard all night on two people. And yet, I'd never felt this well, this complete before.

Jesusa, after touching her face and her arms and her legs and finding only smooth skin and beginning to cry, leaned down and kissed me.

"I have," Tomás said, "a very strange compulsion to do that, too." He kept his tone light, but there was real confusion behind it.

I sat up and kissed him, savoring the healing that had taken place so far. Invisible healing as well as shrinkage of visible tumors. His optic nerve was being restored—against the original genetic advice of his body. Insanely one bit of

119

genetic information said the nerve was complete and the genes controlling its development were not to become active again. Yet his genetic disorder went on causing the growth of more and more useless, dangerous tissue on such finished organs and preventing them from carrying on their function.

Tomás had grown patches of hair on his face overnight. When I touched one of them, he smiled. "I have to shave," he said. "I'd grow a beard if I could, but when I tried, Jesusa said it looked like an alpaca sheared by a five-year-old-child."

I frowned. "Alpaca?"

"A highland animal. We raise them for wool to make clothing."

"Oh." I smiled. "I think your beard will grow more evenly when I've finished with you," I said.

"Do you think you'll ever do that?" he asked. "Finish with us?"

My free head and body tentacles tightened flat to my skin with pleasurable sexual tension. "No," I said softly. "I don't think so."

He had to be told everything. He and Jesusa and I talked and rested all that day, then lay together to share the night. The next morning we began several days of walking— drifting, really—back toward my family's camp. We were in no hurry. I taught them to find and make safe use of wild forest foods. They talked about their people and worried about them. Jesusa talked with real horror about the breaking apart of the planet, but Tomás seemed less concerned.

"It isn't real to me," he said simply. "It will happen long after I'm dead. And if you're telling us the truth, Jodahs, there's nothing we can do to prevent it."

"Will you stay with me?" I asked.

He looked at Jesusa, and Jesusa looked away. "I don't know," he said softly.

"If you stay with me, you'll almost certainly live past the time of separation."

He stared at me, frowning, thinking. They both had their silent, thoughtful times.

We wandered downstream, walking and resting and enjoying one another for seven days. Seven very good days.

Tomás's tumors vanished and the sight of his eye returned. His hearing improved. He looked at himself in the water of a small pond and said, "I don't know how I'll get used to being so beautiful."

Jesusa threw a handful of mud at him.

On the morning of our eighth day together, I was more tired than I should have been. I didn't understand why until I realized that the flesh under my arms itched more than usual, and that it was swollen a little. Just a little.

I was beginning my second metamorphosis. Soon, in the middle of the forest, far from even our temporary home, I would fall into a sleep so deep that Tomá and Jesusa would not be able to awaken me.

9

"Will you stay with me?" I asked Tomás and Jesusa as we ate that morning. I had not asked either of them that question since we began to travel together. I had slept in a cocoon of their bodies every night. Perhaps that had helped bring on the change. Oankali ooloi usually made the final change after they had found mates. Mates gave them the security to change. Mates would look after them while they were helpless and be there for them when they awoke. Now, looking at Jesusa and Tomás, I felt afraid, desperate. They had no idea how much I needed them.

Jesusa looked at Tomás, and Tomás spoke.

"I want to stay with you. I don't really know what that will mean, but I want it. There's no place else for me. But you want us both, don't you?"

"Want?" I whispered, and shook my head. "I need you both very much."

I think that surprised them. Jesusa leaned toward me. "You've known Human beings all your life," she said. "But we've never known anyone like you. And . . . you want me to have children with my brother."

Ah. "Touch him."

"What?"

I waited. They had not touched one another since their first night with me. They were not aware of it, but they were avoiding contact.

Tomás reached out toward Jesusa's arm. She flinched, then kept still. Tomás's hand did not quite reach her. He frowned, then drew back. He turned to face me.

"What is it?"

"Nothing harmful. You *can* touch her. You won't enjoy it, but you can do it. If she were drowning, you could save her."

Jesusa reached out abruptly and grasped his wrist. She held on for a moment, both of them rigid with a revulsion they might not want to recognize. Tomás made himself cover her repellent hand with his own.

As abruptly as they had come together, they broke apart. Jesusa managed to stop herself from wiping her hand against her clothing. Tomás did not.

"Oh, god," she said. "What have you done to us?"

I got up, went around her to sit between them. I could still walk normally, but even those few steps were exhausting.

I took their hands, rested each of them on one of my thighs so that I would not have to maintain a grip. I linked into their nervous systems and brought them together as though they were touching one another. It was not illusion. They were in contact through me. Then I gave them a bit of illusion. I "vanished" for them. For a moment, they were together, holding one another. There was no one between them.

By the time Jesusa finished her scream of surprise, I was "back," and more exhausted than ever. I let them go and lay down.

"If you stay," I said, "what you do, you'll do through me. You literally won't touch one another."

"What's the matter with you?" Tomás asked. "You didn't feel the same just now."

"Oh, I'm not the same. I'm changing. Now. I'm maturing."

They did not understand. I saw concern and questioning on their faces, but no alarm. Not yet.

"My final metamorphosis is beginning now," I said. "It will last for several months."

Now they looked alarmed. "What will happen to you?" Jesusa asked. "What shall we do for you?"

"I'm sorry," I told her, "I had no idea it was so close. The first time, I had several days' warning. If it had happened that way this time, I would have been able to go into the river and get home without your help. I can't do that now."

"Did you think we would abandon you?" she demanded. "Is that why you asked us again to stay?"

"Not that you would walk away and leave me here, no. But that . . . you wouldn't wait."

"A few months?"

"As much as a year."

"We have to get you back to your people. We can't find enough food. . . ."

"Wait. Can you . . . will you make a raft? There are young cecropia trees just above the sandbar. Farther inland, there are plenty of lianas. If you can put something together while I'm awake, we can go downriver to my family's camp. I won't let you pass it. Then . . . if you want to leave me, my family won't try to hold you."

Jesusa moved to sit near my head. "Will you be all right if we leave?"

I looked at her for a long time before I could make myself answer. "Of course not."

She got up and walked a short distance away from me, kept her back to me. Tomás moved to where she had been and took my hand.

"We'll build the raft," he said. "We'll get you home." He thought for a moment. "I don't see why we can't stay until you finish your metamorphosis."

I closed my eyes, and I said nothing. Was that how Nikanj had done it a century before? Lilith had been with it when its second metamorphosis began. Had it been tempted to say, "If you stay with me now, you'll never leave?" Or had it simply never thought to say anything? It was Oankali. It had probably never thought to say anything. It wouldn't have been harboring any sexual feeling for her at that point. It had enjoyed her because she was so un-Oankali—different and dangerous and fascinating.

I felt those things myself about these two, but I felt more. As Nikanj had said, I was precocious.

I said nothing at all to Tomás. Someday he would curse me for my silence.

He went to Jesusa and said, "If we stay, we'll have a chance to see how their families work."

"I'm afraid to stay," she said.

"Afraid?"

She picked up the machete. "We should get started on the raft."

"Jesusita, why are you afraid?"

"Why aren't you?" she said. She looked at me, then at him. "This is an alien thing Jodahs wants of us. Certainly it's an un-Christian thing, an un-Human thing. *It's the thing we've been taught against all our lives.* How can we be accepting it or even considering it so easily?"

"Are you?" he asked quietly.

"Of course I am. So are you. You've said you want to stay."

"Yes, but—"

"Something is not right. Jodahs sleeps with us and heals us and pleasures us—and asks only for the opportunity to go on doing these things." She paused, shook her head. "When I think of leaving Jodahs, finding other Human beings, or perhaps going to the colony on Mars, my stomach knots. It wants us to stay and I want to stay and so do you, *and we shouldn't*! Something is wrong."

I fell asleep at that point. It was not deliberate, but it could not have been better timed. Second metamorphosis, I had been told, was not one long sleep as the first one had been. It was a series of shorter sleeps—sleeps several days long.

I frightened them. Jesusa thought first that I was faking, then that I was dead. Only when they were able to get some reaction from my body tentacles did they decide I was alive and probably all right. They carried me down to the river and left me under a tree while they found other, smaller trees to chop down with their machete. Slow, hard work. I perceived and remembered everything in latent memories, stored away for consideration later when I was conscious.

They took good care of me, moving me when they moved, keeping me near them. Without realizing it, they became a torment to me when they touched me, when I could smell them. But they were a much worse torment when they went too far away. My only salvation was the certainty that they would not abandon me and the knowledge that this, uncomfortable as it was, was normal. It would be the same if I were being cared for by a pair of Oankali or a pair of constructs. Nikanj had warned me. Helpless lust and unreasoning anxiety were just part of growing up.

I endured, grateful to Jesusa and Tomás for their loyalty.

The raft took four days to finish. Not only was the machete not the best tool for the job, but Jesusa and Tomás had never built such a thing before. They were not sure what would work and they would not load me onto a craft that would come apart in the water or one they could not control. They spent time learning to control it with long poles and with paddles. They worried that in some places the river might be too deep for poles. They worried about hostile people, too. We would be very visible on the river. People with guns could pick us off if they wanted to. What could we do about that?

I awoke as they were loading me and baskets of food onto the raft. Figs, nuts, bean pods with edible pulp, and several baked applesauce tubers.

"Are you all right?" Tomás asked when he saw my eyes open. He was carrying me toward the raft. I felt as though I could sink into him, merge with him, become him. Yet I felt as though he were days away from me and beyond my reach completely.

"Don't worry," he said, "I won't drop you. Jesusa might, but I won't."

"Don't say that!" Jesusa said quickly. "Jodahs may not know you're joking."

Tomás put me down on the raft. They had made a pallet for

me there of large leaves covering soft grasses. I made myself relax and not clutch at Tomás as he put me down.

He sat down next to me for a moment. "Is there anything you need? You haven't eaten for days."

"People don't eat much during metamorphosis," I said. "On the other hand, eating can take my mind off . . . other things. Do you see the bush there with the deep green leaves?"

He looked around, then pointed.

"Yes, that one. Pull several branches of young leaves from it. I eat the leaves."

"Truly? They're good for you?"

"Yes, but not for you, so don't ever eat them. I can digest them and use their nutrients."

"Eat some nuts."

"No. You eat the nuts. Bring me the leaves."

He obeyed, though slowly.

I ate the first few leaves while he watched incredulously. "I don't understand enough about you," he said.

"Because I eat leaves? I can eat almost anything. Some things are more worth the effort than others."

"More than that. Something I've been trying to figure out. How do you . . . ? I don't mean to offend you, but I can't figure this out on my own." He hesitated, looked around to see where Jesusa was. She was out of sight among the trees. "How do you shit?" he demanded. "How do you piss? You're all closed up."

I laughed aloud. My Human mother had been with Nikanj for almost a year before she asked that question. "We're very thorough," I said. "What we leave behind would make poor fertilizer—except for our ships. We shed what we don't need."

"The way we shed hair or dead skin?"

"Yes. At home, the ship or the town would take it as soon as it was shed. Here, it's dust. I leave it behind when I sleep—when I sleep normally, anyway. People in metamorphosis leave almost nothing behind."

"I've never seen anything."

"Dust."

"And water?"

I smiled. "Easiest to shed when I'm in it, though I can sweat as you do."

"And?"

"That's all. Think Tomás. When did you last see me drink water? I can drink, of course, but normally I get all the moisture I need from what I eat. We use everything that we take in much more thoroughly than you do."

"Why aren't you ever covered in mud?"

"I do one thing at a time."

"And . . . our children would be like you?"

"Not at first. Human-born children look very Human at first. They eliminate in Human ways until metamorphosis." I changed the subject abruptly. "Tomás, I'm going to stay awake through as much of this trip as I can. I should be able to warn you if we're near people so that we can at least stay close to the opposite shore. And I'll have to stop you at my Family's camp. You won't be able to see it from the river."

"All right," he said.

"If I do fall asleep, make camp. Wait for me to wake up. This is a very long river, and I'm not up to backtracking."

"All right," he repeated.

Jesusa arrived then. She had found a cacao tree the night before, and today had climbed it again for one last harvest. I had pointed a cacao tree out to her as we traveled together, and she had discovered she especially liked the pulp of the pods. She put her basket, stuffed with pods, onto the raft, then helped Tomás push off. They poled us into the current not far from shore.

"Listen," I said to them once the raft was moving easily. Both glanced around to show me they were listening.

"If we're attacked or we have to abandon the raft for any reason, push me off into the water—whether I'm awake or not. I can breathe in the water and nothing that lives there will be interested in eating me. Get me out later if you can. If you can't, don't worry about me. Get yourselves out and keep each other safe. I'm much harder to kill than you are."

They didn't argue. Jesusa gave me an odd look, and I remembered her shooting me. Her gun had not been salvageable. The metal parts had been too damaged. Was she remembering how hard I was to kill—or how I had destroyed their most powerful weapon? After a time, she left poling the raft to Tomás. He seemed to have no trouble letting the current carry us and preventing us from drifting too close to either bank, where fallen trees and sandbars made progress slow and dangerous.

Jesusa sat with me and fed me cacao pulp and did not talk to me at all.

10

We drifted for days on the river.

I could not help with paddles or poles. It took all the energy I had just to stay awake. I could and did sit up and spot barely submerged sandbars for them and keep them aware of the general depth of the water. I kept quiet about the animals I could see in the water. The Humans could see almost nothing through the brown murk, but we often drifted past animals that would eat Human flesh if they could get it. Fortunately the worst of the carnivorous fish preferred slower, quieter waters, and were no danger to us.

It was the people who were dangerous.

Twice I directed Jesusa and Tomás away from potentially hostile people—Humans grouped on one side of the river or the other. Resisters still fought among themselves and sometimes robbed and murdered strangers.

I didn't scent the third group of Humans in time. And, unlike the first two, the third group spotted us.

There was a shot—a loud crack like the first syllable of a phrase of thunder. We all fell flat to the logs of the raft, Jesusa losing her pole as she fell.

She was wounded. I could smell the blood rushing out of her.

I lost myself then. I was not fully conscious anymore, but my latent memories told me later that I dragged myself toward her, my body still flat against the logs. From shore, the Humans fired several more times, and Tomás, unaware of Jesusa's injury, cursed them, cursed the current that was not moving us beyond their reach quickly enough, cursed his own broken rifle. . . .

I reached Jesusa, unconscious, bleeding from the abdomen, and I locked on to her.

I was literally unconscious now. There was nothing at work except my body's knowledge that Jesusa was necessary to it, and that she would die from her wound if it didn't help her. My body sought to do for her what it would have done for itself. Even if I had been conscious and able to choose, I could not have done more. Her right kidney and the large blood vessels leading to it had been severely damaged. Her colon had been damaged. She was bleeding internally and poisoning herself with bodily wastes. Fortunately she was unconscious or her pain might have caused her to move away before I could lock into her. Once I was in, though, nothing could have driven me off.

We drifted beyond the range and apparently beyond the interest of the resisters. I was regaining consciousness as Tomás crawled back to us. I saw him freeze as he noticed the blood, saw him look at us, saw him lunge toward us, rocking the raft, then stop just short of touching us.

"Is she alive?" he whispered.

It was an effort to speak. "Yes," I answered after a moment. I couldn't manage anything else.

"What can I do to help?

One more word. "Home."

I was of no use at all to him after that. I had all I could do to keep Jesusa unconscious and alive while my own body insisted on continuing its development and change. I could not heal Jesusa quickly. I wasn't sure I could heal her at all. I had stopped the blood loss, stopped her bodily wastes from poisoning her. It seemed a very long time, though, before I was able to seal the hole in her colon and begin the complicated process of regenerating a new kidney. The wounded one was not salvageable. I used it to nourish her—which involved me breaking the kidney down to its useful components and feeding them to her intravenously. It was the most nutritious meal she had had in days. That was part of the problem. Neither she nor I was in particularly good condition. I worried that my efforts at regeneration would trigger her genetic disorder, and I tried to keep watch. It occurred to me that I could have left her with one kidney until I was through my metamorphosis and able to look after her properly. That was what I should have done.

I hadn't done it because on some level, I was afraid Nikanj would take care of her if I didn't. I couldn't stand to think of it touching her, or touching Tomás.

That one thought drove me harder than anything else could have. It almost caused me to let us pass my family's home site.

The scent of home and relatives got through to me somehow. "Tomás!" I called hoarsely. And when I saw that I had his attention, I pointed. "Home."

He managed to bring us to the bank some distance past my family's cabin. He waded to shore and pulled the raft as close to the bank as he could.

"There's no one around," he said. "And no house that I can see."

"They didn't want to be easily visible from the river," I said. I detached myself from Jesusa and examined her visually. No new tumors. Smooth skin beneath her ragged, bloody, filthy clothing. Smooth skin across her abdomen.

"Is she all right?" Tomás asked.

"Yes. Just sleeping now. I've lost track. How long has it been since she was shot?"

"Two days."

"That long . . . .?" I focused on him with sensory tentacles and saw evidence of the load of worry and work that he had carried. I could think of nothing sufficient to say to him. "Thank you for taking care of us."

He smiled wearily. "I'll go look for some of your people."

"No, they'll notice my scent if they haven't already. They'll be coming. Help Jesusa off, then come back for me. She can walk."

I shook her and she awoke—or half awoke. She cringed

away when Tomás waded into the shallow water and reached for her. He drew back. After a while, she got up slowly, swayed, and followed Tomás's beckoning hand.

"Come on, Jesusita," he whispered. "Off the raft." He walked beside her through the water and up the bank where the ground was dry enough to be firm. There, she sat down and seemed to doze again.

When he came back for me, he held something in his fingers—held it up for me to see. An irregularly shaped piece of metal smaller than the end joint of his smallest finger. It was the bullet I had caused Jesusa's body to expel.

"Throw it away," I said. "It almost took her from us."

He threw it far out into the river.

11

"Some of my family is coming now," I said. Tomás had put me on the bank beside Jesusa. He had sat down beside me to rest. Now he became alert again.

"Tomás," I said softly.

He glanced at me.

"You won't feel comfortable about letting them get close to you or letting them surround you. Jesusa won't either. My family will understand that. And no one will touch you— except the children. You won't mind their touch."

He frowned, gave me a longer look. "I don't understand."

"I know. It has to do with your being with me, letting me heal you, letting me sleep with you. You'll feel . . . drawn to be with Jesusa and me and strongly repelled by others. The feeling won't last. It's normal, so don't let it worry you."

Lilith, Nikanj, and Aaor came out of the trees together. Aaor. It was awake and strong. The family must only have been waiting for me to get home. Exile—true exile—had been that close.

The three stood near enough to speak normally, but not near enough to make Tomás uncomfortable.

"I'm going to have to learn not to worry about you," Lilith said, smiling. "Welcome back." She had spoken in Oankali. She switched to Spanish, which meant she had heard me talking to Tomás. "Welcome," she said to him. "Thank you for caring for our child and bringing it home." She inserted the English "it" because in English the word was truly neuter. Spanish did not have a word that translated exactly. Spanish-speaking people usually handled the ooloi gender by ignoring it. They used masculine or feminine, whichever felt right to them—when they had to use anything. I filled in my own "its" once I knew they understood.

I took Tomás's hand, felt it grip mine desperately, almost painfully, yet his face betrayed no sign of emotion.

"These are two of my parents," I told him, gesturing with my free hand. "Lilith is my birth mother and Nikanj is my same-sex parent. This third one is Aaor, my paired sibling." I enjoyed the sight of it for a moment. It was gray-furred now and, oddly, not that unusual-looking. Perhaps the other siblings helped it stay almost normal. "Aaor has been closer to me than my skin at times," I said. "I think it turned out to be more like me than it would have preferred."

Aaor, who was restraining itself with an obvious effort, said, "When I touch you, Jodahs, I won't let you go for at least a day."

I laughed, remembering its touch, realizing that I was eager to touch it, too, and understand exactly how it had changed. We would not be the same—Human-born and Oankali-born. Examining it would teach me more about myself by similarity and by contrast. And it would want even more urgently to know where I had found Jesusa and Tomás. If its own sense of smell had not recognized them as young and fertile—as mine had not when I met them—Nikanj would have let it know.

"I'll tell you everything," I said. "But put us somewhere dry, first, and feed us." I meant, and all three of them knew it, that Tomás and Jesusa should be given a dry place and food.

Nikanj rested a sensory arm on Aaor's shoulders and some of the straining eagerness went out of Aaor.

"What are you called?" Nikanj asked Tomás. It spoke very softly, yet that soft voice carried so well. Did I sound that way?

Tomás leaned forward, responding to the voice, then was barely able to keep himself from drawing back. He had never seen an Oankali before, and Nikanj, an adult ooloi, was especially startling. He stared, and then was ashamed and looked away. Then he stared again.

"What are you called?" Nikanj repeated.

"Tomás," he answered finally. "Tomás Serrano y Martín." He had not told me that much. He paused, then said, "This is Jesusa, my sister." He touched her hair the way my Human parents sometimes touched one another's hair. "She was shot."

Nikanj focused sharply on me.

"She's all right," I said. "She's exhausted because she hasn't been eating well for a while—and you know how hard I had to make her body work." I turned and shook her. "Jesusa," I whispered. "You're all right. Wake up. We've reached my family." I kept my hand on her shoulder, shook her again gently, wishing I could give her the kind of comfort I would have been able to give only a few days before. But I had had all I could do to save her life.

She opened her eyes, looked around, and saw Nikanj. She turned her face from it and whimpered—a sound I had not heard from her before.

"You're safe," I told her. "These people are here to help us. You're all right. No one will harm you."

She realized finally what I was saying. She fell silent and became almost still. She could not stop her trembling, but she looked at me, then at Lilith, Aaor, and Nikanj. She made herself look longest at Nikanj.

"Excuse me," she said after a moment. "I . . . haven't seen anyone like you before."

Nikanj's many sensory tentacles flattened smooth to its body. "I haven't seen anyone like you for a century," it said.

At the sound of its voice, she looked startled. She turned to look at me, then looked back at Nikanj. I introduced it along with Lilith and Aaor.

"I'm pleased to meet you," Jesusa lied politely. She watched Nikanj, fascinated, not knowing that it held its position of amusement, of smoothness, extra long for her benefit. I went smooth every time I laughed, but my few sensory tentacles were not that visible even when they were not flattened. And I did laugh. Nikanj did not.

"I'm amazed and pleased," Nikanj said. And to me in Oankali, it said, "Where are they from?"

"Later," I said.

"Will they stay, Oeka?"

"Yes."

It focused on me, seemed to expect me to say more. I kept quiet.

Aaor broke the silence. "You can't walk, can you?" it said in Spanish. "We'll have to carry you."

Tomás stood up quickly. "If you'll show me the way," he said, "I'll carry Jodahs." He hesitated for a moment beside Jesusa. "Sister, can you walk?"

"Yes." She stood up slowly, holding her ragged bloody clothing together. She took a tentative step. "I feel all right," she said, "but . . . so much blood."

Aaor had turned to lead the way back to the cabin. Tomás lifted me, and Jesusa walked close to him. I spoke to her from his arms. "You'll have good food to eat here," I told her. "You'll probably be a little hungrier than usual for a while because you're still regrowing part of yourself. Aside from that, you're well."

She took my dangling hand and kissed it.

Tomás smiled. "If you really fell well, Jesusita, give it one more for me. You don't know what it brought you back from."

She looked ahead ad Nikanj. "I don't know what it's brought me back to," she whispered.

"No one will hurt you here," I told her again. "No one will touch you or even come near you. No one will keep you from coming to me when you want to."

"Will they let me go?" she asked.

I turned my head so that I could look at her with my eyes. "Don't leave me," I said very softly.

"I'm afraid. I don't see how I can stay here with your . . . family."

"Stay with *me*."

"Your . . . your relative. The Oankali one. . . ."

"Nikanj. My ooloi parent. It will never touch you." I would get that promise from it before I slept again.

"It's . . . ooloi, like you."

Ah. "No, not like me. It's Oankali. No Human admixture at all. Jesusa, by birth mother is as Human as you are. My Human father looks like a relative of yours. Even when I'm adult, I won't look the way Nikanj does. You'll never have reason to fear me."

"I fear you now because I still don't understand what's happening."

Tomás spoke up. "Jesusa, it saved you. It could hardly move, but it saved you."

"I know," she said. "I'm grateful. More grateful than I can say." She touched my face, then moved her hand to my hair and let her fingers slide expertly around the base of a group of sensory tentacles.

I shuddered with sudden pleasure and frustrated need.

"I'll try to stay until your metamorphosis is over," she said. "I owe you that and more. I promise to stay that long."

My mother turned her head and looked at Jesusa, then at me, looked long at me.

I met her gaze, but said nothing to her.

After a time, she turned back to the path. Her scent, as it reached me, said she was upset, under great stress. But like me, she said nothing at all.

12

We were given food. For a change, I actually needed it. Healing Jesusa had depleted my resources. I had no strength at all, and Jesusa fed me as she fed herself. She seemed to take some comfort in feeding me.

Jesusa and Tomás were given clean, dry clothing. They went to the river to wash themselves and came back to the house clean and content. They ate parched nuts and relaxed with my family.

"Tell us about your people," Aaor said as the sun went down and Dichaan put more wood on the fire. "I know there are things you don't want to tell us, but . . . tell us how your people came to exist. How did your fertile ancestors find one another?"

Jesusa and Tomás looked at each other. Jesusa looked apprehensive, but Tomás smiled. It was a tired, sad smile.

"Our first postwar ancestors never found one another," he said. "I'll tell you if you like."

"Yes!"

"Our elders were people who joined together because they could communicate," he said. "They all spoke Spanish. They were from Mexico and Peru and Spain and Chile and other countries. The First Mother was from Mexico. She was fifteen years old and traveling with her parents. There were others with them who knew this country and who said it would be best to live higher in the mountains. They were on the way up when the First Mother and her own mother were attacked. They had left the group to bathe. The Mother never saw her attackers. She was hit from behind. She was raped—probably many times.

"When she regained consciousness, she was alone. Her mother was there, but she was dead. The First Mother was badly injured. She had to crawl and drag herself back to her people. They cared for her as best they could. Her father couldn't help her. He left her to others. He was so angry at what had been done to her and to her mother that eventually he left the group. The Mother awoke one morning and he was gone. She never saw him again.

"The people had already begun to make homes for themselves in the place they had chosen when they realized the Mother would have a child. No one had thought it was possible. People had tried to accept their sterility. They said it was better to have no children than . . . than to have un-Human children." Tomás looked down at his hands. When he raised his head, he found himself looking directly at Tino.

"My people said the same thing before I left them," Tino said. "They believed it. But it's a lie."

Tomás looked at Lilith, his gaze questioning.

"You know it's a lie," Lilith said quietly.

Tomás looked at me, then continued his story. "The people worried that the Mother's child might not be Human. No one had seen her attackers. No one knew who or what they had been."

Nikanj spoke up. "They could not have believed we would send them away sterile, then change our minds and impregnate one of them while killing another." Even with its soft mature-ooloi's voice, it managed to sound outraged.

Tomás was already able to look at it, speak to it. It had been careful not to notice when he studied it as he ate. Now he said, "They said you could do almost anything. Some of them said your powers came from the devil. Some said you *were* devils. Some were disgusted with that kind of talk. To them, you were only the enemy. They didn't believe you had raped the Mother. They believed the Mother could be their tool to defeat you. They took her in and cared for her and fed her even when they didn't have enough to eat themselves. When her son was born, they helped her care for him and they showed him to everyone so that the people could see that he was perfect and Human. They called him Adan. Her name was María de la Luz. When Adan was weaned, they cared for him. They encouraged his mother to work in the gardens and help with the building and be away from her son. That way, when the time came, when Adan was thirteen years old, they were able to put mother and son together. By then, both had been taught their duty. And by then, everyone had realized that the Mother was not only fertile but mortal—as they seemed not to be. By the time her first daughter was born, the Mother looked older than some of those who had helped her raise her son.

"The Mother bore three daughters eventually. She died with the birth of her second son. That son was . . . seriously deformed. He had a hole in his back. People say you could see the spine. And he had other things wrong with him. He died and was buried with the Mother in a place . . . that is sacred to us. The people built a shrine there. Some have seen the Mother when they went there to think or to pray. They've seen her spirit." Tomás stopped and looked at the three Oankali. "Do you believe in spirits?"

"We believe in life," Ahajas said.

"Life after death?"

Ahajas smoothed her tentacles briefly in agreement. "When I'm dead," she said, "I will nourish other life."

"But I mean—"

"If I died on a lifeless world, a world that could sustain some form of life if it were tenacious enough, organelles within each cell of my body would survive and evolve. In perhaps a thousand million years, that world would be as full of life as this one."

". . . it would?"

"Yes. Our ancestors have seeded a great many barren worlds that way. Nothing is more tenacious than the life we are made of. A world of life from apparent death, from dissolution. That's what we believe in."

"Nothing more?"

Ahajas became smooth enough with amusement to reflect firelight. "No, Lelka. Nothing more."

He did not ask what "Lelka" meant, though he couldn't have known. It meant mated child—something parents called their adult children and the mates of their children. I would have to ask her not to call him that. Not yet.

"When I was little," Tomás said, "I planted a tree at the Mother's shrine." He smiled, apparently remembering. "Some people wanted to pull it up. It grew so well, though, that no one touched it. People said the Mother must like having it there." He stopped and looked at Ahajas.

She nodded Humanly and watched him with interest and approval.

"The Mother had twenty-three grandchildren," he continued. "Fifteen survived. Among these were several who were deformed or who grew deformed. They were fertile, and not all of their children had the deformities. The deformed ones could not be spared. Sometimes smooth children with only a few dark spots on their skin had deformed young. One of our elders said this was a disorder that had been known before the war. He had known a woman who had it and who looked much the way I did before Jodahs healed me."

Everyone turned at once and focused on me.

"Ask me when his story is finished," I said. "I don't know a name for the disease anyway. I can only describe it."

"Describe it," Lilith said.

I looked at her and understood that she was asking me for more than a description of the disorder. Her face was set and grim, as it had been since Jesusa promised to stay with me through metamorphosis. She wanted to know what reason there might be apart from her love for me for not telling the Humans how bound to me they were becoming. She wanted to know why she should betray her own kind with silence.

"It was a genetic disorder," I said. "It affected their skin, their bones, their muscles, and their nervous systems. It made tumors—large ones on Tomás's face and upper body. His optic nerve was affected. The bones of his neck and one arm were affected. His hearing was affected. Jesusa was covered head to foot in small very visible tumors. They didn't impair her ability to move or to use her senses."

"I was very lucky," Jesusa said quietly. "I looked ugly, but people didn't care, because I could have children. I didn't suffer the way Tomás did."

Tomás looked at her. The look said more than even a shout

of protest could have. "You suffered," he said. "And if not for Jodahs, you would have made yourself go back and suffer more. For the rest of your life."

She stared at the floor, then into the fire. There was no shyness in the gesture. She simply did not agree with him. The corners of her mouth turned slightly downward. As her brother began speaking again, I took her hand. She jumped, looked at me as though I were a stranger. Then she took my hand between her own and held it. I didn't think she had noticed that across the room from us Tino was holding one of Nikanj's sensory arms in exactly the same way.

"Sometimes," Tomás was saying, "people have only brown spots and no tumors. Sometimes they have both. And sometimes their minds are affected. Sometimes there are other troubles and they die. Children die." He let his voice vanish away.

"No more!" Lilith said. "That misery will soon be over for them."

Tomás turned to face her. "You must know they won't thank me or Jesusa for that. They'll hate us as traitors."

"I know."

"Was it that way for you?"

Lilith looked downward for a moment, moving only her eyes. "Has Jodahs told you about the Mars colony?"

"Yes."

"It didn't exist as an alternative for me."

"My people may not see it as an alternative either."

"If they're wise, they will." She looked at Nikanj. "Their disorder does sound like something that was around before the war, if it matters. In the United States, people called it *neurofibromatosis*. I don't know the Spanish name for it. It could have occurred as a mutation in one or more of the Mother's children if no one had it until the third generation. I remember reading about a couple especially horrible prewar cases. Sometimes the tumors became malignant. That would be a special attraction to Jodahs, I think. Ooloi can see great unused potential in that kind of thing."

"See it and smell it and taste it," Aaor said.

Everyone focused on it.

"I can change to look the way Jodahs does," it said.

"There must be two more or at least one more sick Human among the Mother's people who would join me."

Silence. Jesusa and Tomás looked startled.

"You don't understand how strongly we're taught against you," Tomas said. "And most of us believe. Jesusa and I came down to the lowlands to see a little of the world before she began to have child after child, and before I became too crippled. No one else we know of had done such a thing. I don't think anyone else would."

"If I could reach them," Aaor said, "I could convince them."

I could see the hunger in it, the desperation. Ayodele and Yedik moved to sit on either side of it and ease its discomfort as best they could. They seemed to do this automatically, as though they had finally adapted to having ooloi siblings.

But Aaor was not comforted. "I'm one more mistake!" it said. "One more ooloi who shouldn't exist. There's no other place on Earth for me to find mates. And if their people are collected and given the choice of Mars, union with us, or sterility where they are, I'll never get near them! Even the ones who choose union with us will be directed to other mates. Mates who are not accidents."

"None of them will accept union," Jesusa said. "I know them. I know what they believe."

"But you don't know us well enough yet," Aaor said. "Did you know what you would do . . . before Jodahs touched you?"

"I know I won't lead you or anyone else to my people," she told it. "If your people can find mine without us as Jodahs said, we can't stop you. But nothing you can say would make us help you."

"You don't understand!" it said, leaning toward her.

"I know that," she admitted, "and I'm sorry."

They said more as I drifted into sleep, but they found no common ground. Throughout the argument, Jesusa never let go of my hand. When Nikanj saw that I had fallen asleep, it said I should be taken to the small room that had been set aside for Aaor's metamorphosis.

"There are too many distractions for it out here," it told Jesusa and Tomás. "Too much stimulation. It should be isolated and allowed to focus inward on the changes its body must make."

"Does it have to be isolated from us?" Tomás asked.

"Of course not. The room is large enough for three, and Jodahs will always need the companionship of at least one person. If you both have to leave it for a while, tell Aaor or tell me. The room is over there." It pointed with a strength hand.

Tomás lifted my unconscious body, Jesusa helping him with me now that I was deadweight. I have a clear, treasured memory of the two of them carrying me into the small room. They did not know then that my memory went on recording everything my senses perceived even when I was unconscious. Yet they handled me with great gentleness and care, as they had from the beginning of my change. They did not know that this was exactly what Oankali mates did at these times. And they did not see Aaor watching them with a hunger that was so intense that its face was distorted and its head and body tentacles elongated toward us.

III

Imago

III

Tango

1

During my metamorphosis, Aaor lost its coat of gray fur. Its skin turned the same soft, bright brown as Jesusa's, Tomás's and my own. It grew long, black Human-looking hair and began to wear it as Tino wore his—bound with a twist of grass into a long tail down his back. I wore mine loose.

"Apart from that," Jesusa told me during one of my waking times, "the two of you could be twins."

Yet she avoided Aaor—as did Tomás. It smelled more like me than anyone else alive. But it did not smell exactly like me. Their Human noses had no trouble perceiving the difference. They didn't know that was what they were perceiving, but they avoided Aaor.

And it did not want to be avoided.

I found its loneliness and need agonizing when it touched me. It awoke me several times as I lay changing. It didn't mean to, but my body perceived it as an unhealed wound, and I could not rest until I had eased its pain and given . . . not healing, but momentary relief. What I gave was inadequate and short-lived, but Aaor came back for it again and again.

Once, lying linked with me, it asked if I could give it one of the young Humans.

I hurt it. I didn't mean to, but what it said provoked reaction before I could control myself. Direct neural stimulation. Pure pain. As pure as any sensation can be. I did manage not to loop the pain between us and keep it going.

Yet afterward, Aaor needed more healing. I kept it with me to give it comfort and ease its loneliness. It stayed until I fell asleep.

I never gave Aaor a verbal answer to its question. It never repeated the question. It seemed to realize that I could no longer separate myself deliberately from Tomás and Jesusa. They could still leave me, but they wouldn't. Jesusa took the promises she gave very seriously. She would not try to leave until I was on my feet again. And Tomás would not leave without her. By the time they were prepared to go, it would be too late.

My only fear was that someone in the family would tell them. My mother believed she should, but she had not, so far. She loved me, and yet, until now, she had been able to do nothing to help me. She had not been able to make herself destroy the only chance I was likely to get of having the mates I needed.

Yet she was weighted with guilt. One more betrayal of her own Human kind for people who were not Human, or not altogether Human. She spoke to Jesusa as a much older sister—or as a same-sex parent. She advised her.

"Listen to Jodahs," I heard her say on one occasion. "Listen carefully. It will tell you what it wants you to know. It won't lie to you. But it will withhold information. Once you've heard what it has to say, get away from it. Get out of the house. Go to the river or a short way into the forest. Do your thinking there about what it's told you, and decide what questions you still need answers to. Then come home and ask."

"Home?" Jesusa whispered so softly I almost failed to hear. They were outside the house, replacing the roof thatch. They were not near my room, but my mother probably knew I could hear them.

"You live here," my mother said. "That makes this home. It isn't a permanent home for any of us." She was good at evasion and withholding information herself.

"Would you go to Mars if you could?" Jesusa asked.

"Leave my family?"

"If you were as I am. If you had no family."

My mother did not answer for a long time. She sighed

finally. "I don't know how to answer that. I'm content with these people. More than content. I lost my husband and my son before the war. They died in an accident. When the war came, I lost everything else. We all did, we elders, as you call us. I couldn't give up and die, but I expected almost nothing. Food and shelter, maybe. An absence of pain. Nikanj said it knew I needed children, so it took seed from the man I had then and made me pregnant. I didn't think I would ever forgive it for that."

"But . . . you have forgiven it?"

"I've understood it. I've accepted it. I wouldn't have believed I could do that much. Back when I met my first mature ooloi, Nikanj's parent Kahguyaht, I found it alien, arrogant, and terrifying. I hated it. I thought I hated all ooloi."

She paused. "Now I feel as though I've loved Nikanj all my life. Ooloi are dangerously easy to love. They absorb us, and we don't mind."

"Yes," Jesusa agreed, and I smiled. "I'm afraid, though, because I don't understand them. I'll go to Mars if I don't stay with Jodahs. I can understand settling a new place. I know what to expect from a Human husband."

"Look at my family, Jesusa—and realize you're only seeing six of our children. This is what you can expect if you mate with Jodahs. There's closeness here that I didn't have with the family I was born into or with my husband and son."

"But you have Oankali mates other than Nikanj."

"You will, too, eventually. With Jodahs, I mean. And your children will look much like mine. And half of them will be born to an Oankali female, but will inherit from all five of you."

After a time, Jesusa said, "Ahajas and Dichaan aren't so bad. They seem . . . very gentle."

"Good mates. I was with Nikanj before they were—like you with Jodahs. That's best, I think. An ooloi is probably the strangest thing any Human will come into contact with. We need time alone with it to realize it's probably also the best thing."

"Where would we live?"

"You and your new family? In one of our towns. I think any one of them would eventually welcome the three of you. You'd be something brand-new—the center of a lot of attention. Oankali and constructs love new things."

"Jodahs says it had to go into exile because it was a new thing."

"Is that what it said, really?"

Silence. What was Jesusa doing? Searching her memory for exactly what I had said? "It said it was the first of its kind," she said finally. "The first construct ooloi."

"Yes."

"It said there weren't supposed to be any construct ooloi yet, so the people didn't trust it. They were afraid it would not be able to control itself as an ooloi must. They were afraid it would hurt people."

"It did hurt some people, Jesusa. But it's never hurt Humans. And it's never hurt anyone when it's had Humans with it."

"It told me that."

"Good. Because if it hadn't, I would have. It needs you more than Nikanj ever needed me."

"You want me to stay with it."

"Very much."

"I'm afraid. This is all so different. . . . How did you ever . . . ? I mean . . . with Nikanj. . . . How did you decide?"

My mother said nothing at all.

"You didn't have a choice, did you?"

"I did, oh, yes. I chose to live."

"That's no choice. That's just going on, letting yourself be carried along by whatever happens."

"You don't know what you're talking about," my mother said.

After that, there was no talk for a while. My mother had not shouted those last words, as some Humans would have. She had almost whispered them. Yet they carried such feeling, they would have silenced me, too—and I did know much of what my birth mother had survived. And it was so much more than she had said that Jesusa would not have wanted to hear it. Yet, in a way, in my mother's voice she had heard it. It was not until I had almost drifted off to sleep that they spoke again. Jesusa began.

"It's flattering to think that Jodahs needs us. It seems so powerful, so able to endure anything. At first I couldn't understand why it even wanted us. I was suspicious."

"It can endure a great deal of physical suffering. And it will have to if you leave it."

"There are other Humans for it to mate with."

"No, there aren't. There's Mars now. Resisters choose to go there. Ordinary resisters are too old for Jodahs anyway. As for the few young Humans born on the ship, they're rare and spoken for."

"So . . . what will happen to Jodahs if we leave?"

"I don't know. Just as I don't know what's going to happen to Aaor, period. It's Aaor that I'm most worried about now."

"It asked me if I would tell it where my people were—tell it alone so that it could go to them and try to persuade two of them to mate with it."

"What was your answer?"

"That they would kill it. They would kill it as soon as they realized what it was."

"And?"

"It said it didn't care. It said Jodahs had us, but it was starving."

"Did you tell it what it wanted to know?"

"I couldn't. Even if I didn't know how my people would greet it, I couldn't betray them that way. They'll already think of me as a traitor when the Oankali come for them."

"I know. Aaor knows, too, really. But it's desperate."

"Tomás says it asked him, too."

"That's unusual. Has it asked you more than once?"

"Three times."

"That goes beyond unusual. I'll talk to Nikanj about it."

"I don't mean to make trouble for it. I wish I could help it."

"It's already in trouble. And right now, Nikanj is probably the only one who can help it."

I stopped fighting sleep and let myself drift off. I would talk to Aaor when I awoke again. It was starving. I didn't know what I could do about that, but there must be something.

2

But I had no chance to talk to Aaor before my second metamorphosis ended. It left home as I had. It wandered, perhaps looking for some sign of Jesusa and Tomás's people.

It found only aged, hostile, infertile resisters who had nothing to offer it except bullets and arrows.

It changed radically: grew fur again, lost it, developed scales, lost them, developed something very like tree bark, lost that, then changed completely, lost its limbs, and went into a tributary of our river.

When it realized it could not force itself back to a Human or Oankali form, could not even become a creature of the land again, it swam home. It swam in the river near our cabin for three days before anyone realized what it was. Even its scent had changed.

I was awake, but not yet strong enough to get up. My sensory arms were fully developed, but I had not yet used them. By the time Oni and Hozh found Aaor in the river, I was just learning to coordinate them as lifting and handling limbs.

Hozh showed me what Aaor had become—a kind of near mollusk, something that had no bones left. Its sensory tentacles were intact, but it no longer had eyes or other Human sensory organs. Its skin, very smooth, was protected by a coating of slime. It could not speak or breathe air or make any sound at all. It had attracted Hozh's attention by crawling up the bank and forcing part of its body out of the water. Very difficult. Painful. Its altered flesh was very sensitive to sunlight.

"I would never have recognized it if I hadn't touched it," Hozh told me. "It didn't even smell the same. In fact, it hardly smelled at all."

"I don't understand that," I said. "It isn't an adult yet. How can it change its scent?"

"Suppressed. It suppressed its scent. I don't think it intended to."

"It doesn't sound as though it intended to become what it has in any way. When it can be brought to the house, tell Ooan to bring it to me."

"Ooan has taken it back into the water to help it change back. Ooan says it almost lost itself. It was becoming more and more what it appeared to be."

"Hozh, are Jesusa and Tomás around the house?"

"They're at the river. Everyone is."

"Ask them to come to me."

"Can you help Aaor?"

"I think so."

It went away. A short time later Jesusa and Tomás came to me and sat on either side of me. I thought about sitting up to say what I had to say to them, but that would have been exhausting, and there were other things I wanted to do with the energy I had.

"You saw Aaor?" I asked them.

Tomás nodded. Jesusa shuddered and said, "It was a . . . a great slug."

"I think we can help it," I said. "I wish it had come to me before it went away. I think we could have helped it even then."

"We?" Tomás said.

"One of you on one side of me and Aaor on the other. I think I can bring you and it together enough to satisfy it. I think I can do that with no discomfort to you." I touched each of them with a sensory arm. "In fact, I hope I can arrange things so that you enjoy it."

Tomás examined my left sensory arm, his touch bringing it

to life as nothing else could. "So you'll give Aaor a little pleasure," he said. "What good will that do?"

"Aaor wants Human mates. It *must* have mates of some kind. Until it can get them, will you share what we have with it?"

Jesusa took my right sensory arm and simply held it. "I couldn't touch Aaor," she said.

"No need. I'll touch it. You touch me."

"Will it be changed back to what it was? Will Nikanj finish changing it before it brings it to us?"

"It will not be a limbless slug when it's brought to us. But it won't be what it was when it left us either. Nikanj will make it a land creature again. That will take days. Nikanj won't even bring it out of the river until it has developed bones again and can support itself. By the time it's able to come to us, we'll be ready for it."

Jesusa let go of my sensory arm. "I don't know whether I can be ready for it. You didn't see it, Jodahs. You don't know how it looked."

"Hozh showed me. Very bad, I know. But it's my paired sibling. It's also the only other being in existence that's like me. I don't know what will happen to it if I don't help it."

"But Nikanj could—"

"Nikanj is our parent. It will do all it can. It did all it could for me." I paused, watching her. "Jesusa, do you understand that what happened to Aaor is what was in the process of happening to me when you found me?"

Tomás moved against me slightly. "You were still in control of yourself," he said. "You were even able to help us."

"I never stayed away from home as long as Aaor has. As it was, I don't think I would have gotten back without you. I would have gone into the water or into the ground for my second metamorphosis. Our changes don't go well when we're alone. I don't know what I would have become."

"You think Aaor is in its second metamorphosis?" Jesusa asked.

"Probably."

"No one said so."

"They would have if you'd asked them. To them it was

obvious. Once we get Aaor stabilized, it can finish its change in here. I'll be up soon."

"Where will we sleep?" Jesusa asked.

With me! I thought instantly. But I said, "In the main room. We can build a partition if you like."

"Yes."

"And we'll have to go on spending some of our time with Aaor. If we don't, its change will go wrong again."

"Oh, god," Jesusa whispered.

"Have the two of you eaten recently?"

"Yes," Tomás said. "We were having dinner with your Human parents when Oni and Hozh found Aaor."

"Good." They could share their meal with me and save me the trouble of eating. "Lie down with me."

They did that willingly enough. Jesusa cringed a little when for the first time I looped a sensory arm around her neck. When she was still, I settled into her with every sensory tentacle on her side of my body. I could not let her move again for a while.

Then with relief that was beyond anything I had ever felt with her, I extended my sensory hand, grasped the back of her neck with it, and sank filaments of it bloodlessly into her flesh.

For the first time, I injected—could not avoid injecting—my own adult ooloi substance into her.

By the neural messages I intercepted, I knew she would have convulsed if she had been able to move at all. She did shout, and for an instant I was distracted by the abrupt adrenaline scent of Tomás's alarm.

With my free sensory arm, I touched the skin of his face. "She's all right," I made myself say. "Wait."

Perhaps he believed me. Perhaps the expression on Jesusa's face reassured him. Whatever the reason, he grew calm and I focused completely on Jesusa. I should have gone into both of them at once, but this first time as an adult, I wanted to savor their individual essences separately.

Adult awareness felt sharper to me, finer and different in some way I had not yet defined. The smell-taste-feel of Jesusa, the rhythm of her heartbeat, the rush of her blood, the texture of her flesh, the easy, right, life-sustaining working of her organs, her cells, the smallest organelles within her cells—all this was a vast, infinitely absorbing complexity. The genetic error that had caused her and her people so much misery was as obvious to me as a single cloud in an otherwise clear sky. I was tempted to begin now to make repairs. Her body cells would be easy to alter, though the alteration would take time. The sex cells, though, the ova, would have to be replaced. Both her parents had the disorder and about three quarters of her own ova were defective. I would have to cause parts of her body to function as they had not since before her birth. Best to save that kind of work until later. Best simply to enjoy Jesusa now—the complex harmonies of her, the built-in danger of her genetically inevitable Human conflict: intelligence versus hierarchical behavior. There was a time when that conflict or contradiction—it was called—both frightened some Oankali so badly that they withdrew from contact with Humans. They became Akjai—people who would eventually leave the vicinity of Earth without mixing with Humans.

To me, the conflict was spice. It had been deadly to the Human species, but it would not be deadly to Jesusa or Tomás any more than it had been to my parents. My children would not have it at all.

Jesusa, solemn and questioning, beautiful on levels she would probably never understand, would surely be one of the mothers of those children.

I enjoyed her for a few moments more, especially enjoyed her pleasure in me. I could see how my own ooloi substance stimulated the pleasure centers of her brain.

"Monitor them very carefully," Nikanj had told me. "Give them as much as they can take, and no more. Don't hurt them, don't frighten them, don't overstimulate them. Start them slowly, and in only a little time, they will be more willing to give up eating than to give you up."

Jesusa had only begun to taste me—me as an adult—and I could see that this was true. She had liked me very much as a subadult. But what she felt now went beyond liking, beyond loving, into the deep biological attachment of adulthood. Literal, physical addiction to another person, Lilith called it. I couldn't think about it that coldly. For me it meant that soon Jesusa would not want to leave me, would not be able to leave me for more than a few days at a time.

It worked both ways, of course. Soon I would not be able to stand long separation from her. And she could hurt me by deliberately avoiding me. From what I knew of her, she would be willing to do this if she thought she had cause—even though she would inflict as much pain on herself as on me. Lilith had done that to Nikanj many times before the Mars colony was established.

Human males could be dangerous, and Human females frustrating. Yet I felt compelled to have both. So did Aaor, no doubt. If Jesusa and Tomás ever turned their worst Human characteristics against me, it would probably be on account of Aaor. I had no choice but to try to help it, and Jesusa and Tomás must help me with it. I did not know whether I could make the experience easy for them.

All the more reason to see that they enjoyed this experience.

Jesusa grew pleasantly weary as I explored her and healed the few bruises and small wounds she had acquired. Her greatest enjoyment would happen when I brought her together with Tomás and shared the pleasure of each of them with the other, mingling with it my own pleasure in them both. When I could make an ongoing loop of this, we would drown in one another.

But that was for later. Now, without apparent movement, I caressed and lulled Jesusa into deep sleep.

"They will never understand what treasure they are," Nikanj had said to me once while it sat with me. "They see our differences—even yours, Lelka—and they wonder why we want them."

I detached myself from Jesusa, lingering for a moment over the salt taste of her skin. I had once heard my mother say to Nikanj, "It's a good thing your people don't eat meat. If you did, the way you talk about us, our flavors and your hunger and your need to taste us, I think you would eat us instead of fiddling with our genes." And after a moment of silence, "That might even be better. It would be something we could understand and fight against."

Nikanj had not said a word. It might have been feeding on

her even then—sharing bits of her most recent meal, taking in dead or malformed cells from her flesh, even harvesting a ripe egg before it could begin its journey down her fallopian tubes to her uterus. It stored some of the eggs and consumed the rest. I would have taken an egg from Jesusa if one had been ready. "We feed on them every day," Nikanj had said to me. "And in the process, we keep them in good health and mix children for them. But they don't always have to know what we're doing."

I turned to face Tomás, and without a word, he lay down beside me, and used his arms to pull me closer to him. When he had kissed me very thoroughly, he said, "Will I always have to wait?"

"Oh, no," I said, positioning him so that he would be comfortable. "Once I've tasted you this way, I doubt that I'll ever be able to keep you waiting again."

I looped one sensory arm around his neck, exposed my sensory hand. I paralyzed him as I had Jesusa, but left him an illusion of movement. "Males in particular need to feel that they're moving," Nikanj had told me. "You'll enjoy them more if you give them the illusion they're climbing all over you."

It was entirely right. And though I had not been able to collect an egg from Jesusa, I collected considerable sperm from Tomás. Much of it carried the defective gene and was useless for procreation. Protein. The rest of it I stored for future use.

Tomás was stronger than Jesusa. He lasted longer before he tired. Just before I put him to sleep, he said, "I never intended to let you get away from me. Now I know you never will."

I used his muscles to move us both close against Jesusa. There, with me wedged between them, the two could sleep and I could rest and take a little more of their dinner. They wouldn't feel it. They could spare it, and I needed it to build strength fast now—for Aaor's sake.

3

Aaor was in its second metamorphosis. When Nikanj brought it to me after several days of reconstruction, it was not yet recognizable. Not like a Human or an Oankali or any construct I had ever seen.

Its skin was deep gray. Patches of it still glistened with slime. Aaor could not walk very well. It was bipedal again, but very weak, and its coordination had not returned as it should have.

It was hairless.

It could not speak aloud.

Its hands were webbed flippers.

"It keeps slipping away," Nikanj said. "I'd brought it almost back to normal, but it has no control left. The moment I release it, it drifts toward a less complex form."

It placed Aaor on the pallet we had prepared for it. Tomás had followed it in. Now he stood staring as Aaor's body retreated farther and farther from what it should have been. Jesusa had not come in at all.

"Can you help it?" Tomás asked me.

"I don't know," I said. I lay down alongside it, saw that it was watching me. Its reconstructed eyes were not what they should have been either. They were too small. They protruded too much. But it could see with them. It was staring at my sensory arms. I wrapped them both around it, wrapped my strength arms around it as well.

It was deeply, painfully afraid, desperately lonely and hungry for a touch it could not have.

"Lie down behind me, Tomás," I said, and saw with my sensory tentacles how he hesitated, how his throat moved

157

when he swallowed. Yet he lay behind me, drew up close, and let me share him with Aaor as I had already shared him with Jesusa.

In spite of my efforts, there was no pleasure in the exercise. Something had gone seriously wrong with Aaor's body, as Nikanj had said. It kept slipping away from me—simplifying its body. It had no control of itself, but like a rock rolling downhill, it had inertia. Its body "wanted" to be less and less complex. If it had stayed unattended in the water for much longer, it would have begun to break down completely—individual cells each with its own seed of life, its own Oankali organelle. These might live for a while as single-cell organisms or invade the bodies of larger creatures at once, but Aaor as an individual would be gone. In a way, then, Aaor's body was trying to commit suicide. I had never heard of any carrier of the Oankali organism doing such a thing. We treasured life. In my worst moments before I found Jesusa and Tomás, such dissolution had not occurred to me. I didn't doubt that it would have happened eventually—not as something desirable, but as something inescapable, inevitable. We called our need for contact with others and our need for mates *hunger*. The word had not been chosen frivolously. One who could hunger could starve.

The people who had wanted me safely shut away on Chkahichdahk had been afraid not only of what my instability might cause me to do but of what my hunger might cause me to do. Dissolution had been one unspoken possibility. Dissolution in the river would be bound to affect—to infect—plants and animals. Infected animals would be drawn to areas like Lo, where ship organisms were growing. So would free-living cells be drawn to such places. Only a very few cells would end by causing trouble—causing diseases and mutations in plants, for instance.

Aaor wanted to continue living as Aaor. It tried to help me bring it back to a normal metamorphosis, but without words, I discouraged its efforts. It had not even enough control to help in its own restoration.

Tomás wanted desperately to withdraw from me and from Aaor. I put him to sleep and kept him with me. His presence would help Aaor whether he was conscious or not.

For a day and a half, the three of us lay together, forcing Aaor's body to do what it no longer wanted to do. By the time Tomás and I got up to go to bathe and eat, Aaor looked almost as it had before it went away. Smooth brown skin, a sensory arm bud under each strength arm, a dusting of black hair on its head, fingers without webbing, speech.

"What am I going to do?" it asked just before we left it with Nikanj.

"We'll take care of you," I promised.

Without a word to each other, Tomás and I went to the river and scrubbed ourselves.

"I don't ever want to do that again," Tomás said as we emerged from the water.

I said nothing. The next day, as Aaor's body shape began to change in the wrong way, Tomás and I did it again. He didn't want to, but he looked at Aaor and me and reluctantly lay down alongside me.

The next time it happened, I called Jesusa. Afterward, at the river, she said, "I feel as though I've been crawled over by a lot of slugs!"

Aaor's body did not learn stability. Again and again, it had to be brought back from drifting toward dissolution. Working with Jesusa or Tomás, I could always bring it back, but I couldn't hold it. Our work was never finished.

"Why does it always feel so disgusting?" Jesusa demanded after a long session. We had washed. Now three of us shared a meal—something we weren't able to do very often.

"Two reasons," I said. "First, Aaor isn't me. Mated people don't want that kind of contact with ooloi who aren't their mates. The reasons are biochemical." I stopped. "Aaor smells wrong and tastes wrong to you. I wish I could mask that for you, but I can't."

"We never touch it, and yet I feel it," Jesusa said.

"Because it needs to feel you. I make you sleep because it doesn't need to feel your revulsion. You can't help feeling revulsion, I know, but Aaor doesn't need to share it."

"What's the second reason?" Tomás asked.

I hugged myself with my strength arms. "Aaor is ill. It should not keep sliding away from us the way it does. It should stabilize the way my siblings used to help me stabilize. But it can't." I looked at his face—thinner than it should have been, though he got plenty to eat. The effects of his sessions with Aaor were beginning to show. And Jesusa looked older than she should have. The vertical lines between her eyes had deepened and become set. When all this was over I would erase them.

She and Tomás looked at one another bleakly.

"What is it?" I asked.

Jesusa moved uncomfortably. "What will happen to Aaor?" she asked. "How long will we have to keep helping it?" She leaned back against the cabin wall. "I don't know how much longer I can stand it."

"If we can get it through metamorphosis," I said, "it might stabilize just because its body is mature."

"Do you think you would have without us?" Jesusa asked.

I didn't answer. After a moment, no answer was necessary.

"What will happen to it?" she insisted.

"Ship exile, probably. We'll take it back to Lo, and it will be sent to the ship. There it may find Oankali or construct mates who can stabilize it. Or perhaps it will finally be . . . be allowed to dissolve. Its life now is terrible. If it has nothing better to look forward to . . ."

They turned simultaneously and looked at each other again. They were paired siblings, after all, though they did not think in such terms. They were like Aaor and me. Between them a look said a great deal. That same look excluded me.

Jesusa took one of my sensory arms between her hands and coaxed out the sensory hand. She seemed to do this as naturally as my male and female parents did it with Nikanj. She rarely touched my strength arms now that my sensory arms had grown.

"Nikanj has talked to us about Aaor," she said softly.

I focused narrowly on her. "Nikanj?"

"It told us what you've just told us. It said Aaor probably would dissolve. Die."

"Not exactly die."

"Yes! Yes, die. It will not be Aaor any longer no matter how many of its cells live. Aaor will be gone!"

I was startled by her sudden vehemence. I resisted the

impulse to calm her chemically because she did not want to be calmed.

"We know more about dying than you do," she said bitterly. "And, I tell you, I know death when I see it."

I put my strength arm around her, but could not think of anything to say.

Tomás spoke finally. "At home, she was made to help with the sick and the dying. She hated it, but people trusted her. They knew she would do what was necessary, no matter how she felt." He sighed. "Like you, I suppose. There must be something wrong with me—to love only serious, duty-bound people."

I smiled and extended my free sensory arm to him.

He came to sit with us and accepted the arm. No intensity now. Only comfort in being together. We'd had little of that lately.

"If Aaor had a chance to mate with a pair of Humans," Jesusa said, "would it survive?"

She felt frightened and sick to her stomach. She spoke as though the words had been beaten out of her. Both Tomás and I stared at her.

"Well, Jodahs? Would it?"

"Yes," I said. "Almost certainly."

She nodded. "What I was thinking is that if you could fix our faces back the way they were, we could go home. I can think of people who might be willing to join us once they know what we've found—what we've learned."

"We'd be locked up and bred!" Tomás protested.

"I don't think any elders or parents would have to see us. You were always good at coming and going without being seen when you thought you might be put to work."

"That was nothing. This is serious." He paused. "With a name like yours, sister, this isn't a role you should play."

She turned her face away from him, rested her head against my shoulder. "I don't want to do it," she said. "But why should Aaor die? We know our people will be taken and moved or absorbed or sterilized. It's too late to prevent that. How can we watch Aaor suffer and know it will probably die and just do nothing? It's true that our people will think badly of us when they find out that we've joined the Oankali. But they *will* find out eventually, no matter what."

"They'll kill us if they get the chance," Tomás said.

Jesusa shook her head. "Not if we look the way we used to look. Jodahs will have to change us back in every way. Even your neck must be stiff again. That will give us a chance to get out again sooner or later, even if we're caught." She thought for a moment. "They can't know yet what we've done, can they, Jodahs?"

"Not yet," I admitted. "Nikanj has avoided sending word to the ship or to any of the towns."

"Because it hoped we would do just what we're doing."

I nodded. "It would not ask either of you. It only hoped."

"And you?"

"I couldn't ask either. You had already refused. We understood your refusal."

She said nothing for a while. She sat utterly still, staring at the floor. Adrenaline flowed into her system, and she began to shake.

"Jesusa?" I said.

"I don't know if I can do it," she said. "You think you understand. You don't. You can't."

I held her and stroked her until she stopped shaking. Tomás touched her hair, reaching across me to do it, and making me want to grab his hand and stop him. Oankali male and female mates had no need to do this. I had to learn to endure it in Human mates.

"Shall we do it?" she asked him suddenly.

He drew back from her, looked from one of us to the other, then looked away.

She looked at me. "Shall we?" she asked.

I opened my mouth to say yes, she should, of course. Then I closed it. "I don't want you to destroy yourself," I said after a while. "I don't want to trade my sibling's life for yours." I felt what she felt. She could not give me multisensory illusions. Humans did not have that kind of control. But I could feel how tightly she held herself, how her stomach hurt her and her muscles ached. I had to keep stopping myself from giving her relief. She didn't need or want that from me now. Both my mother and Nikanj had warned me that not every pain should be immediately healed. Her body language would tell me when she wanted relief.

"I won't die," she whispered. "I'm not that fragile. Or maybe . . . not that lucky. If I can save your sibling, I will. But I think it would be easier for me to break several of my bones."

Now she and I both looked at Tomás.

He shook his head. "I hate that place," he said softly. "Full of pain and sickness and duty and false hope. I meant to die rather than see it again. You both know that."

I nodded. Jesusa made no move at all. She watched him.

"Yet I love those people," he said. "I don't want to do this to them. Isn't there any other way?"

"None that anyone's thought of," I said. "If you can do this, you'll save Aaor. If you can't, we'll get it to the ship and . . . hope for the best."

"We've already betrayed our people," Jesusa said softly. "We did that with you, Jodahs. All we're doing now is arguing about whether to bring two more of our people out early or let them all wait until the Oankali arrive."

"Is that all?" Tomás said with bitter irony.

"Will you go with me?" she asked.

He sighed. "Didn't I promise you I'd get you back there?" He ran a hand through his own hair. After a moment he got up, and went outside.

4

There were complications.

We couldn't leave until Aaor's metamorphosis ended. Jesusa and Tomás thought I would give them back their disfigurement and they would go back to the mountains alone. They couldn't have done that, even if I had been willing to let them try. They couldn't leave me now.

I never told them they couldn't leave. They found out as Lilith had. When they had had all they could take of Aaor for awhile, when they realized I could not be talked out of going with them to their mountain home, they went away on their own. They went together into the forest and stayed for several days. It was a foretaste for me of what I would suffer when they died.

I panicked when I realized they were gone. Tomás was supposed to spend the night with Aaor and me. The moment I thought about him, though, I realized he wasn't in camp. Neither was Jesusa. Their scent was beginning to fade.

Why? Where had they gone? Which way had they gone? I focused all my concentration on picking up their scent trail, finding out where their scent was strongest and freshest. Once I discovered the path they had taken into the forest, I would follow them.

Ahajas stopped me.

She was large and quiet and immensely comfortable to be near. Oankali females tended to be that way. I knew that sometimes after a session with Aaor, Nikanj went to her and literally seemed to grow into her body. She was so much larger, it looked like a child against her.

Now she blocked my path.

"Let them come back to you," she said quietly.

I stared at her with my eyes while my sensory tentacles all focused to the path Jesusa and Tomás had taken.

"I saw them leave," she said. "They took packs and machetes. They'll be all right, and in a few days, they'll be back."

"Resisters could capture them!" I said.

"Yes," she said. "But it isn't likely. They were on their own for a long time before they met you."

"But they—"

"They are as able as any Humans to take care of themselves. Lelka, you should have told them how they were bound to you."

"I was afraid to. I was afraid they'd do this."

"They probably would have. But now when they begin to

need you and feel desperate and afraid, they won't know why."

"That's why I want to go after them."

"Speak to Lilith first. She used to do this, you know. Nikanj had to learn very young that she would stretch the cord until it almost strangled her. And if Nikanj went after her, she would curse it and hate it."

I knew that about Lilith. I went to her and stood near her for a while. She was drawing with black ink or dye on bark cloth. In Lo, other Humans had treasured her drawings— scenes of Earth before the war, of animals long extinct, of distant places, cities, the sea. . . . She did paintings, too, sometimes with dyes from plants. She had done little of that during our exile. Now she was returning to it, stripping bark from the limb of a nearby fig tree, preparing it and making her dye and her brushes and sharp sticks. She had told me once that it was something she did to calm herself. Something she did to make herself feel Human.

She patted the ground next to her, and I went over and cleared a space and sat down.

"They're gone," I said.

"I know," she said. She was drawing an outdoor family meal with all of us gathered and eating from gourd dishes and Lo bowls. All. My parents, my siblings—even Aaor as it had looked before it went into the forest—and Jesusa and Tomás. Everyone was completely recognizable, though it seemed to me they shouldn't have been. They were made up only of a few black lines.

"Your mates will never trust me or Tino again," she said. "That will be our reward for keeping quiet about what was happening to them."

"Shall I go after them?"

"Not now. In a few days. Go when your own feelings tell you they're suffering, maybe turning back. Meet them somewhere between here and wherever they've gone. Can you track them well enough to do that?"

"Yes."

"Do it, then. And don't expect them to behave as though they're glad to see you for any reasons except the obvious biological need."

"I know."

"They won't love or even like you for quite a while."

"Or trust me," I said miserably.

"That won't last. It's us they'll distrust and resent."

I moved around to face her. "They'll know you kept silent for me."

She smiled a bitter smile. "Pheromones, Lelka. Your scent won't let them hate you for long. They can hate us, though. I'm sorry for that. I like them. You're very lucky to have them."

I did as she said. And when I brought home my silent, resentful mates, they did as she had said they would. Tino and Tomás seemed to find some common ground by the time Aaor had completed its metamorphosis, but Jesusa held an unyielding grudge. She hardly spoke to my mother from then on. And when it was time for us to go, and she learned that Aaor had to go with us, she almost stopped speaking to me. That was another battle. Aaor did have to go. If we left it behind with only Nikanj to help it, it would not survive. I suspected it was surviving now only because of our combined efforts and its new hope of Human mates to bond with. I suspected, too, that Jesusa understood this. She never threatened to change her mind, to refuse us and leave Aaor to its fate. She was gentler with Aaor than she was with me. Contact with it through me was still torment for her, but its illness reached something in her that perhaps nothing else could. I, on the other hand, was both her comfort and torment. She stopped touching me. She accepted my touch, even enjoyed it as much as she ever had. But she stopped reaching out to me.

"You did wrong," Tomás told me when he had been watching us for a while. "If she wasn't so good at punishing you, I'd have to think of a way to do it myself."

"But you don't mind," I said. He had felt only relief when I met them in the forest and brought them home. Jesusa had been full of resentment and anger.

"She minds," he said. "She feels trapped and betrayed. I mind that."

"I know. I'm sorry. I was more afraid of losing you than you can imagine."

"I can see Aaor," he said. "I don't have to imagine."

"No. It was the two of you I wanted. Not just to avoid pain."

He looked at me for a moment, then smiled. "She'll forgive you eventually, you know. And she'll be very suspicious of why she's done it. And she'll be right. Won't she?"

I looped a sensory arm around his neck and did not bother to answer.

The rainy season was just ending when the four of us prepared to leave camp. Aaor was strong again—able to walk all day and live on whatever it ran across. And if we slept with it every two or three nights, it could hold its shape. Yet with us all around, it was hideously lonely, empty, almost blank. It could follow and care for itself—just barely. I had to touch it sometimes to rouse it. It was as though it were lost within itself, and only surfaced when we were in contact. It rarely spoke.

When we were ready to go, Nikanj stood between my Oankali parents to give me final advice and to say goodbye.

"Don't come back to this place," it said. "In a few months, we'll return to Lo. We'll give you plenty of time, but we need to go home. Once we get there, everyone will have to know about your mates and their village. Lo will signal the ship and the Humans will be picked up. If the four of your succeed, you'll be six by then, and perhaps you'll be back at Lo yourselves." It focused on me for a time without speaking, and I could not help thinking that if we weren't careful, we might not live to get back to Lo. I might never see my parents again. Nikanj must have been thinking the same thing.

"Lelka, I have memories to give you," it said. "Let me pass them to you now. I think it's time."

Genetics memories. Viable copies of cells that Nikanj had received from its own ooloi parent or that it had collected itself or accepted from its mates and children. It had duplicated everything it possessed and now it would pass the whole inheritance on to me. It was time. I was a mated adult.

Yet as Nikanj stepped away from Ahajas and Dichaan and reached for me with all four arms, I didn't feel like an adult. I was afraid of this final step, this final touch. It was as though Nikanj were saying, "Here's your birthright, my final gift/duty/pleasure to you." Final.

But Nikanj said nothing at all. When it touched me, I pulled back, resisting. It simply waited until I was calmer. Then it spoke. "You must have this before you go, Lelka." It paused. "And you must pass it on to Aaor as soon as Aaor is mated and stable. Who knows when the two of you will see me again?"

I made myself step into its embrace and at once I felt myself held and penetrated, held absolutely still, but not paralyzed. Nikanj had a gentler touch than I had yet managed. And it still gave pleasure. Even to me. Even now.

Then the world around me seemed to flare brilliant white. I could no longer see beyond myself. All my senses turned inward as Nikanj used both sensory hands to inject a rush of individual cells, each one a plan by which a whole living entity could be constructed. The cells went straight into my newly mature yashi. The organ seemed to gulp and suckle the way I had once at my mother's breast.

There was immense newness. Life in more varieties than I could possibly have imagined—unique units of life, most never seen on Earth. Generations of memory to be examined, memorized, and either preserved alive in stasis or allowed to live their natural span and die. Those that I could re-create from my own genetic material, I did not have to maintain alive.

The flood of information was incomprehensible to me at first. I received it and stored it with only a few bits of it catching my attention. There would be plenty of time for me to examine the rest. I wouldn't lose any of it, and once I understood it, I wouldn't forget it.

When the flood ended and Nikanj was sure I could stand alone, it let me go.

"Now," it said, "except for the lack of Oankali or construct mates, you're an adult."

I felt confused, stuffed with information, overwhelmed with new sensation, stupefied, unable to do much more than hold myself up. I heard what Nikanj said, but the meanings of the words did not reach me for what seemed to be a long time. I felt it touch me once more with a sensory arm, then draw me to it and walk me over to Tomás, who was making a pack of the Lo cloth hammock and the other things my parents had given me.

Tomás got up at once and took me from Nikanj. He was, I recalled later, careful not to touch Nikanj, but no longer concerned about its nearness. Mated adults behaved that way—at ease with one another because they understood where they belonged and what they should and should not do.

"What did you do to it?" Tomás asked.

"Passed it information it might need on this dangerous trip with you. It's a little like a drunk Human right now, but it will be all right in a few moments."

Tomás looked at me doubtfully. "Are you sure? We were about to leave."

"It will be fine."

I recalled all this later, the way I recalled things I perceived while I was asleep. Tomás sat me down next to him, finished putting his pack together and rolling it. Then he took one of my sensory arms between his hands and said, "If you don't wake up, we'll leave you here and you can come running after us when you're sober."

He was amused, but he wasn't joking. He would leave without Aaor and me and let us catch up as best we could. Jesusa would certainly go along with him.

I groped for him, smelling for him rather than seeing him, hardly able to focus on him at all. He gave me his hand readily enough, and I locked on to it, focused so narrowly on it that I began to see and hear him normally through the incredible confusion of information Nikanj had given me. That information was a weight demanding my attention. It would not begin to "lighten" until I began to understand it. To understand it all could take years, but I must at least begin now.

"It's not really like being drunk," I said when I could speak. "It's more like having billions of strangers screaming from inside you for your individual attention. Incomprehensible . . . overwhelming . . . no word is big enough. Let me stay close to you for a while."

"Nikanj said it just gave you information," he protested.

"Yes. And if I began now and continued for the rest of our

lives, I could only explain a small fraction of it aloud to you. Ooan should have waited until we came back."

"Can you travel?" he asked.

"Yes. Just let me stay close to you."

"I thought that was settled. You'll never get away from me."

5

There was no end to the forest. The trees and smaller plants changed. Some varieties vanished, but the forest continued. It was a heavy coat of green fur on the hills and later on the nearly vertical cliffs of the mountains. There were places where we could not have gotten through without machetes.

There were old trails, ledges along cliff faces that perhaps dated back to a time before the war. Below us, a branch of the river cut through a deep, narrow gorge. Above us the mountains were green and sheer, bordering a blue and white band of sky that broadened ahead of us. The water ran high and fast below us, green and white, breaking over huge rocks. I might survive a fall to it, but it was unlikely that any of the others would.

But my Human mates were in their own country, sure-footed and confident. I had wondered whether they would be able to find their way home. They had traveled this route only once, nearly two years before. But Jesusa in particular was at home as soon as the landscape became more vertical than horizontal. Most often she broke trail for us just because she obviously loved the job and was better at it than any of us could have been. When our trail, narrow ledge that it was, vanished, she was usually the first to spot it above us or below or beginning again some distance away. And if she spotted it, she led the climb toward it. She never waited to see what the rest of us wanted to do—she simply found the best way across. The first time I saw her spread flat against the mountain, finding tiny hand- and footholds in the vegetation and the rock, making her way upward like a spider, I froze in absolute panic.

"She's part lizard," Tomás said, smiling. "It's disgusting. I'm not clumsy myself, I've never even see her fall."

"She's always done this?" Aaor asked.

"I've seen her go up naked rock," Tomás said.

I looked at Aaor and saw that it, too, had reacted with fear. This trip had begun to do it good. The trip had forced it to use its body and focus attention on something other than its own misery. It had made the safety of the two Humans its main concern. It understood the sacrifice they were making for it, and the sacrifice they had already made.

It was last across the gulf, holding on with both feet and all four arms. "I make a better insect than you do," it told Tomás as it reached the rest of us and safety.

Tomás laughed as much with surprise as with pleasure. I don't think he had ever heard Aaor even try to make a joke before.

There were times when we could descend to the river and walk alongside it or bathe in it. Jesusa and Tomás caught fish occasionally and cooked and ate them while Aaor and I took ourselves as far away as we could and focused on other things.

"Why do you let them do that?" Aaor demanded of me the second time it happened. "They shouldn't be hungry."

"They're not," I agreed. "Jesusa told me they lost most of their supplies coming out of the mountains—accidentally dropped them into those rapids we passed two days ago."

"That was then! They don't have to kill animals and eat them now!" Aaor sounded petulant and miserable. It brushed away my sensory arm when I reached out to it, then changed its mind and grasped the sensory arm in its strength hands.

I extended my sensory hand and reached into its body to understand what was wrong with it. As always, it was like reaching into a slightly different version of myself. It was feeling sick—nauseated, disgusted, oddly Human, yet unable to cope with the Humanity of Jesusa and Tomás.

"When you have Human mates," I told it, "you have to remember to let them be Human. They've killed fish and eaten them all their lives. They know we hate it. They need to do it anyway—for reasons that don't have much to do with nutrition."

Aaor let me soothe it, but still said, "What reasons?"

"Sometimes they need to prove to themselves that they still own themselves, that they can still care for themselves, that they still have things—customs—that are their own."

"Sounds like an expression of the Human conflict," Aaor said.

"It is," I agreed. "They're proving their independence at a time when they're no longer independent. But if this is the worst thing they do, I'll be grateful."

"Will you sleep with them tonight?"

"No. And they know it."

"They—" It stopped, froze utterly still, and signaled me silently. "There are other Humans nearby!"

"Where?" I demanded, silent and frozen myself, trying to catch the sight or the scent.

"Ahead. Can't you smell them?" It gave me an illusion of scent, faint and strange and dangerous. Even with this prompting, I could not smell the new Humans on my own, but Aaor was completely focused on them.

"Males," it said. "Three, I think. Maybe four. Headed away from us. No females."

"At least they're headed away," I whispered aloud. "Do any of them smell anything like Tomás? I can't tell from what you gave me."

"They all smell very much like Tomás. That's why I can't tell how many there are. Like Tomás, but including a certain odd element. The genetic disorder, I suppose. Can't you smell them?"

"I can now. They're so far away, though, I don't think I would have noticed them on my own. They have a dead animal with them, did you notice?"

Aaor nodded miserably.

"They've been hunting," I said. "Now they're probably

heading home. Although I don't smell anything that could be their home. Do you?"

"No," it said. "I've been trying. Maybe they're just looking for a place to camp—a place to cook the animal and eat it."

"Whatever their intentions, we'll have to be careful tomorrow." I focused on it. "You've never been shot, have you?"

"Never. People always aim at *you* for some reason."

I shook my head. "You're picking up Tomás's sense of humor. I don't know what your new mates will think of that." I paused. "Being shot hurts more than I would want to show you. I could probably handle the pain better now, but I wouldn't want to have to. I wouldn't want you to have to."

It moved closer to me and linked into me with its sensory tentacles. "I'm not sure I could survive being shot," it said. "I think part of me might, but not as me."

"You can't know that for sure."

It said nothing, but there was no tenacity to it, no feeling that it could withstand abrupt shock and pain. It thought it would dissolve. It was probably right.

"They've finished eating their fish," I said. "Let's go back."

We detached from one another and it turned wearily to follow me. "Do you know," it said, "that before we left home, Ooan still said it couldn't find the flaw in us, couldn't see why we needed mates so early—needed, not just wanted? And why we focus so on Humans." It paused. "Do you want other mates?"

"Oankali mates," I said. "Not construct."

"Why?"

"I think . . . I feel as though it will balance the two parts of me—Human and Oankali. I don't know what the Oankali will think about that, though."

"If they ever accept us and if you find two that you like, don't let them make their decision from a distance."

I smiled. "What about you? Humans and Oankali?"

It rested one strength arm around my shoulders. It almost never touched me with its sensory arms, though it accepted my own gladly. It behaved as though it were not yet mature.

"What about me?" it repeated. "I can't plan anything. It's hard for me to believe from one day to the next that I'm even going to survive." It made a fist with its free strength hand, then relaxed the hand. "Most of the time I feel as though I could just let go like this and dissolve. Sometimes I feel as though I should."

I slept with it that night. I couldn't do as much for it alone, but it couldn't have tolerated Jesusa or Tomás until they had digested their meal. I couldn't imagine it not existing, truly gone, never to be touched again—like never being able to touch my own face again.

Two days later, Jesusa and Tomás told me to give them back the marks of their genetic disorder. We had crawled up the nearly nonexistent trail on the mountain and back down again to the river. We had crossed the trail of the hunters we had scented earlier. There were four of them and they were still ahead of us. And now, when the wind was right, I could scent more Humans. Many more. Aaor's head and body tentacles kept sweeping forward, controlled by the tantalizing scent.

"The more Human you can make yourselves look, the less likely you are to be shot if you're seen," Tomás told us. He was looking at Aaor as he spoke. Then he faced me. "I've seen you both change by accident. Why can't you change deliberately?"

"I can," I said. "But Aaor's control is just not firm enough. It already looks as Human as it can look."

He drew a deep breath. "Then this is as close as it should get. You should change us and camp here."

"We can't even see your town from here," Aaor protested.

"And they can't see you. If you round that next bend, though, part of our settlement will be visible to you. But the way is guarded. You would be shot."

Aaor seemed to sink in on itself. We had made a fireless camp. My mates were on either side of me, linked with me. Aaor was alone. "You should change yourself and go with them," it said. "They'll function better if they not separated from you. I can survive alone for a few days."

"If we're caught, we'll be separated," Jesusa said. "We'll be shut up in separate places. We'll be questioned. I would probably be married off very quickly." She stopped. "Jodahs, what will happen if someone tries to have sex with me?"

I shook my head. "You'll fight. You won't be able to help fighting. You'll fight so hard, you might win even if the male is much stronger. Or maybe you'll just make him hurt or kill you."

"Then she can't go," Tomás said. "I'll have to do it alone."

"Neither of you should go," I said. "If hunters come out this far, we should wait. We have time."

"That will get you a man," Jesusa said. "Maybe several men. But women don't hunt."

"What do females do?" I asked. "What might bring them out away from the protection of the settlement?"

Jesusa and Tomás looked at one another, and Tomás grinned. "They meet," he said.

"Meet?" I repeated, uncomprehending.

"The elders tell us who we must marry," he said. "But they can't tell us who we must love."

I knew Humans did such things: marry here and mate there and there and there. . . . There was nothing in Human biology to prevent this. In fact, Human biology encouraged male Humans to have liaisons with more than one female. The male's investment of time and energy in fathering children was much smaller than the female's. Still, the concept felt alien to me. To have a mating and somehow put it aside. Most construct males never had true mates. They went wherever they found welcome and everyone knew it. There was no permanent bonding, no betrayal, no biological wrongness to contend with.

"Do your people meet this way because they would like to be mated?" I asked.

"Some of them," Tomás said. "Others only feel a temporary attraction."

"It would be good to get a pair for Aaor who already care for one another."

"We thought that, too," Jesusa said. "We meant to go to the village and bring away the people we would have been married to. But they wouldn't be coming out here to be together. They're brother and sister, too. A brother and two sisters, really."

"It would be better, safer to go after people who have already slipped away from your village. Is there a place where such people often meet?"

Tomás sighed. "Change us back tonight. Make us as ugly as we were, just in case. Tomorrow night, we'll show you some of the places where lovers meet. If you go there at all, it will have to be at night."

But the next night we were spotted.

6

We did not know we had been seen. As we rounded the final bend before the mountain people's village, we kept hidden in the trees and undergrowth. All we could see of their village were occasional stonework terraces cut into the sides of forested mountains. Crops grew on the terraces—a great deal of corn, some large melons, more than one species of potato, and other things that I did not recognize at all—foods neither I nor Nikanj had ever collected or stored memories of. These were surprisingly distracting—new things just sitting and waiting to be tasted, remembered. Yashi, between my hearts and protected now by a broad, flat slab of bone that no Human would have recognized as a sternum, did twist—or rather, it contracted like a long-empty Human stomach. Any perception of new living things attracted it and distracted me. I looked at Aaor and saw that it was utterly focused on the village itself, the people.

Its desperation had sharpened and directed its perceptions.

The Humans had built their village well above the river, had stretched it along a broad flattened ridge that extended between two mountains. We could not see it from where we were, but we could see signs of it—a great deal more terracing high up. These terraces could not be reached from where we were, but there was probably a way up nearby. All we could see between the canyon floor and the terraces was a great deal of sheer rock, much of it overgrown with vegetation. It was nothing I would have chosen to climb.

The scent of the Humans was strong now. Aaor, perhaps caught up in it, stumbled and stepped on a dry stick as it regained its balance. The sharp snap of the wood was startling in the quiet night. We all froze. Those stalking us did not freeze—or not quickly enough.

"Humans behind us!" I whispered.

"Are they coming?" Tomás demanded.

"Yes. Several of them."

"The guard," Tomás said. "They'll have guns."

"You two get away!" Jesusa said. "We'll have a better chance without you. Wait for us at the cave we passed two days ago. Go!"

The guard meant to catch us against their mountains. We were trapped now, really. If we ran to the river, we would have to go around them or through them, and probably be shot. There was nowhere for us to go except up the sheer cliff. Or down like insects to hide in the thickest vegetation. We could not get away, but we could hide. And if the guard found Jesusa and Tomás, perhaps they would not look for us.

I pulled Aaor down with me, fearing for it more than I feared for any of us. It was probably right in suspecting that it could not survive being shot.

In the darkness, Humans passed on either side of where Aaor and I lay hidden. They knew the terrain, but they could not see very well at night. Jesusa and Tomás led them a short distance away from us. They did this by simply walking down the slope toward the river until they walked into the arms of their captors.

Then there was shouting—Jesusa shouting her name, Tomás demanding that he be let go, that Jesusa be let go, guards shouting that they had caught the intruders.

"Where are the rest of you?" a male voice said. "There were more than two."

"Make a light, Luis," Jesusa said with deliberate disgust. "Look at us, then tell me when there has been more than one Jesusa and more than one Tomás."

There was silence for a while. Jesusa and Tomás were walked farther from us—perhaps taken where the moonlight would show more of their faces. Their tumors looked exactly as they had when I met them, so I wasn't worried about them not being recognized. But still, they had said they would be separated, imprisoned, questioned.

How long would they be imprisoned? If they were separated, they wouldn't be able to help one another break free. And what might be done to them if they gave answers that their people did not believe? They had, with obvious distaste for lying, created a story of being captured by a small group of resisters and held by separate households so that neither knew all the details of the other's captivity. Resisters actually did such things, though most often, their captives were female. Tomás would say he had been made to work for his captors. He had done planting, harvesting, hauling, building, cutting wood, whatever needed to be done. Since he had actually done these things while he was with us, he could give accurate descriptions of them. He would say that his sister was held hostage to ensure his good behavior while his captivity kept her in line. Finally the two had been able to get together and escape their resister captors.

This could have happened. If Jesusa and Tomás could tell it convincingly, perhaps they would not be imprisoned for long.

The two had been recognized now. There were no more hostile cries—only Jesusa's anguished "Hugo, please let me go. Please! I won't run away. I've just run all the way home. Hugo!"

The last word was a scream. He was touching her, this Hugo. She had known they would touch her. She had not known until now how difficult it would be to endure their touch. She could touch other females in comfort. Tomás could touch males. They would have to protect one another as best they could.

"Let her alone!" Tomás said. "You don't know what she's

been through." His voice said she had already been released. He was only warning.

"Everyone said you two were dead," one guard told them.

"Some *hoped* they were dead," another voice said softly. "Better them than all of us."

"No one will die because of us," Tomás said.

"We haven't come home to die," Jesusa said. "We're tired. Take us up."

"Does everyone know them?" the softer voice asked. It sounded almost like an ooloi voice. "Does anyone dispute their identity?"

"We could strip them down here," someone said. "Just to be sure."

Tomás said, "Bring your sister down, Hugo. We'll strip her, too."

"My sister stays home where she belongs!"

"And if she didn't, how would you want her treated? With justice and decency? Or should she be stripped by seven men?"

Silence.

"Let's go up," Jesusa said. "Hugo, do you remember the big yellow water jar we used to hide in?"

More silence.

"You know me," she said. "We were ten years old when we broke that jar, and I got caught and you didn't and I never told. You know me."

There was a pause, then the Hugo voice said, "Let's take them up. Someone will probably have some dinner left over."

They were taken away.

Aaor and I followed to see the path they would use and to see as much as we could of the guards.

Of the seven, four were obviously distorted by their genetic disorder. They had large tumors on their heads or arms. They looked different enough to be shot on sight by lowland resisters.

We followed as long as there was forest cover, then watched as they went up a pathway that was mostly rough stone stairs leading up the steep slope to the village.

When we could no longer hear them, Aaor pulled me close

to it and signaled silently, "We can't just go wait in the cave. We have to get them out!"

"Give them time," I said. "They'll try to find a pair of Humans for you."

"How can they? They'll be shut up, guarded."

"Most of these guards were young and fertile. And perhaps Jesusa will be given female guards. What are guards but villagers doing a tiresome, temporary duty?"

Aaor tried to relax, but its body was still tense against mine. "Seeing them walk away was like beginning to dissolve. I feel as though part of me has walked away with them."

I said nothing. Part of me *had* walked away with them. Both they and I knew what it would be like to be separated for a while—worse, to be kept apart by other people who would do all they could to stand between us. I would not begin to miss them physically for a few days, but with my uncertainty, my realization that I might not get them back, I had all I could do to control myself. I sat down on the ground, my body trembling.

Aaor sat next to me and tried to calm me, but it could not give what it did not feel in itself. The Humans could have caught us easily then—two ooloi sitting on the ground shuddering helplessly.

We recovered slowly. We were in control of our bodies again when Aaor said silently, "We can't give them more than two days to work—and that might not be long enough for them to do anything."

I could last longer than two days, but Aaor couldn't. "We'll give them the time," I said. "We'll get as close as we can and rest alert for two days."

"Then we'll have to get them out if they can't escape on their own."

"I don't want to do that," I said. "Tomás was talking as much to us as to his people when he said no one would die because of him and Jesusa. But if we try to get them out, we could be forced to kill."

"That's why it's best to go in while we're still in control of ourselves. You know that, Jodahs."

"I know," I whispered aloud.

7

We went up a steep, heavily forested slope, crawling up, clinging like caterpillars. Being six-limbed had never been quite so practical.

We climbed to the level of the terraces, and lay near them, hidden, during the next day. When night came, we explored the terraces and compulsively tried bits of the new foods we found growing there. By then, our skins had grown darker and we were harder for the Humans to see—while we could see everything.

We climbed higher up one of the mountains that formed a corner of the settlement. Just over halfway up, we reached the Human settlement with its houses of stone and wood and thatch. This was a prewar place. It had to be. Parts of it looked ancient. But it did not look like a ruin. All the buildings were well kept and there were terraces everywhere, most of them full of growing things. Away from the village, there was an enclosure containing several large animals of a kind I had not seen before—shaggy, long-necked, small-headed creatures who stood or lay at ease around their pen. Alpacas?

We could smell other, smaller animals caged around the village, and we could smell fertile, young Humans everywhere. Even above us on the mountain, we could smell them. What would they be doing up there?

How many were up there? Three, my nose told me. A female and two males, all young, all fertile, two afflicted with the genetic disorder. Why couldn't it just be those two for Aaor? What would we do with the third one if we went up? Why hadn't Jesusa and Tomás told us about people living in such isolation? Except for their being one too many of them, they were perfect.

"Up?" I said to Aaor.

It nodded. "But there's an extra male. What do we do with him?"

"I don't know yet. Let's see if we can get a look at them before they see us. Separating them might be easier than we think."

We climbed the slope, noticing, but for the most part not using, the long serpentine path the Humans had made. There had been Humans on it that day. Perhaps there would be Humans on it the next day. Perhaps it led to a guard post, and the guard changed daily. Anyone on top would have a fine view of all approaches from the mountains or the canyon below. Perhaps the people at the top stayed longer than a day and were resupplied from below at regular intervals—though there were a few terraces near the top.

We went up quietly, quickly, eating the most nutritious things we could find along the way. When we reached the terraces, we stopped and ate our fill. We would have to be at our best.

On a broad ledge near the top, we found a stone cabin. Higher up was a cistern and a few more terraces. Inside the cabin, two people slept. Where was the third? We didn't dare go in until we knew where everyone was.

I linked with Aaor and signaled silently. "Have you spotted the third?"

"Above," it said. "There is another cabin—or at least another living place. You go up to that one. I want these two." It was utterly focused on the Human pair.

"Aaor?"

It focused on me with a startlingly quick movement. It was as tight as a fist inside.

"Aaor, there are hundreds of other Humans down there. You'll have a life. Be careful who you give it to. I was very lucky with Jesusa and Tomás."

"Go up and keep the third Human from bothering me."

I detached from it and went to find the second cabin. Aaor would not hear anything I had to say now, just as I would not have heard anyone who told me to beware of Jesusa and

Tomás. And if the Humans were young enough, they could probably mate successfully with any healthy ooloi. If only Aaor were healthy. It wasn't. It and the Humans it chose would have to heal each other. If they didn't, perhaps none of them would survive.

I found not a cabin higher up on the mountain, but a very small cave near the top. Humans had built a rock wall, enclosing part of it. There were signs that they had enlarged the cave on one side. Finally heavy wooden posts had been set against the stone and from these a wooden door had been hung. The door seemed more a barrier against the weather than against people. Tonight the weather was dry and warm and the door was not secured at all. It swung open when I touched it.

The man inside awakened as I stumbled down into his tiny cave. His body heat made him a blaze of infrared in the darkness. It was easy for me to reach him and stop his hands from finding whatever they were grasping for.

Holding his hands, I lay down alongside him on his short, narrow bed and wedged him against the stone wall. I examined him with several sensory tentacles, studying him, but not controlling him. I stopped his hoarse shouting by looping one sensory arm around his neck, then moving the coil up to cover his mouth. He bit me, but his blunt Human teeth couldn't do any serious harm. My sensory arms existed to protect the sensitive reproductive organs inside. The flesh that covered them was the toughest flesh to be found on my body.

The male I held must have been more at home in his tiny cave than most people would have been. He was tiny himself—half the size of most Human males. Also, he had some skin disease that had made a ruin of his face, his hands, and much of the rest of his body. He was hairless. His skin was as scaly as those of some fish I'd seen. His nose was distorted—flattened from having been broken several times—and that enhanced his fishlike appearance. Strangely he was free of the genetic disorder that Jesusa, Tomás, and so many of the other people of the village had. He was grotesque without it.

I examined him thoroughly, enjoying the newness of him.

By the time I had finished, he had stopped struggling and lay quietly in my arms. I took my sensory arm from his mouth, and he did not shout.

"Do you live here because of the way you look?" I asked him.

He cursed me at great length. In spite of his size, he had a deep, hoarse, grating voice.

I said nothing. We had all night.

After a very long time, he said, "All right. Yes, I'm here because of the way I look. Got any more stupid questions?"

"I don't have time to help you grow. But if you like, I can heal your skin condition."

Silence.

"My god," he whispered finally.

"It won't hurt," I said. "And it can be done by morning. If you're afraid to stay here after you're healed, you can come with us when we leave. Then I'll have time to help you grow. If you want to grow."

"People my age don't grow," he said.

I brushed bits of scaly, dead skin from his face. "Oh, yes," I said. "We can help people your age to grow."

After another long pause, he said, "Is the town all right?"

"Yes."

"What will happen to it?"

"Eventually my people will come to it and tell your people they don't have to live in distorted bodies or in isolation or in fear. Your people have been cut off for a long time. They don't realize there's another, larger colony of healthy, fertile Humans living and growing without Oankali."

"I don't believe you!"

"I know. It's true, though. Shall I heal you?"

"Can I . . . see you?"

"At sunrise."

"I could make a fire."

"No."

He shook his head against me. "I should be more afraid than this. My god, I should be pissing on myself. Exactly what the hell are you anyway?"

"Construct. Oankali-Human mixture. Ooloi."

"Ooloi . . . The mixed ones—male and female in one body."

"We aren't male or female."

"So you say." He sighed. "Do you mean to hold me here all night?"

"If I'm to heal you, I'll have to."

"Why are you here? You said your people would come eventually. What are you doing here now?"

"Nothing harmful. Do you want hair?"

"What?"

I waited. He had heard the question. Now let him absorb it. Hair was easy. I could start it as an afterthought.

He put his head against my chest. "I don't understand," he said. "I don't even understand . . . my own feelings." Much later he said, "Of course I want hair. And I want skin, not scales. I want hair, and I want height. I want to be a man!"

My first impulse was to point out that he was a man. His male organs were well developed. But I understood him. "We'll take you with us when we go," I said.

And he was content. After a while, he slept. I never drugged him in the way ooloi usually drugged resisters. Once he had passed his first surprise and fear, he had accepted me much more quickly than Jesusa and Tomás had—but I had been only a subadult when I met them. And adult ooloi—a construct ooloi—ought to be able to handle Humans better. Or perhaps this man—I had not even asked his name, nor he mine—was particularly susceptible to the ooloi substance that I could not help injecting. In his Human way, he had been very hungry, starving, for any touch. How long had it been since anyone was willing to touch him—except perhaps to break his nose again. He would need an ooloi to steer him away from breaking a few noses himself once he was large enough to reach them. He had probably been treated badly. He did not veer from the Human norm in the same way as other people in the village, and Humans were genetically inclined to be intolerant of difference. They could overcome the inclination, but it was a reality of the Human conflict that they often did not. It was significant that this man was so ready to leave his home with someone he had been taught to think of as a devil—someone he hadn't even seen yet.

8

By morning, I had given the cave Human a smooth, new skin and the beginnings of a full head of hair.

"It will take me longer to repair your nose," I told him. "When I have, though, you'll be able to breathe better with your mouth closed."

He took a deep breath through his mouth and stared at me, then looked at himself, then stared at me again. He rubbed a hand over the fuzz on his head, then held the hand in front of him and examined it. I had not allowed him to awaken until I'd gotten up myself, opened the door to the dawn, and found the short, thick gun he had been reaching for the night before. I had emptied it and thrown it off the mountain. Then I awoke the man.

Seeing me alarmed him, but he never once reached toward the hiding place of the gun.

"What's your name?" I asked him.

"Santos." His voice now was a harsh whisper rather than a harsh growl. "Santos Ibarra Ruiz. How did you do this? How is it possible?" He rubbed the fingers of his right hand over his left arm and seemed to delight in the feel of it.

"Did you think you were dreaming last night?" I asked.

"I haven't had time to think."

"Who will come up here today?"

He blinked. "Here? No one."

"Who will visit the cabin below?"

"I don't know. I lose track with them. Are you going down there?"

"Eventually. Have your breakfast if you like."

"What are you called?"

"Jodahs."

He nodded. "I've heard that some of your kind had four arms. I didn't believe it."

"Ooloi have four arms."

He stared for some time at my sensory arms, then asked, "Are you really going to take me away with you and make me grow?"

"Yes."

He smiled, showing several bad teeth. I would fix those, too—have him shed them and grow more.

Later that morning we went down to the stone cabin. The male and female there were sharing their breakfast with Aaor. Santos and I startled them, but they seemed comfortably at home with Aaor. And Aaor looked better than it had since its first metamorphosis. It looked stable and secure in itself. It looked satisfied.

"Will they come with us?" I asked in Oankali.

"They'll come," it answered in Spanish. "I've begun to heal them. I've told them about you."

The two Humans stared at me curiously.

"This is Jodahs, my closest sibling," Aaor said. "Without it I would already be dead." It actually said, "my closest brother-sister," because that was the best either of us could do in Spanish. No wonder people like Santos thought we were hermaphroditic.

"These are Javier and Paz," Aaor said. "They are already mates."

They were also close relatives, of course. They looked as much alike as Jesusa and Tomás did, and they looked like Jesusa and Tomás—strong, brown, black-haired, deep-chested people.

Santos and I were given dried fruit, tea, and bread. Javier and Paz seemed most interested in Santos. He was their relative, too, of course.

"Do you feel well, Santos?" Paz asked.

"What do you care?" Santos demanded.

Paz looked at me. "Why do you want him? Wish him a good day, and he'll spit on you."

"He needs more healing than I can give him here," I said. I turned my head so that he would know I was looking at him. "He'll have less reason to spit when I'm finished with him, so maybe he'll do less spitting. Perhaps then I'll find mates for him."

He watched me while I spoke, then let his eyes slide away from me. He stared, unseeing, I think, at the rough wooden table.

"Will others come up here today?" I asked Paz.

"No," she said. "Today is still our watch. Juana and Santiago will come tomorrow to relieve us."

Santos spoke abruptly, urgently. "Are you really going with them?"

"Of course," Paz said.

"Why? You should be afraid of them. You should be terrified. When we were children they told us the devil had four arms."

"We're not children anymore," Javier said. "Look at my right hand." He held it up, pale brown and smooth. "I have a right hand again. It's been a frozen claw for years, and now—"

"Not enough!"

Javier opened his mouth, his expression suddenly angry. Then, without speaking, he closed his mouth.

"I want to go," Paz said quietly. "I'm tired of telling myself lies about this place and watching my children die." She pushed very long black hair from her face. As she sat at the table, most of her hair hung to the floor behind her. "Santos, if you had seen our last child before it died, you would thank God for the beauty you had even before your healing."

Santos looked away from her, shamefaced but stubborn. "I know all that," he said. "I don't mean to be cruel. I do know. But . . . we have been taught all our lives that the aliens would destroy us if they found us. Why did our belief and our fear slip away so quickly?"

Javier sighed. "I don't know." He looked at Aaor. "They're not very fearsome, are they? And they are . . . very interesting. I don't know why." He looked up. "Santos, do you believe we are building a new people here?"

Santos shook his head. "I've never believed it. I have eyes. But that's no reason for us to consent to go away with people we've been taught were evil."

"Did you consent?" Paz asked.

". . . yes."

"What else is there, then?"

"Why are they here!" He turned to me. "Why are you here?"

"To get Human mates for Aaor," I said. "And now I have to get my own Human mates back. They are—"

"Jesusa and Tomás, we know," Paz said. "Aaor said they were imprisoned below. We can show you where they're probably being held but I don't know how you can get them out."

"Show us," I said.

We went outside where the stone village lay below us, spread like a Human-made map. The buildings seemed tiny in the distance, but they could all be seen. The whole flattened ridge was visible.

"See the round building there," Javier said, pointing.

I didn't see it at first. So many gray buildings with gray-brown thatched roofs, all tiny in the distance. Then it was clear to me—a stone half-cylinder built against a stone wall.

"There are rooms in it and under it," Paz said. "Prisoners are kept there. The elders believe people who travel must be made to spend time alone to be questioned and prove they are who they say they are, and that they have not betrayed the people." She stopped, looked at Javier. "They would say that we've betrayed the people."

"We didn't bring the aliens here," he said. "And why do the people need us to produce more dead children?"

"They won't say that if they catch us."

"What will they do to you?" I asked.

"Kill us," Paz whispered.

Aaor stepped between them, one sensory arm around each. "Jodahs, can we take them out, then come back for Jesusa and Tomás?"

I stared down at the village, at the hundreds of green terraces. "I'm afraid for them. The longer we're separated, the more likely they are to give themselves away. If only they had told us . . . Paz, did people watch the canyon from up here before Jesusa and Tomás left home?"

"No," she said. "We do this now *because* they left. The elders were afraid we would be invaded. We made more guns and ammunition, and we posted new guards. Many new guards."

"This isn't really a good place to watch from," Javier said. "We're too high and the canyon is too heavily forested. People would have to almost make an effort to attract our attention. Light a fire or something."

I nodded. We had made cold camps for days before we reached the village. Yet we had been spotted. New guards. More vigilance. "You have to help us get you away from here," I said. "You know where the guards are. We don't want to hurt them, but we have to get you away and I have to get Jesusa and Tomás out."

"We can help you get away," Paz said. "But we can't help you reach Tomás and Jesusa. You've seen that they're guarded and in the middle of town."

"If they're where you say, I can get almost to them by climbing around the slope. It looks steep, but there's good cover."

"But you can't get Jesusa and Tomás out that way."

I looked at her, liking the way she stood close to Aaor, the way she had put one hand up to hold the sensory arm that encircled her throat. And, though she was a few years older, she was painfully like Jesusa.

I spoke in Oankali to Aaor. "Take your mates tonight and get clear of this place. Wait at the cave down the canyon."

"You didn't desert me," Aaor said obstinately in Spanish.

"I can reach them," I said. "Alone and focused, I can come up through the terraces and avoid the guards—or surprise them and sting them unconscious. And no door will keep me from Jesusa and Tomás. I can take them down the slope to the canyon. You've seen them climb. Especially Jesusa. I'll carry Tomás on my back if I have to—whether he wants me to or not. So tonight, you take your mates to safety.

And take Santos for me. I intend to keep my promise to him."

After a while, Aaor nodded. "I'll come back for you if you don't meet us."

"It might be better for you if you didn't," I said.

"Don't ask the impossible of me," it said, and guided its mates back into the stone cabin.

9

We meant to leave late that night—Aaor with the Humans down their back-and-forth pathway, then down terraces and a neglected, steep, overgrown path to the canyon floor. I meant to go down the other side of the mountain and work my way around as close as possible to the place where Jesusa and Tomás were being held.

It would have worked. The mountain village would be free of us and able to continue in isolation until Nikanj sent a shuttle to gas it and collect the people.

But that afternoon a party of armed males came up the trail to the stone cabin.

We heard them, smelled their sweat and their gunpowder long before we saw them. There was no time for Aaor to change Javier and Paz, give them back the deformities it had taken from them.

"Were their faces distorted?" I asked Aaor.

It nodded. "Small tumors. Very visible."

And nowhere to hide. We could climb up to Santos's cave, but what good would that do? If villagers found no one in the cabin, they would be bound to check the cave. If we began to climb down the other side of the mountain, we could be picked off. There was nothing to do but wait.

"Four of them?" I asked Aaor.

"I smell four."

"We let them in and we sting them."

"I've never stung anyone."

I glanced toward its mates. "Didn't you make at least one of them unconscious last night?"

Its sensory tentacles knotted against his body in embarrassment, and its mates looked at one another and smiled.

"You can sting," I said. "And I hope you can stand being shot now. You might be."

"I feel as though I can stand it. I feel as though I could survive almost anything now."

It was healthy, then. If we could keep its Humans alive, it would stay healthy.

"Is there a signal you should give?" I asked Javier.

"One of us should be outside, keeping watch," he said. "They won't be surprised that we're not, though. On this duty, I think only the elders watch as much as they should. I mean, Jesusa and Tomás left two years ago and there's been no trouble. Until now."

Laxity. Good.

The cabin was small and there was nowhere in it to hide. I sent the three Humans up the crooked pathway to Santos's cave. Vegetation was thick even this near the summit, and once they went around one of the turns, they could not be seen from the stone cabin. They would not be found unless someone went up after them. Aaor and I had to see that no one did. We waited inside the cabin. If we could get the newcomers in, there was less chance of accidentally killing one of them by having him fall down the slope.

I touched Aaor as I heard the men reach our level. "For Jesusa and Tomás's sake," I said silently, "we can't let any of them escape."

Aaor gave back wordless agreement.

"Javier!" called one of the newcomers before he reached the cabin door. "Hey, Javier, where are you?"

The cabin windows were high and small and the walls were thick. It would have been no easy matter to look in and see whether anyone was inside, so we were not surprised when one of the Humans kicked the door open.

Human eyes adjust slowly to sudden dimness. We stood

behind the door and waited, hoping at least two of the men would stumble in, half blind.

Only one did. I stung him just before he would have shouted. To his friends he seemed to collapse without reason. Two of them called to him, stepped up to help him. Aaor got one of them. I just missed the other, struck again, and caught him just outside the door.

The fourth was aiming his rifle at me. I dived under it as he fired. The bullet plowed up the ground next to the face of one of his fallen friends.

I held him with my strength hands, took the gun from him with my sensory arms, emptied it, and threw it far out so that it would clear the slope and fall to the canyon floor. Aaor was getting rid of the others in the same way.

The man in my strength arms struggled wildly, shouting and cursing me, but I did not sting him. He was a tall, unusually strong male, gray-haired and angular. He was one of the sterile old Humans—one of the ones the people here called elders. I wanted to see how he responded to our scent when he got over his first fear. And I wanted to find out why he and the three fertile young males had come up. I wanted to know what he knew about Jesusa and Tomás.

I dragged him into the cabin and made him sit beside me on the bed. When he stopped struggling, I let go of him.

His sudden freedom seemed to confuse him. He looked at me, then at Aaor, who was just dragging one of his friends into the cabin. Then he lurched to his feet and tried to run.

I caught him, lifted him, and sat him on the bed again. This time, he stayed.

"So those damned little Judases did betray us," he said. "They'll be shot! If we don't return, they'll be shot!"

I got up and shut the door, then touched Aaor to signal it silently. "Let's let our scent work on them for a while."

It consented to do this, though it saw no reason. It turned one of the males over and stripped his shirt. The male's body and face were distorted by tumors. His mouth was so distorted it seemed unlikely that he could speak normally.

"We have time," Aaor said aloud. "I don't want to leave them this way."

"If you repair them, they won't be able to go home," I reminded it. "Their own people might kill them."

"Then let them come with us!" It lay down next to the male with the distorted mouth and sank a sensory hand and many sensory tentacles into him.

The elder stared, then stood up and stepped toward Aaor. His body language said he was confused, afraid, hostile. But he only watched.

After a while, some of the tumors began to shrink visibly, and the elder stepped back and crossed himself.

"Shall we take them with us, once we've healed them?" I asked him. "Would your people kill them?"

He looked at me. "Where are the people who were in this house?"

"With Santos. We were afraid they might be shot by accident."

"You've healed them?"

"And Santos."

He shook his head. "And what will be the price for all this kindness? Sterility? Long, slow death? That's what your kind gave me."

"We aren't making them sterile."

"So you say!"

"Our people will be here soon. You will have to decide whether to mate with us, join the Human colony on Mars, or stay here sterile. If these males choose to mate with us or to go to Mars, why should they be sterilized? If they decide to stay here, others can sterilize them. It isn't a job I'd want."

"Mars colony? You mean Humans without Oankali are living on Mars? The planet Mars?"

"Yes. Any Humans who want to go. The colony is about fifty years old now. If you go, we'll give you back your fertility and see that you're able to father healthy children."

"No!"

I shrugged.

"This is our world. Your people can go to Mars."

"You know we won't."

Silence.

He looked again at what Aaor was doing. Several of the smallest visible tumors had already vanished. His expression, his body language were oddly false. He was fascinated. He did not want to be. He wanted to be disgusted. He pretended to be disgusted.

He was more than fascinated. He was envious. He must have experienced the touch of an ooloi back before he was released to become a resister. All Humans of his age had been handled by ooloi. Did he remember and want it again, or was it only our scent working on him? Oankali ooloi frightened Humans because they looked so different. Aaor and I were much less frightening. Perhaps that allowed Humans to respond more freely to our scent. Or perhaps, being part Human ourselves, we had a more appealing scent.

When I had checked the two Humans on the floor, seen that they were truly unconscious and likely to stay that way for a while, I took the elder by the shoulder and led him back to the bed.

"More comfortable than the floor," I said.

"What will you do?" he asked.

"Just have a look at you—make sure you're as healthy as you appear to be."

He had been resisting for a century. He had been teaching children that people like me were devils, monsters, that it was better to endure a disfiguring, disabling genetic disorder than to go down from the mountains and find the Oankali.

He lay down on the bed, eager rather than afraid, and when I lay down beside him, he reached out and pulled me to him, probably in the same way he reached out for his human mate when he was especially eager for her.

10

By the time it began to get dark, our captives had become our allies. They were Rafael, whose tumors Aaor had healed and whose mouth Aaor had improved, and Ramón, Rafael's brother. Ramón was a hunchback, but he knew now that he didn't have to be. And even though we had had not nearly enough time to change him completely, we had already straightened him a little. There was also Natal, who had been deaf for years. He was no longer deaf.

And there was the elder, Francisco, who was still confused in the way Santos had been. It frightened him that he had accepted us so quickly—but he had accepted us. He did not want to go back down the mountain to his people. He wanted to stay with us. I sent him up to bring Santos, Paz, and Javier back to us. He sighed and went, thinking it was a test of his new loyalty. He was the only one, after all, who had not needed our healing.

Not until he brought them back did I ask him whether he could get Jesusa and Tomás out.

"I could talk to them," he said. "But the guards wouldn't let me take them out. Everyone is too nervous. Two of the guards last night swear they saw four people, not two. That's why we were sent up here. Some people thought Paz and Javier might have seen something, or worse, might be in trouble." He looked at Paz and Javier. They had come in and gone straight to Aaor, who coiled a sensory tentacle around each of their necks and welcomed them as though they had been away for days.

Jesusa and Tomás *had* been away from me for two days. I was not yet desperate for them, but I might be in two more days if I didn't get them out. Knowing that made me uneasy, anxious to get started. I left the too-crowded cabin and went to sit on the bare rock of the ledge outside. It was dusk, and the two brothers, Rafael and Ramón, had gotten into the cabin's food stores and begun to prepare a meal.

Francisco and Santos came out with me and settled on either side of me. We could see the village below through a haze of smoke from cooking fires.

"When will you leave?" Santos asked.

"After dark, before moonrise."

"Are you going to help?" he asked Francisco

Francisco frowned. "I've been trying to think of what I could do. I think I'll go down and just wait. If Jodahs needs help, if it's caught, perhaps I can give it the time it needs to prove it isn't a dangerous animal."

Santos grinned. "It is a dangerous animal."

Francisco looked at him with distaste.

"You should be looking at Jodahs that way. Its people will come and destroy everything you've spent your life building."

"Go back up to your cave, Santos. Rot there."

"I'll follow Jodahs," Santos said. "I don't mind. In fact, it's a pleasure. But I'm not asleep. These people probably won't kill us, but they'll swallow us whole."

Francisco shook his head. "How's your breathing these days, Santos? How many times have you had that nose of yours broken? And what has it taught you?"

Santos stared at him for a moment, then screeched with laughter.

I looped a sensory arm around Santos's neck, pulled him against me. He didn't try to say anything more. He didn't really seem to be out to do harm. He just enjoyed having the advantage, knowing something a century-old elder didn't know—something I had overlooked, too. He was laughing at both of us. He kept quiet and held still, though, while I fixed his nose. In the short time I had, I couldn't make it look much better. That would mean altering bone as well as cartilage. I did a little of that so he could breathe with his mouth closed if he wanted to. But the main thing I did was repair nerve damage. Santos hadn't just been hit on the nose. He had been thoroughly beaten about the head. His body could "taste" and enjoy the ooloi substance I could not help giving when I penetrated his skin. That had won him over to me. But he could smell almost nothing.

"What are you doing to him?" Francisco asked with no particular concern. His sense of smell was excellent.

"Repairing him a little more," I said. "It keeps him quiet, and I promised him I'd do it. Eventually he'll be almost as tall as you are."

"Seal up his mouth while you're at it," Francisco said. "I'll walk down now."

"Do you still want to come with us?"

"Of course."

I smiled, liking him. It seemed I couldn't help liking the people I seduced. Even Santos. "You'll go to Mars, won't you?"

"Yes." He paused. "Yes, I think so. I might not if you were looking for mates. I wish you were."

"Thank you," I said. "If you change your mind, I can help you find Oankali or construct mates."

"Like you?"

"Your ooloi would be Oankali."

He shook his head. "Mars, then. With my fertility restored."

"Absolutely."

"Where shall I meet you once you've gotten Tomás and Jesusa out?"

"Follow the trail downriver. Come as quickly as you can, but come carefully. If you can't get away, remember that my people will be coming here soon anyway. They won't hurt you, and they will send you to Mars if you still want to go."

"I'd rather leave with you.

"You're welcome to come with us. Just don't get killed trying to do it. You're much older than I am. You're supposed to have learned patience."

He laughed without humor. "I haven't learned it, little ooloi. I probably never will. Watch for me on the river trail."

He left us, and I sat repairing Santos until it was time for me to go. I left him with a fairly good sense of smell.

"Don't make trouble," I told him. "Use that good mind of yours to help these people get away."

"Francisco wouldn't have minded what you're doing to us," he said. "I figured it out, and I don't mind."

"I'll do experiments when my mates' lives are not at stake. Until we're away from this place, Santos, try to be quiet unless you have something useful to say."

I went into the cabin and told Aaor I was leaving.

It left its mates and the meal it had been eating. It had used more energy than I had in healing the Humans. It probably needed food.

Now it settled all four of its arms around me and linked. "I will come back if you don't follow us," it said silently.

"I'll follow. Francisco is going to help me—if necessary."

"I know. I heard. And I still inherit Santos."

"Use his mind and push his body hard. This trip should do that. You should start down now, too."

"All right."

I left it and headed down the mountain, using the path when it was convenient, and ignoring it otherwise. The Humans with Aaor would find it dark and would have to be careful. For me it was well lit with the heat of all the growing plants. I had to climb down past the flattened ridge on which the village had been built. I had to travel along the broad, flat part of the ridge below the level of sight of any guard watching from the village. I had to come up where terraces filled with growing things would conceal me for as long as possible.

11

When I reached the village, I lay on a terrace until the sounds of people talking and moving around had all but ceased. I calculated by hearing and smell where the guards patrolled. I tried to hear Jesusa or Tomás, or her people talking about them, but there was almost nothing. Two males were wondering what they had seen in their wanderings. A female was explaining to a sleepy child that they had been "very, very bad" and were locked up as punishment. And somewhere far from where I lay, Francisco was explaining to someone that five guards on the mountain were enough, and that he wanted to sleep in his own bed, not on a stone floor.

He was not questioned further. No doubt being an elder gave him a few privileges. I wondered how long my influence on him would last, and how he would react to its ending. Best not to find out. I had deliberately not told him about the cave where we were to meet. Willingly or unwillingly, he might lead others to it.

There was a scream suddenly and the sound of a blow. I had lain frozen for some time before I realized it had nothing to do with us. Nearby, a male and female were arguing, cursing each other. The male had hit the female. He did this again several times and she went on screaming. Even Human ears must have been full of the terrible sound.

I crept out of the terraces and into the village.

I was close to Jesusa and Tomás, close to the building I had been shown from the mountain. I could not go straight to it. There were houses in the way and two more high stone steps that raised the level of the ground. The flattened ridge was not as flat as it had seemed. Stone walls had been built here and there to retain the soil and create the level platforms on which the houses had been built. In that way, the houses as well as the crops were terraced.

There were pathways and stairs to make movement easy, but these were patrolled. I avoided them.

Crouching beneath one of these tiers, I caught Jesusa's scent. She was just ahead, just above, and there was a faint scent of Tomás as well.

But there were two others—armed males.

I stood up carefully and peered over the wall of the tier. From where I was, all I could see were more walls—walls of buildings. There were no people outside.

I climbed up slowly, looking everywhere. Someone came out of a doorway abruptly and walked away from me down the path. I flattened my body against a wall of large, smooth stones.

Around me, people slept with slow, even breathing. The angry male, still some distance from me, had stopped beating his mate. I did not stand away from the wall until the person from the doorway—a pregnant female—had crossed the path and taken the stairs down to a lower level.

Farther along the pathway I was confined to, I recognized the round building—a half-cylinder of smooth gray rock. Both Jesusa and Tomás were inside, though I did not think they were together. I walked toward it, all my sensory tentacles in prestrike knots and my sensory arms coiled against me. If I could do this without noise, we could get away, and it might be morning before anyone knew we were gone.

The building had heavy wooden doors.

In time, I could smash them, but only with a great deal of noise. Someone would shoot me long before I'd finished.

I uncoiled one sensory arm and probed the door. Filaments of my sensory hand could penetrate it as easily as they could penetrate flesh. A wooden door set in a wooden frame, held shut by a massive wooden crossbar that rested in a cradle of iron. Very simple. The iron cradle consisted of four flattened, upturned prongs, two fastened to the door with several metal screws and two fastened to the doorframe.

Quickly, carefully, I rotted the wood that held the prong

screws on the door. Through my sensory hand, I injected a corrosive, and the wood began at once to disintegrate. I could not have destroyed the door this way, but getting rid of the small sections of wood that held the screws was no trouble. In effect, I digested them.

After a time, the heavy crossbar slid to the floor.

The two men just inside shouted in surprise, then cursed and made several quick, noisy movements. They came together to examine the door and ask each other what could have caused it to fall apart that way.

When I hit the door, they were exactly where I wanted them to be. The door knocked them down before they could raise their rifles. I stung first one, then the other, with a lashing motion of sensory arms. Both collapsed unconscious. It could only have been reflex that caused one of them to fire his gun.

The bullet glanced off one rock wall and spent itself against another.

And suddenly, everywhere, there were voices.

Jesusa was so close. . . . But there was no time.

I stepped out through the doorway, meaning to disappear for a while, try again later.

Outside, there was a forest of long wood-and-metal rifles. People had leaped from sleep onto their pathway, some of them naked, but all of them armed.

I jumped back behind the heavy door and slammed it as people fired into it. I grabbed the crossbar and kicked and jammed it into a prop. It wouldn't hold long against their guns and their bodies, but it would give me a moment.

What to do? They would kill me before I could speak. They would kill me as soon as they reached me. If I went into the area where Jesusa was confined, they might kill her, too.

I reached for the two guards and forced them conscious. I dragged them to their feet, made them stand on either side of me, made them breathe in as much as they could of me.

They struggled a little at first. Then I looped my sensory arms around them and injected my ooloi substance into them. I had to quiet them before the door gave way.

"Save your lives," I said softly. "Don't let your people shoot you. Make them listen!"

At that moment the door gave way.

People poured into the room, ready to shoot. I held the two guards in front of me, held them with only my strength hands visible. The less alien I seemed now, the more likely I was to live for a few more moments.

"Don't shoot us!" the guard under my right hand shouted.

"Don't shoot!" the other echoed. "It isn't hurting us."

"It's an alien," someone shouted.

"Oankali!"

"Four-arms!"

"Kill it!"

"No!" my prisoners screamed together.

"It can sting people to death! Kill it!"

"There's no need to kill me!" I said. I tried consciously to sound the way Nikanj did when it both frightened Humans and got them to cooperate. "I don't want to hurt you, but if you shoot me, I may lose control and kill several of you before I die."

Silence.

"I mean you no harm."

Again the curse, and it was, unmistakably, a curse. "Four-arms!"

And from someone else. "They strike like snakes!"

"I didn't come to strike anyone," I said. "I mean you no harm."

"What do you want here!" one of them demanded.

I hesitated and someone else answered for me.

"Isn't it obvious what the thing wants? The prisoners, that's what! It's come for them!"

"I've come for them," I agreed softly.

People began to look uncertain. I was reaching them—probably more with my scent than with anything I was saying. All I had to do was keep them here a little longer. They might go in and get Jesusa and Tomás for me. The two in my hands would probably do that now if I asked it of them. But I still needed them—for just a while longer.

"If you kill me," I said, "my people will find out about it. And those who shoot me will never live on a planet or know freedom again. Ask your elders. They remember."

People began to look at one another doubtfully. Some of

them lowered their guns and stood not knowing what to do. There had always been a fear among Humans that we could read their thoughts. No doubt that was why they had feared letting even one of their people go down into the lowland forest. Most had never understood that it was their bodies we read—inside and out. And if we were alert and competent— more so than I had been with Santos—their bodies kept few secrets.

"Who will speak for you?" I asked the crowd. If they had been Oankali or construct, I would never have asked such a question. I could have made my case to anyone, and the people would have joined person-to-person or through their town organisms, and there would have been a consensus.

But these people were Human. I had to find their leaders. Two males stepped forward out of the crowd.

"Elders?" I asked.

One of them nodded. The other only stared at me in obvious disgust.

"I mean no harm," I said. "Harm will only be done if you shoot me. Do you accept that?"

"Perhaps," the one who had nodded said.

I shrugged. "Examine your own memories." And I kept quiet and left them to their memories. Meanwhile, without drawing attention to the gesture, I took my hands from the two men in front of me. They didn't move.

"Why do you want Jesusa and Tomás?" demanded the disgusted elder.

"They are my mates."

There was a sudden rush of surprised muttering from the people. I heard disbelief and questioning, threats and cursing, honor and disgust.

"Why should you be surprised?" I asked. "Why did you think I wanted them? Why else would I be willing to risk your killing me?" I paused, but no one spoke. "We care for our mates as deeply as you do for yours," I said.

"It would be better for them to be killed than to be given to you," the disgusted elder said.

"Your people almost destroyed themselves," I said, "and you still haven't had enough killing?"

"Your people want to kill us!" someone said from the crowd.

I spoke into renewed muttering. "My people are coming here, but they won't kill. They didn't kill your elders. They plucked them out of the ashes of their war, healed them, mated with those who were willing, and let the others go. If my people were killers, you wouldn't be here." I paused to let them think, then I continued. "And there wouldn't be a Human colony on the planet Mars where Humans live and breed totally free of us. The Humans there are healthy and thriving. Any Human who wants to join them will be given healing and restored fertility if necessary, and transportation."

What happened next was totally irrational, yet somehow, later, I felt that I should have anticipated it.

The disgusted elder's face twisted with anger and revulsion. He cursed me, called on his god to damn me. Then he fired his gun.

One of the two Human guards whom I had held, and then released, jumped between the elder's gun and me.

An instant later, the guard lay dying and the two elders struggled for possession of the disgusted one's rifle.

I saw the murderous elder subdued by his companion and two deformed young people. Then I was on the floor beside the injured man. "Keep them off me," I told the remaining guard. "His heart is damaged. I can save him, but only if they let me alone."

I paid no more attention to what they did. The injured guard needed all my attention. By the definition of most Humans, he was already dead. The large-caliber bullet fired at close range had gone through his heart and come out of his back just missing his spine. I had all I could do to keep him alive while I repaired the heart. The Humans would not murder me. The moment for that had passed.

12

I was hungry when I finished the healing. I was almost weak with hunger. And the scent of Jesusa and Tomás so nearby was tormenting. I could not let the Humans keep them from me much longer.

I began to pay attention to my immediate surroundings again and found myself locking into the eyes of the man I had just healed.

"I was shot," he said. "I remember . . . but it doesn't hurt."

"You're healed," I said. I hugged him. "Thank you for shielding me."

He said nothing. He sat up when I did and looked around at the people who had gathered around us and sat down. We were the center of a ring of elders and aged fertiles—people who looked ancient, but were not nearly as old as the youthful-looking elders. There were no females present.

"Give me something to eat," I told them. "Plant material. No meat."

No one moved or spoke.

I looked at the guard I had just healed. "Get me something, please."

He nodded. No one stopped him for going out, though everyone was armed.

I sat still and waited. Eventually the Humans would begin to talk to me. They were playing a game now, trying to make me uneasy, trying to put me at more of a disadvantage than I was. A small, Human, hierarchical game. They might not let my guard back in. Well, I was uncomfortably hungry, not desperately hungry. And I didn't know their game well enough to play it. At some time they would probably take pleasure in telling me what they intended to do to me. I was in no hurry to hear that. I didn't expect to like it.

I almost slept. My guard came back with a dish of cooked beans and some grain and fruit that I did not recognize. A good meal. I thanked him and sent him away because I was afraid he would speak for me and get into trouble.

Sometime later, Francisco came in. There were three more elders with him. From their looks, they were probably the oldest males in the village. They were gray-haired, and their faces were deeply lined. One of them walked with a severe limp. The other two were gaunt and bent. They had probably been old before the war.

These four sat down facing me, and Francisco spoke quietly. "Are you all right?"

I looked at him, trying to guess what his situation was. Why had he come? It was too late for him to play the part he had promised to play. He was holding himself very tightly, yet trying hard to seem relaxed. I decided not to recognize him—for now.

"My mates are still imprisoned," I said.

"We'll let you see them soon. We want you to know first what we've decided."

I waited.

"You've said your people will be coming here."

"Yes."

"You'll wait here for them." His body inclined toward me, full of repressed tension. It was important to him that I accept what he was saying.

I kept quiet, turned my face away from him so that I could watch him without making him feel watched. There was no triumph in him, no slyness, no sign that he was doing anything more than telling me what his people had decided—and perhaps hoping that I didn't give him away.

"The guards have captured your companion," Francisco said in the same quiet way. "It will be brought here soon."

"Aaor?" I asked. "Is it injured? Is anyone injured?"

"Nothing serious. Your companion was shot in the leg, but it seems to have healed itself. One of our people whom you've tampered with was injured slightly."

"Who? Which one?"

"Santos Ibarra Ruiz."

Of course. I shook my head. Someone in the group of elders groaned. "Is he all right?" I asked.

"Our guards heard him arguing with someone in your companion's party," Francisco said. "What they investigated and took prisoners, Santos bit one of them. He was clubbed. He's all right except for a few bruises and a headache."

Santos had given Aaor away. Who but Santos would? How many lives had he endangered or destroyed?

"What will happen to the Humans we've . . . tampered with?" I asked.

"We haven't decided yet," Francisco said. "Nothing probably."

"They should be hanged," someone muttered. "Supposed to be on watch. . . ."

"They were taken by surprise," Francisco said. "If I hadn't decided to come down and sleep in my own bed, I could have been taken myself."

So that was why he was still free. He had convinced his people that we had arrived after he left. That story might protect him and enable him to help the others. His body expressed his discomfort with the lie, but he told it well.

"Will you keep Aaor here, too?" I asked.

"Yes. It won't be hurt unless it tries to escape. Neither will you. Our people feel that having you here will assure their safety when your people arrive."

I nodded. "Was this your idea?"

The elder with the limp spoke up. "It doesn't matter to you whose idea it was! You'll stay here. And if your people don't come . . . perhaps we'll be able to think of something to do with you."

I turned to face him. "Use me to heal your leg," I said softly. "It must pain you."

"You'll never get your poisonous hands on me."

I would. Of course I would. If they kept Aaor and me here, nothing would stop them for using us to rid them of their many physical problems.

"This wasn't my idea," Francisco said. "My only idea was

that you shouldn't be shot. A great many people here would like to shoot you, you know."

"That would be a serious mistake."

"I know." He paused. "Santos was the one who suggested keeping you here."

I did not shout with laughter. Laughter would have made the elders even more intensely suspicious than they were. But within myself, I howled. Santos was making up for his error. He knew exactly what he was doing. He knew his people would use Aaor's and my healing ability and breathe our scents, and finally, when our people arrived, his would meet them without hostility. In that way, I would, as Francisco had said, assure the mountain people's safety. People who did not fight would be in no danger at all, would not even be gassed once the shuttle caught Aaor's and my scents.

"Bring Aaor," I said.

"Aaor is coming." Francisco paused. "If you try anything, if you frighten these people in any way at all, they *will* shoot you. And they won't stop shooting until there's nothing living left of you."

I nodded. There would be a great deal that was living left of me, but it would certainly not survive *as* me. And it might do harm here—as a disease. It was best for us to die on a ship or in one of our towns. Our substance would be safely absorbed into the larger organism. If it were not absorbed, the Oankali organelles in it would find things to do on their own.

Aaor was brought in by young guards. I looked at its legs for traces of a bullet wound, but could see none. The Humans had let it heal itself completely before they brought it in.

It walked over and sat down beside me on the stone floor. It did not touch me.

"They want us to stay here," it said in Spanish.

"I know."

"Shall we?"

"Yes, of course."

It nodded. "I thought so, too." It pulled its mouth into something less than a smile. "You were right about being shot. I don't want to go through it again."

"Where are your mates?"

"At their home not far from here—under guard."

I faced Francisco again. "We agree to stay here until our people come, but Aaor should live with its mates. And I should live with mine."

"You'll be imprisoned here in this tower!" one of the gaunt old elders said. "Both of you! You'll stay here under guard. And you'll have no mates!"

"We'll live in houses as people should," I said softly.

Someone spat the words "Four-arms!" and someone else muttered, "Animals!"

"We'll live with the people you know to be our mates," I continued. "If we don't, we'll become . . . very dangerous to ourselves and to you."

Silence.

My scent and Aaor's probably could not convert these people quickly without direct contact, but our scents could make everyone more likely to believe what we said. We could persuade them to do what they knew they really should do.

"You'll live with your mates," Francisco said above much muttering. "Most of us accept that. But wherever you live, you will be guarded. You must be."

I glanced at Aaor. "All right," I said. "Guard us. There's no need for it, but if it comforts you, we'll put up with it."

"Guards to keep people from accepting your poison!" muttered the lame elder.

"Give me my mates now," I said very softly. People leaned forward to hear. "I need them and they need me. We keep one another healthy."

"Let it be with them," Aaor supplemented. "Let them comfort one another. They've been apart for days now."

They argued for a while, their hostility slowly decreasing like a wound healing. In the end Francisco himself freed Jesusa and Tomás. They came out of their prison rooms and took me between them, and the elders and old fertiles watched with conflicting emotions of fear, anger, envy, and fascination.

13

We stayed.

We healed the people in spite of our guards. We healed our guards.

Young people came to us first, and went away without their tumors, sensory losses, limps, paralysis. . . . People brought their children to us. Jesusa, Tomás, and I shared a stone house with Aaor, Javier, and Paz. Once we were settled, Jesusa went out and found all the people she remembered as having deformed or disabled children. She badgered them until they began to bring their children to us. The small house was often full of healing children.

And Santos began to grow. I gave him a handsome new nose and he went right on talking too much and risking getting it broken again. But people seemed less inclined to hit him.

The first elder to come to us was female with only one leg. The stump of her amputated leg pained her and she hoped I could stop the pain. I sent her to Aaor because I had more people to heal then I could manage. Over a period of weeks, Aaor grew her a new leg and foot.

After that, everyone came to us. Even the most stubborn elders forgot how much they hated us once we'd touched them. They didn't suddenly begin to love us, but they stopped spitting as we walked by, stopped muttering curses or threats at us, stopped pointing their guns at us to remind us of their power and their fear. They let us alone. That was enough.

Their people, however, did begin to love us and to believe what we told them and to talk to us about Oankali and construct mates.

14

The shuttle, when it arrived, landed down in the canyon. There it could drink from the river and eat something other than the mountain people's crops. No one was gassed. There was no panic on the part of the Humans. It was a measure of the Humans' trust that they let Aaor and me and our mates go down to meet the newcomers. At the last moment, Francisco decided to come with us, but only because, as he had admitted, his long years had not taught him patience.

Seven families had come with the shuttle. Most were from Chkahichdahk, since that was where shuttles lived when they were not in use. They had stopped at Lo, however, to pick up my parents. The first person I spotted in the small crowd was Tino—and I came much nearer him than I should have to grabbing him and hugging him. Too Human a reaction. I hugged Nikanj instead, though Nikanj did not particularly want to be hugged. It tolerated the gesture and used it as an opportunity to sink its sensory tentacles into me and examine me thoroughly. When it had finished, without a word, it reached for Aaor and examined it. It held Aaor longer, then focused on Javier and Paz. They were watching with obvious curiosity but without alarm. They had already passed the stage of extreme avoidance of everyone except Aaor. Now, like Jesusa and Tomás, they were simply careful.

Neither of them had ever seen an Oankali before. They were fascinated, but they were not afraid.

Nikanj flattened its sensory tentacles to that glittering smoothness it could achieve when it was gleefully happy. "Lelka," it said, "if you will introduce us to your mates, we

212

may begin to forgive you for staying here and not letting us know you were all right."

"I'm not sure I'll forgive it," Lilith said. But she was smiling, and for a time, everything else had to wait until Javier and Paz were welcomed into the family and the rest of us rewelcomed and forgiven. I saw Jesusa reach out to my mother for the first time since their break. The two embraced and I felt my own sensory tentacles go smooth with pleasure.

"The mountain Humans decided to keep us," Aaor was explaining to the rest of the family. "Since their only alternative as they saw it was to kill us, we were willing to stay."

"Is this one of them?" Ahajas asked, looking at Francisco.

I introduced him and he, too, met her with curiosity but no fear.

"Would you have killed them?" she asked with odd amusement.

Francisco smiled, showing very white teeth. "Of course not. Jodahs captured me long before it captured most of my people."

Ahajas focused on me. "Captured?"

"No one has captured him," I said. "He wants to go to the Mars colony."

Ahajas went very smooth. "Do you want that?"

"I did." Francisco shook his head. "Maybe I still do."

I looked at him, surprised. He had been one of the holdouts—very certain. Now that the shuttle was here, he was less certain. "Shall we find mates for you?" I asked.

He looked at me, then did something very Oankali. He turned and walked away. He walked quickly, would have gone back to the steep road and up to the village if Ahajas had not spoken.

"Does he have a female mate, Lelka?" she asked me.

I nodded. "Inez. She's an old fertile." She had joined Francisco after bearing nine children. Now she was past the age of childbearing. Francisco had brought her to me once and asked me to check her health. She turned out to be one of the healthiest old fertiles I had ever touched, but I understood that Francisco's real purpose had been to share her with me—and me with her. Yet he had truly wanted to emigrate. Until now.

"Jodahs," Ahajas said, "I think there are mates for him here, now. Bring him back."

I went after Francisco, caught him, took him by the arms. "My Oankali mother says there are people here, now, who might mate with you."

He stood still for a moment, then abruptly tried to wrench free. I held him because his body language told me that he wanted to be held more than he wanted to be let go. He was afraid and confused and ashamed and powerfully drawn to the idea of potential Oankali mates.

After his first effort, he would not shame himself by continuing to struggle against me. I let him go when he truly wanted it. Then I took his right hand loosely and led him back toward Ahajas, who waited with a mated group of strangers—three Oankali. Francisco began to sweat.

"I would give anything at all to have you instead," he told me.

"You already have all I can give you," I said. "If you like these new people, their ooloi can give you much more." I paused. "Do you think Inez will consent to have her fertility restored? Maybe she's tired of having children."

He laughed, momentarily decreasing the level of his tension. "She's been after me to see whether I could get you to make changes in us. She wants to have at least one child with me."

"A construct child?"

"I don't know—although if I'm willing after resisting for a century . . ."

"Take these new people up to see her. Talk to her, and to them."

He stopped me, turned me to face him. "You've done this to me," he said. "I would have gone to Mars."

I said nothing.

"I can't even hate you," he whispered. "My god, if there had been people like you around a hundred years ago, I couldn't have become a resister. I think there would be no resisters." He stared at me a moment longer. "Damn you,"

he said slowly, sadly. "Goddamn you." He walked past me
and went to Ahajas and the waiting Oankali family.

"They are your ooan relatives," Lilith said, and I looked at
her with amazement. She had somehow managed to approach
me without my noticing.

"You were preoccupied," she said. She wanted very much
to touch me and made no effort to hide it. She looked at me
hungrily. "You and Aaor are beautiful," she said. "Are you
both really all right?"

"We are. We need Oankali mates, but other than that we're
fine."

"And that man, Francisco, is he typical of the people
here?"

"He's one of the old ones. The first one I met."

"And he loves you."

"As you said once: pheromones."

"At first, no doubt. By now, he loves you."

". . . yes."

"Like João. Like Marina. You have a strange gift, Lelka."

I changed the subject abruptly. "Did you say those people
with Francisco were my ooan relatives? Nikanj's relatives?"

"Nikanj's parents."

I turned to look at them, remembering their names. I had
heard them all my life. The ooloi was Kahguyaht, large for an
ooloi—as big as Lilith, who was large for a Human female.
Kahguyaht had not given such large size to Nikanj. Its male
mate, Jdahya, was of an ordinary size. The placement of his
sensory tentacles gave him an oddly Human look. They hung
from his head like hair. They were placed on his face in a way
that could be mistaken for Human eyes, ears, nose. He was
the first Oankali Lilith had ever met. She was looking at him
now and smiling. "Francisco will like him," she said.

Francisco would like them all if he let himself. He was
talking now with Tediin, Kahguyaht's huge female mate—
again, bigger than average. She did not look in the slightest
Human. He was laughing at something she had said.

"There are people waiting to meet you, Jodahs," Lilith
said.

Oh, yes. They were waiting to meet me and examine me

and decide whether I should be allowed to go on running around loose. They were already meeting Aaor.

Three ooloi were investigating Aaor. Two waited to meet me. My ooan parents would be busy for a while with Francisco, but these others must be satisfied. I went to them wearily.

15

It wasn't bad being examined by so many. It wasn't uncomfortable. After a time even my ooan family left Francisco to poke and probe us. They took us into the shuttle. Through the shuttle, Oankali and constructs of all sexes could make easy, fast, nonverbal contact with us and with one another. The group had the shuttle fly out of the canyon and up as high as necessary to communicate with the ship. The ship transmitted our messages and those of its own inhabitants to the lowland towns and their messages to us. In that way, the people came together for the second time to share knowledge of construct ooloi who should not exist, and to decide what to do with us.

The shuttle left children and most Humans back in the canyon. Both could have come and participated through their ooloi, but for them the experience would be jarring and disorienting. Everything was too intense, went too fast, was, for the Humans, too alien. Linking into the nervous system of a shuttle, a ship, or a town even through an ooloi was, according to Lilith, one of the worst experiences of her life. Yet she and Tino went up with us, and absorbed what they could of the complex exchange.

The demands of the lowlanders and the people of the ship were surprisingly easy for me to absorb and understand. I could handle the intensity and the complexity. What I wasn't sure I could handle was the result. The whole business was like Lilith's rounded black cloud of hair. Every strand seemed to go its own different way, bending, twisting, spiraling, angling. Yet together they formed a symmetrical, recognizable shape, and all were attached to the same head.

Oankali and construct opinion also took on a recognizable shape from apparent chaos. The head that they were attached to was the generally accepted belief that Aaor and I were potentially dangerous and should either go to the ship or stay where we were. The lowland towns were apologetic, but they still felt unsure and afraid of us. We represented the premature adulthood of a new species. We represented true independence—reproductive independence—for that species, and this frightened both Oankali and constructs. We were, as one signaler remarked, frighteningly competent ooloi. We must be watched and understood before any more of us were made—and before we could be permitted to settle in a lowland town.

Continued exile, then. The mountains. We would not go to Chkahichdahk. The people knew that. We let them know it again, Aaor and I together.

"There will be two more of you," someone signaled from far away. I separated out the signal in my memory and realized that it had come from far to the east and south on the other side of the continent. There, an ooloi in a Mandarin-speaking Jah village was reporting its shameful error, its children going wrong. Both were in metamorphosis now. Both would be ooloi.

"Bring them here as soon as they can travel," I signaled. "They'll need mates quickly. It would be best if they had chosen mates already."

"This is first metamorphosis," the signaler protested.

"And they are construct! Bring them here or they'll die. Put them on a shuttle as soon as you can. For now, let them know that there are mates for them here."

After a time, the signaler agreed.

This produced confusion among the people. One mistake simply focused attention on the ooloi responsible. Two mistakes unconnected, but happening so close together in time after a century of perfection, might indicate something other than ooloi incompetence.

There was much communication about this, but no conclusion. Finally Aaor interrupted.

"This will probably happen again," it said. "An ooloi subadult who doesn't want to go to the ship should be sent here. The Humans who want to stay here should be left here and let alone. They want mates and I think there are Oankali and constructs who are willing to come here to mate with them."

"I believe we will be staying," Kahguyaht signaled. "We've found resisters who might mate with us." It paused. "I don't believe they would even consider us if they hadn't spent these last months living near Jodahs and Aaor."

"Your ooan children," someone signaled.

Kahguyaht signaled very slowly. "Where is the flaw in what I've said?"

No response. I doubted that anyone really believed Kahguyaht was expressing misplaced family pride. It was simply telling the truth.

"Aaor and I want Oankali mates," I signaled. "We want to start children. I think once we've done that, once you've examined our children, you'll know that we're not dangerous."

"You are dangerous," several people signaled. "There's no safe way to begin a new species."

"Then help us. Send us mates and young construct ooloi. Watch us all you like, but don't hinder us."

"Have you planted a town?" someone on Chkahichdahk asked.

I signaled negative. "We didn't know we would be staying here . . . permanently."

"Plant a town," several people signaled. "How can you think of having children with no town to hold them?"

I hesitated, focused on Kahguyaht. It spoke aloud within the shuttle. "Plant a town, Lelka. In less than a hundred years, my mates and I will be dead. You should plant the town that you and your mates and children will leave this world in."

"If I plant a town," I signaled the people, "will Aaor and I be permitted Oankali mates? Will Oankali and construct mates come to the Humans here?"

There was a long period of discussion. Some people were more concerned about us than others. Some, clearly, would have nothing to do with us until we had been stable for several more years, and clearly done no harm. They were in the minority. The majority decided that as long as we stayed where we were, anyone who wanted to join us could do so.

"Plant a town," they told us. "Prepare a place. People will come."

A few of them signaled such eagerness that I knew they would be with us as soon as they could get a shuttle. Humans who wanted mates were rare enough and desirable enough to make people dare to face any danger they thought Aaor and I might present. And Aaor and I were interesting enough in our newness to seduce Oankali who needed ooloi mates. People seeking mates were more vulnerable to seduction than they would be at any other time in their lives. They would come.

16

Sometime later, when the visiting families and the mountain Humans had begun to get together and curiously examine one another, I prepared to plant the new town.

I sorted through the vast genetic memory that Nikanj had given me. There was a single cell within that great store—a cell that could be "awakened" from its stasis within yashi and stimulated to divide and grow into a kind of seed. This seed could become a town or a shuttle or a great ship like Chkahichdahk. In fact, my seed would begin as a town and eventually leave Earth as a great ship. It would never be a shuttle, though it would be parent to shuttles.

Over the next few days, I found the cell, awakened it,

nourished it, and encouraged it to divide. When it had divided several times, I stopped it, separated one cell from the mass, and returned that cell to stasis. This was work that only an adult ooloi could do, and I found that I enjoyed it immensely.

I took the remaining mass—the seed—still within my body to the place that the Humans and the visiting families had agreed was good for people and towns. Several of the visitors and Humans traveled with me by shuttle, since the chosen place was well upriver from the mountain village. There were scattered stone ruins at the new place where the canyon broadened into a large valley. Plenty of land, plenty of water, easy access to many needed minerals. Less easy access to others, according to what the shuttle's senses told us when it had landed and tasted the new place. But whether or not the town had to develop a longer and more complex root system than most towns, everything it needed with within its reach. Including us. Here the town could grow and always have the companionship of some of us. It would need that companionship as much as we did during our metamorphoses. Yet we were planting it too far from the mountain people's crops for it to be tempted to reach them and eat them before it was big enough to feed the people itself. While it was young, it would be particularly voracious. And it would need the space the valley afforded it to grow and mature before it had to deal with mountains.

"This could be a good place to live," one of the elders commented as she left the shuttle and looked around. She was the woman whose leg Aaor had regenerated. She had decided with most of her people to stay on Earth.

"There's room here for many more people," Jesusa said, looking at me. She wanted a child even more than I did. It was hard for her to wait for Oankali mates. At least now we knew there were potential mates coming.

I chose a spot near the river. There I prepared the seed to go into the ground. I gave it a thick, nutritious coating, then brought it out of my body through my right sensory hand. I planted it deep in the rich soil of the riverbank. Seconds after I had expelled it, I felt it begin the tiny positioning movements of independent life.